Trading the urban pace of Edinburgh for a tiny village overlooking a breathtaking blue loch was a great move for budding photographer Sylvie Carmichael and her artist husband, Seamus—until a dangerous crime obscures the view . . .

Sylvie's bucolic life along the heather-covered moors of the Highlands is a world away from the hectic energy of the city. But then a London buyer is killed after purchasing a long-lost Scottish masterpiece from Seamus's gallery—and the painting vanishes. As suspicion clouds their new life, and their relationship, Sylvie's search for answers plunges her into an unsolved mystery dating back to Cromwellian Scotland through World War I and beyond. And as she moves closer to the truth, Sylvie is targeted by a murderer who's after a treasure within a treasure that could rewrite history . . . and her own future.

Also by Amy M. Reade

The Malice Series
The House on Candlewick Lane
Highland Peril

Novels
Secrets of Hallstead House
The Ghosts of Peppernell Manor
House of the Hanging Jade

Lyrical Press books are published by
Kensington Publishing Corp. 119 West 40th Street New York, NY 10018

All Kensington titles, imprints, and distributed lines are available at special quantity discounts for bulk purchases for sales promotion, premiums, fund-raising, and educational or institutional use.

To the extent that the image or images on the cover of this book depict a person or persons, such person or persons are merely models, and are not intended to portray any character or characters featured in the book. Special book excerpts or customized printings can also be created to fit specific needs. For details, write or phone the office of the Kensington

Special Sales Manager:
Kensington Publishing Corp.
119 West 40th Street
New York, NY 10018
Attn. Special Sales Department. Phone: 1-800-221-2647.

First Electronic Edition: September 2017
eISBN-13: 978-1-5161-0015-6
eISBN-10: 1-5161-0015-8

First Print Edition: September 2017
ISBN-13: 978-1-5161-0018-7
ISBN-10: 1-5161-0018-2

Printed in the United States of America

Highland Peril

Amy M. Reade

LYRICAL UNDERGROUND
Kensington Publishing Corp.
www.kensingtonbooks.com

For John

Acknowledgments

As always, I must thank my first reader, my husband, John for his invaluable advice and support. And thank you to my kids, who offer nothing but encouragement as I continue along this journey I've chosen. And thank you to the rest of my family, for always keeping the faith.

I would also like to thank the editors, artists, and talented professionals at Kensington Publishing for all their hard work in bringing my words to print. And in particular, I offer a huge thanks to my editor, Martin Biro.

Glossary

bairn: child

braw: fine, great

cullen skink: classic Scottish soup made with smoked fish (usually haddock), potatoes, and onions

dinnae: don't

ghillie brogues: shoes specially made for bagpipers or for wearing with kilts. They are generally black, with no tongue and long laces.

haggis: often referred to as Scotland's national dish, it is a combination of meat, oatmeal, onions, spices, and salt. The meat is frequently sheep's heart, liver, and lungs.

ken: *v.,* to know

kirk: church

scunner: a person who engenders disdain; someone who causes disgust

sgian dubh: (Gaelic) "black knife." This traditional kilt accessory is a small knife, often with a decorative handle and leather sheath, which is worn tucked inside the top of a man's hose.

sporran: pouch used to store small personal items, usually worn with a pocketless kilt

torch: flashlight

wynd: alley or narrow lane

Prologue

1652 Scotland

"Quickly, Elizabeth!" the woman whispered, the urgency in her voice unmistakable.

"I'm hurrying, m'lady," the maid replied with a grunt, gathering her skirts in one hand and tripping across the rocks behind her mistress. The waves crashed far below at the base of the jagged cliff as the North Sea grew angrier in the keening wind.

The bundle of flax was as heavy as an anvil. Elizabeth repeatedly changed hands to hold the neck of the burlap bag and her skirts simultaneously, being sure to keep the contents of the bag from spilling onto the ground.

"Over here, Elizabeth," Christian whispered. "Don't go any closer to the edge." Christian was in the lead, making her way through the tall grass in the darkness, her steps guided only by the few distant torches burning on the side of the mammoth castle facing the sea.

Elizabeth followed the sound of Christian's voice, straining to hear above the wind. Twice she had to stop, but only for a moment, to catch her breath. She didn't know how Christian was managing with two bags.

The women had a long distance to walk before they would meet the Reverend Grainger's coach. They were headed several miles through the woods, from Castle Dunnottar to a road that would take them to the village of Kinneff. It would be a difficult walk, fraught with danger, not only because of the rock-strewn path and the precipitous drop to the sea, but because the English army was nearby, and who knew what wild animals and ill-meaning men lurked in the darkness.

Elizabeth hurried to catch up, almost dragging the heavy bag along beside her. Her mistress stopped for a moment, waiting for her to draw near. "Stay close behind me. Do not say a word to anyone."

Elizabeth nodded, not sure if Christian could see her face in the darkness. She clenched and unclenched her hands, trying to uncramp them. She bent to the side to retrieve her bag, but her foot bumped it and tipped it over. The neck of the bag had come untied and some of the flax spilled onto the ground with a quiet shushing sound. Elizabeth looked up, barely able to see Christian moving forward toward the English encampment.

"Elizabeth!" came the hoarse whisper. "You must hurry!"

Several moments later Elizabeth, panting with exertion, caught up to Christian. "What have you been doing? You must move more quickly. If I had known you would be so slow, I would have done this myself."

"I'm sorry, m'lady," Elizabeth mumbled.

Elizabeth knew her mistress could not have made such a journey by herself with three bags of flax. Christian needed her help, and was likely grateful for it. The two women, each lugging her heavy load, continued through the grass, thankful for the wind that cooled their faces and for the cloud-filled night, which helped them move away from the castle unnoticed.

Christian finally spoke. "Do you hear that? I believe there is a horse ahead. Perhaps it is my husband's coach."

"Who's there?" a voice shouted. Both women froze. Each knew instinctively to remain absolutely still and wait for the English soldier atop his steed to continue on his way. Though Christian had discussed with the mistress of Castle Dunnottar the possibility of being discovered by the English, she had not discussed it with Elizabeth. But Elizabeth knew what they had just accomplished, and she knew they had risked their lives this night. They were not about to reveal their presence on this desolate cape high above the heaving sea.

In spite of the cool breeze, a droplet of sweat made its way down Elizabeth's face and dripped onto the ground. She would have sworn she heard it hit the ground with a deafening roar. Of course the soldier could not hear her sweating. She wondered if her mistress was sweating, too, nearby in the darkness.

After a few moments of silence, save for the wind billeting around them, Christian and Elizabeth heard the soldier on his horse move away through the waving grass. He wasn't trying very hard to be quiet. He probably assumed he had startled an animal foraging for food.

The two women continued on their way, stopping only to listen for sounds above the wind. There were none. The soldier had disappeared.

Elizabeth heaved the bag onto her back, where it would not make any noise dragging along the dry ground. Another hour, and the night sky remained blacker than ever. Finally she heard a noise—the sound of a horse. Elizabeth strained her eyes to see ahead into the darkness, but she could see nothing but the even darker form of her mistress standing in front of her.

"Over here," Christian whispered, barely audible. Elizabeth followed the sound of her voice. They had arrived at the dirt track several miles north of the village of Kinneff. Elizabeth set down her heavy sack. The horse's soft whinny carried on the wind and Christian crept closer to the sound. Just a moment later there was the trill of a bird—a labored sound that seemed out of time and place in the darkness.

"My husband is here," Christian whispered. She made a similar trilling sound with her throat. Elizabeth tugged the sack along the ground until she could see the outline of the small coach and the horse in front of it. A tall figure stood near the horse. Reverend Grainger. He stepped forward and took hold of one of the bags his wife was carrying. He hoisted it onto the seat of the coach and then did the same with the second bag. Christian clambered up into the coach and turned around to watch as her husband took Elizabeth's bag by the neck and swung it up with the others. He climbed up onto the seat and took the reins; Elizabeth took her place behind the coach. She would walk the rest of the way.

A short distance down the road, the coach stopped. The only noise Elizabeth could hear was from the wind, but the Reverend had heard muted voices up ahead. He turned in his seat and hissed a warning to the two women. "*Shh!* I will speak to them."

The coach drew up to a group of three soldiers, one of whom was holding a torch for light. One of the men ordered them to stop as they approached. Reverend Grainger pulled on the reins. The horse, seemingly having taken on the nervous temperament of the Reverend and the two women with him, stomped his feet and neighed.

"What are you doing?" asked one of the soldiers, his English accent strong.

"I received word that my good wife was taken ill whilst visiting Castle Dunnottar, and I have been to fetch her and her maidservant."

The soldier with the torch leaned closer to the side of the coach. "What is in the bags?"

"The bags contain flax that my wife and her maidservant will use to make poultices for my parishioners."

"Let me have a look."

Christian obediently opened the necks of the three bags of flax and the soldier ran his hand through the seeds, letting them fall back into the bags like gold pieces in a treasure chest.

"Where are you going?"

"To Kinneff."

"Proceed."

Without further discussion, Reverend Grainger flipped the reins and the horse clopped forward toward Kinneff. Elizabeth knew, without hearing, that the couple in the coach had just heaved great sighs of relief.

Before arriving at Kinneff, the coach slowed. Elizabeth knew what was happening; it had all been part of the hastily arranged plan. She must never know what was to happen to the contents of the bags, so she was being sent away forever to protect herself, her employers, and Scotland.

Christian climbed down from the coach and Reverend Grainger came around from the front. Elizabeth stood before them and bowed her head.

"Elizabeth, you have been a good and faithful servant, but as you are aware, we can no longer risk having you in our employ. Nor can you risk remaining in our company. The time has come for you to depart to destinations unknown. We will not ask whither you go, and we demand that you do not reveal to us the arrangements you have made or your whereabouts."

With these words Reverend Grainger pulled a small bag from under his cloak. Elizabeth knew how many coins the bag contained—she had agreed to the amount in advance of the trip to Castle Dunnottar. The coins jingled softly as the Reverend handed the bag to Elizabeth, then her former employers watched as she wordlessly turned away from the road and walked straight into the wood nearby, her future plans known only to her and one other person.

It would be the last time she would ever see the Reverend Grainger and Christian Fletcher.

At long last the coach arrived at the Kinneff Church. Christian longed for sleep, but there was still much work to do. She and her husband reached for the bags of flax on the floor of the coach. They pulled the bags along the ground to the rear of the church, their eyes darting in all directions to see whether any figures lurked in the dark.

Reverend Grainger pulled a huge iron key from inside his cloak, where he always kept it. With a grating noise that seemed much louder than it really was, the key found its way inside the lock of the church door and Reverend Grainger pushed open the heavy door. He led the way to the nave, where he lit a small torch. A tiny flame sprang to life, providing just enough light to see as he knelt down and used his fingertips to pry a wooden board from the floor. It came up without a sound. Christian reached for a tall pile of neatly folded linen cloths and slid the pile closer to where she and her husband squatted on the floor of the almost-dark church.

The first bag was one Christian had been carrying since the women's departure from Castle Dunnottar. She plunged her arm into the flax and slowly and carefully pulled out the object, which had been hidden among the seeds.

It was solid silver, gleaming dully in the light from the torch. Atop its length was a crystal globe and a lustrous Scottish pearl.

The Sceptre of Scotland. It had been used at the coronation of Queen Mary of Scots.

Christian handled it as though it were holy, running her fingertips up its length and around the globe and pearl. Not a breath could be heard in the church. The flame sputtered.

"Wife, wrap the Sceptre, and do so with haste," the Reverend Grainger cautioned. Laying out a length of linen, Christian placed the Sceptre on the floor with extreme gentleness, then wrapped it in several lengths of cloth until it was sufficiently padded. Having completed her task, she handed the Sceptre to her husband, who took it with equal care and placed it in the hollow space where the floorboard had been.

Christian reached into the other bag she had carried from the castle. Again she plunged her arm into the seeds of flax and pulled out the first of two objects hidden inside. She gazed at it, her tears glistening in the feeble torchlight. She put her hand back into the bag and drew out the second object.

The objects, together as one just hours ago, made up the Sword of Scotland. The Sword, with its silver gilt handle, intricate carvings, and scabbard of velvet and silver, might someday be restored to its original grandeur. Christian was no doubt remembering her sadness as she watched the Commander of the Castle, George Ogilvie, break the sword into two pieces in order to safeguard its continued existence. Christian would not allow the Sword, nor its brethren regalia, to fall into the hands of the Cromwellian forces.

These objects, too, were carefully wrapped in linen cloths and laid under the floorboard of the kirk.

Christian then turned to the bag that Elizabeth had carried. Reaching into the flax seeds with both hands, she drew out the final piece of the Scottish Regalia.

The Crown of Scotland.

She had entrusted this, the most awe-inspiring piece of the Honours of Scotland, to Elizabeth because she knew the maid would more likely be ignored if they had been stopped and questioned by Cromwell's troops.

Drawing an almost imperceptible breath, she ran her fingers around the circlet of the Crown, feeling each jewel and precious stone in turn. In the hushed light of the torch, she frowned and ran her fingers around the circlet again, then reached to take the torch from her husband.

Holding the torch close to her face and bringing the Crown nearer, she peered anxiously at the circlet. She turned it and studied the stones, then looked up at Reverend Grainger with an expression of pained confusion.

"There are two stones missing from this circlet. I am sure the jewels and the stones were all there when we departed from the castle. Have my eyes deceived me?"

"Where are the other gems?" asked her husband.

"I do not know. We must find them. Quickly—help me search through the flax to ensure they are not within the seeds."

Handful by tedious handful, Christian and Reverend Grainger took every flax seed out of the bag, spreading them on the floor of the kirk. The Reverend would normally have left such a menial task to his wife, but this was a matter crucial to the survival of the Scottish Regalia.

The jewels were not among the seeds.

"Elizabeth. She stole the jewels," Christian said in a low, deadly voice.

Hadn't Elizabeth stopped repeatedly on the path from Castle Dunnottar to adjust the bag in her worthless hand? She must have dislodged the jewels when she stopped, leaving them behind for retrieval at a later time.

"The wretch!" Christian hissed. "Where can the jewels be?"

"We do not have the luxury of looking for them right now. We must reunite the Crown with the other regalia before the English realize they are missing and come looking for them."

Christian, her hands fumbling and clumsy, quickly wrapped the Crown in swaths of linen, then she and her husband placed the Crown lovingly under the floorboard. They gazed for one long moment at the relics under the kirk floor before Reverend Grainger replaced the board. Helping his wife to her feet, he looked at her with alarm and intensity in his eyes.

"What are we going to tell people when the relics are unearthed?"

"I do not know," she replied. "Perhaps we can locate Elizabeth and force her to tell us where she has hidden the jewels."

"She has promised to disappear and never to reveal her whereabouts to us."

"There must be someone who knows where she is. Perchance a family member? I seem to recall Elizabeth having a sister."

But Elizabeth had planned carefully, despite the short time she had to do so. She had disappeared, along with her sister, and once they reached their destination they would never tread upon Scottish soil again. Oliver Cromwell was in control of the land of the Scots. Christian and her husband, the Reverend Grainger, went about their daily duties—she working in the house and in the garden, he exemplifying the ways of God and keeping his flock on the path to righteousness.

One night Christian crept out of their home and through the darkness to the kirk, looking over her shoulder all the while to make sure she hadn't been seen or followed by an English soldier. Once inside with the door safely bolted behind her, she walked in silence to the place where the Honours of Scotland were still hidden. Kneeling down, she pried up the floorboard and laid it to her side. She reached into the hole and gently pulled out the bundles wrapped in linen, gazing at them with urgent reverence. She must hurry. She had brought with her another bundle of linens. She unwrapped the relics one by one and rewrapped them in the fresh, clean linens.

She replaced the wooden floorboard, then slipped out the back of the kirk and returned home by a different path, still in darkness, still watching and listening for Cromwell's soldiers.

During the long years of the war with England, Christian stole away in the darkness of the night often to rewrap the Honours in clean cloths, and to satisfy herself that they were safe under the kirk floor.

Though Christian and the Reverend rarely spoke about the gems Elizabeth had somehow removed from the Honours, on the nights that she rewrapped the relics her husband would wait for her in the darkness. In the quiet of their bedroom, they would wonder softly when the theft would be discovered. Their clandestine attempts to locate Elizabeth had failed, and they wondered if they would be held responsible. But when the morning came they would resume their daily duties once again, deferring any further discussion of the Honours until the next time Christian would visit the kirk in the darkness.

* * * *

After Elizabeth left Christian and the Reverend Grainger, she waited in the wood and watched them drive away, the deep charcoal night settling around her in the stillness. But she could not afford to tarry. Joan would be waiting for her.

She hastened to her sister's house, which sat along a faint dirt track on the other side of the wood. Elizabeth knew the way, even in the darkness.

Holding her skirt and feeling for the trees, which reached out to block her way, she scanned the path in front of her for the candle that Joan had promised to leave burning. Before long she saw a tiny pinprick of light. A nervous, churning feeling began to seep into her body. She and Joan would never be able to return to Kinneff or the surrounding countryside after this night. Her deception would be discovered in a few short hours—she and Joan needed to vanish before then.

As the pinprick of light grew into a dull flame, Elizabeth quickened her steps. She peered through the darkness, which seemed to have intensified as she drew closer to the house. Would Joan be wavering in her commitment to join her? Would she resent Elizabeth for putting them both into the precarious situation of having to flee Scotland?

Elizabeth knocked one time on the thin wooden door of Joan's house, the sisters' agreed-upon signal for Joan to open the door. If anyone else had knocked on her door in the dead of night, Joan would have feared bandits. Or worse.

Joan opened the door and, taking Elizabeth's arm, pulled her younger sister into the house without ceremony. She slammed the door.

"Are ye ready?" Elizabeth asked, breathless from her trek through the wood.

"Aye."

"Then extinguish the flame and let us leave."

"Do ye have the gems hidden in the folds of thy frock?"

"Nay. I had to bury them closely under the ground outside the castle."

"What?" Joan hissed. "How are we to retrieve them?"

"When we stop at dawn, I will draw a map to allow thee to find them. I will not forget where I hid the pouch, along the ground near the castle, but if danger or death should befall me, thou will be able to find the gems and live in comfort into thy dotage."

"Are ye sure the mistress and the Reverend Grainger know nothing of this?"

"I am sure."

"Let us go." Joan reached for two small bundles, which lay on the floor beside the door. She handed one to Elizabeth, kept one for herself, and blew out the candle.

The sisters stole away to the north, along the edge of a stream that flowed through the wood. They were walking toward the land belonging to Castle Dunnottar, where they would retrieve what Elizabeth had hidden not so many hours before. As the dawn brushed the sky with strokes of the lightest pink, they turned away from the water and plunged deeper into the nearby wood. There they would take turns sleeping and staying alert for robbers or other threats. Though Joan had made sure to place a sharpened knife in each of the bundles, both sisters knew they would be doomed if ever they were required to defend themselves.

Elizabeth slept first. She slept lightly, waking with each slight noise in the underbrush. But she slumbered again quickly each time, secure in the trust she placed in Joan to alert her if any danger should present itself.

When she awoke with a clearer head, she motioned for Joan to lie down. Though it would be uncomfortable on the ground with just leaves on which to rest her head, Elizabeth knew Joan would be able to sleep quickly. While Joan slept, Elizabeth reached into her bundle and pulled out the quill and small inkwell she had asked Joan to include. Tearing a small piece of cloth from her apron, she used the ink-dipped quill to draw a rough map to the gems. She hoped such a map would not be necessary—for if it were, it would mean she had met her demise.

Once Joan awoke, the sisters ate a small meal of cheese and soft bread in the pleasant cool and dim light of the wood. They spoke little, since their voices would carry on the wind. Elizabeth knew her mistress and Reverend Grainger would not send anyone to look for her because of the circumstances under which the gems had been taken from the castle, but she feared that others meaning harm would come upon them if their voices were heard. They dared not light a fire for cooking, so, aside from the inkwell and quill, the bundles the sisters carried contained little more than food they could eat easily and without flame. The weather was still mild, so neither Elizabeth nor Joan worried about cold while they slept on the ground.

Once the ink dried on the cloth, Elizabeth rolled up the map and tucked it into her waistband.

"If anything should happen to me," she whispered to Joan, "thou will find the map here at my waist. Use it to find the gems and build a life of comfort for thyself."

Joan nodded solemnly. She hoped she would never have to use the map, because she did not like to think of life without Elizabeth. She was the timid one—Elizabeth was the brave one. She knew she would likely not survive if Elizabeth came to harm.

As night fell, the sisters secured their bundles and set off quietly through the wood. They stayed within the relative safety of the trees until darkness enveloped them in its velvety shroud. Elizabeth longed to walk by the water so she could drink, but she would be patient and wait a bit longer. The wind blew the clouds to and fro, sometimes blocking out the moon and stars, sometimes allowing the nighttime illumination to guide the sisters' steps.

"'Tis not far now," Elizabeth said to her sister in a low voice.

She thought she heard Joan respond, but when she turned around to ask her to repeat what she had said, she realized that the only steps she heard were her own. Joan had stopped moving.

"Why are you not following me?" Elizabeth hissed.

Joan did not reply. An icy spear of anxiety ripped through Elizabeth's body. Peering through the darkness, she could see by the faint light of the moon that Joan was standing quite close by, stock-still.

"Whatever is the matter?" Elizabeth asked in her quietest whisper.

She could barely make out Joan shaking her head. Then Elizabeth heard it, too. A twig snapping.

They were not alone in the wood.

Was it a man or an animal? Elizabeth could not know. She took one tentative step backward toward Joan, then another, then another. In a moment she had clasped Joan's hand, which was trembling and clammy. Joan squeezed Elizabeth's hand, whether for reassurance or for a signal of danger, Elizabeth did not know.

It took Elizabeth a moment to realize she had stopped breathing. She took in a deep breath as quietly as she could, clenching the muscles in her torso. She listened and heard it again. Another twig snapping.

Joan dropped Elizabeth's hand and fell to the ground, curling into a ball, her head tucked inside her arms.

Elizabeth was torn between joining Joan on the ground, standing to face whomever—or whatever—was nearby, and running farther into the wood. Before she could decide, she heard the distinctive *click* of a musket.

The danger came from man, the most dangerous animal of all.

Fully aware that the sisters were within the lines of entrapment formed by Cromwell's soldiers, Elizabeth made a quick decision. Raising her voice, she spoke into the darkness.

"Hullo? Who's there?"

"State your name," came a man's deep voice.

"My name is Jane, m'lord, and this is my sister, Margaret. We have become lost and we are hungry. Perchance you could assist us?" Elizabeth could sense Joan looking up from her place on the ground.

"Whither are you going?" the soldier asked in a gruff voice.

"To Edinburgh."

"Thee and thy sister are going in the wrong direction. Turn around now and haste ye to the south. 'Tis the land of Castle Dunnottar you have chanced upon."

"Might ye have a bit of food you could spare?" Elizabeth asked, her courage a thing of wonder to Joan.

"I do not," the soldier said. "Now go, before someone else sees you."

Knowing how lucky they were to have escaped capture—or worse—by Cromwell's soldier, Elizabeth and Joan turned and walked quickly through the wood in the direction from which they had come.

When they reached the spot where they had spent the previous day, they stopped.

"What shall we do now?" Joan asked, her voice tremulous.

"I do not know," Elizabeth replied. "We must try to remain calm. We will figure out a way to get back onto Castle Dunnottar land."

"But the soldiers…they will see us," Joan said.

"We will figure out a way," Elizabeth repeated.

But as the day grew long the sisters were forced into the realization that there was no way to get back to Castle Dunnottar without the near-certainty of being discovered and captured.

They could not return to Joan's house because the mistress and the Reverend Grainger might be looking for them there. They could not return to the town of Kinneff for the same reason. As understanding dawned on them, Elizabeth felt the stirrings of fear. She and Joan had made an irreversible choice, and they must now continue with their plan to leave Scotland, with or without the gems that would ensure their comfort for the rest of their days.

The sisters could not stay idle in the wood. They were sure to be seen by soldiers or people from Kinneff, who would certainly wonder what they were doing there. All they could do was make their way south, as the soldier had directed.

They continued walking night after long night and sleeping in hiding places during the days. Rarely did they see other people, but when the forests thinned and they came upon a hamlet or a village, they walked quickly and quietly through the lanes and alleys while curious villagers were asleep.

Their supply of food, which Joan had so carefully prepared, soon vanished. The sisters were forced to resort to eating berries and grasses from the woods as they walked at night. Occasionally they would come upon a pen of goats or sheep, and they would take a drink of milk, praying the noises made by the goats would not wake the sleeping farmer.

Many days later the sisters reached a bustling town. Daring to venture in from the woods in a dire search for food, they took care to behave as the townsfolk would. They walked arm in arm, smiling and chatting as though they belonged. Although they received a few curious glances, they were left to themselves. Because they were still in Scotland, they weren't afraid to speak aloud on the streets. They would not be persecuted for their manner of speech as long as they were still inside their homeland. The farther they traveled south, however, the more difficult it would become to allow their voices to be heard in public. Once in England, they would have to be very careful who they spoke to.

* * * *

It was many weeks before Elizabeth and Joan reached England, and when they arrived they found that Scots were reviled and unwanted. They roamed the countryside looking for accommodation and employment, and it was several months before both young women found work—Elizabeth in a tannery and Joan in a manor house as a laundress. Both women worked every day from before dawn until after dark and found their work difficult, demanding, and exhausting.

At night the sisters would talk about the gems they had left behind in Scotland. They would wonder aloud whether the gems had been found. They would speak wistfully about how their lives could have been different if only they had not been thwarted in their attempts to recover them.

Though Joan never married, Elizabeth eventually wed the tanner for whom she worked. Theirs was not a happy marriage, however, and Elizabeth would visit Joan often and bemoan her lot in life. The sisters always planned to someday follow the map drawn by Elizabeth long ago, but they never left England. They led meager lives, the sisters who were once full of hope and expectation.

Joan died a young woman, childless and alone save for Elizabeth. She never knew the sadness that followed Elizabeth for the rest of her short life.

As the war between England and Scotland came to an end, Reverend Grainger and Christian were finally able to unearth the Honours from the hiding place where they had lain unmolested during Cromwell's siege. When it was discovered that several gems were missing from the Honours, a great hue and cry went up. The couple were questioned many times about the provenance of the gems, and both insisted they had been stolen by their former employee, Elizabeth. When the authorities went in search of Elizabeth and her sister, they found to their great dismay that Elizabeth and Joan had disappeared, along with any information about the whereabouts of the gems. The trail the sisters left went cold at the English border. Authorities surmised that Elizabeth and Joan had changed their identities and disappeared, never to be seen again in Scotland.

CHAPTER 1

As much as I love Seamus, he can make me crazy.

Don't get me wrong—living in the Scottish Highlands suits me better than I ever dreamed it would when he first suggested we leave Edinburgh. I enjoy working in the antique shop and I don't even mind running the gallery when he's been bitten by the painting bug and can't tear himself away from his latest creation.

But when he asked me to "whip up a wee snack" for him and a client, I had to put my foot down.

"I'm not your maid, Seamus. Whip something up yourself."

He spread his big hands out, pleading. "Please, Sylvie. I don't have time."

"Neither do I. Just take him over to the pub."

"It's pouring out. There's no need to go out in this weather when we have stuff to eat here. I promised him real Scottish food."

"Well, that's your problem. You know I can't cook anything, let alone anything Scottish."

"Just slice up some of the haggis in the fridge and fry it."

"I'll burn it. Remember what happened last time?"

He nodded, grimacing. "It was as hard as a rock."

"Why do we need to feed him, anyway? What's so special about him?"

"Keep your voice down," Seamus cautioned, looking over his shoulder through the door to the shop. "He's up from London. Looking for a painting that reminds him of his childhood. There's one he seems to like, but it's expensive and I'm trying to butter him up."

"Well, you'll have to butter him up without haggis, I'm afraid."

"Fine. Just get us a couple drams, would you?"

I glared daggers at my husband. "All right. But if you sell that painting, you have to take me shopping in Edinburgh."

He smiled. "You know I will, love."

"You're lucky I'm so nice."

He chuckled as he walked back into the shop, shaking his red head. "Care for a dram?" I heard him ask the man from London.

I went into the house and poured two measures of whisky, put them on a tray, and carried them back into the shop. Seamus was pointing out a small detail on a painting when I walked in.

"Ah, here's the whisky, along with my wife. Sylvie, I'd like you to meet Florian McDermott. He grew up in the Highlands and lives in London now. He's looking for a special painting. Florian, meet Sylvie."

I set my tray down and shook hands with the man, who was wispy and pale. His hand was cold in mine, though his eyes were warm.

"I'm looking for a painting that reminds me of my childhood in the Highlands," Florian explained.

"You must have fond memories of your childhood."

"What makes you think that?" Florian asked.

"Um, I guess…"

"It was awful."

I was at a loss for words. I looked to Seamus for help.

He just smiled and reached for the two glasses. Handing one to Florian, he raised his own in the air and said in a booming voice, "Here's tae ye!"

Florian raised his glass in silence, nodded, took a tiny sip of the whisky, and began to cough. He hacked away while Seamus grabbed his glass and I hurried for the pitcher of ice water I kept in the gallery. He was still coughing when I returned. He drank the water right from the pitcher, though I had meant for him to add it to the whisky to cut its strength.

"Are ye all right, man?" Seamus asked. Florian gasped for air, nodding, his previously pale face now a mask of hot pink.

"Sorry about that," he gasped. "It was a bit stronger than I expected."

"A *bit* stronger?" Seamus asked. "It must have gone down your throat like flame. I'm sorry. If I'd known, I would have had Sylvie get you something milder."

I glared at him. *If I'd known, I would have made you get your own whisky,* I thought.

"No, no. I just wasn't expecting it, that's all," Florian assured us. "I'm not much of a drinker."

"Ginger ale for you?" Seamus asked.

"No, thank you. I think I'd like to go back to the bed and breakfast where I'm staying and think about this for tonight."

"No problem at all," Seamus replied. He handed Florian a business card. "I look forward to hearing from you."

Florian nodded, his face returning to its former ghostly hue. He left without another word.

"He's a strange one, that's certain," Seamus said after Florian had disappeared from view.

"Did he say why he wants to get a painting to remember something he thought was awful?"

Seamus shrugged. "He didn't make much sense."

"Quite a loon," I said.

"I don't care if he's from outer space as long as he buys that painting. I've had it for three years now and nothing I can say will convince anyone to buy it. It's just too expensive."

"Why not lower the price?"

"Because it's by William Leighton Leitch, a famous Scot painter. So it's worth a lot of money. It's just a matter of waiting for the right buyer to come along."

"Well, maybe you've finally snared the right person."

He chucked me under the chin. "I didn't *snare* him. I just let the painting do the talking."

I smiled at my big, burly husband. "That painting must have quite a way with words, then."

He busied himself in the back of the shop while I returned to the gallery. No one had come in while we were speaking to Florian. We didn't get a lot of visitors, but when we did it was usually a serious buyer who came specifically to buy one of Seamus's paintings.

When we lived in Edinburgh, Seamus painted urban scenes with great success. In Bide-A-Wee house, where we lived with my sister, Greer, and her little girl, Ellie, until our marriage, Seamus had made part of the sunny, bright living room into a studio. He sold paintings online and in Edinburgh galleries. He had also been invited to show several of his paintings in some of the smaller London galleries, where they nevertheless had a larger audience and fetched higher prices. Once we were married we moved into our own flat near Bide-A-Wee and he continued painting there, until the weekend we went camping with friends—against my better judgment—in the mountains of the Scottish Highlands.

Seamus was hooked. The raw, rugged beauty of that part of Scotland appealed to both the artist and the outdoorsman in him, and he couldn't wait to leave Edinburgh and head north. He longed for a change from the scenery of the city.

But I didn't want to go. I loved the city, with its moods, weather, wonderful and sometimes quirky inhabitants, and its cultural events and history.

We were at loggerheads—a rather inauspicious way to begin married life.

But repeat trips to the Highlands on our days off and Seamus's constant discussion of how wonderful life would be if we moved finally began to wear me down. I found myself looking online at homes for sale. I began to actually look forward to our day trips and short overnights to the mountains.

But what clinched it for me, what made me finally agree to leave Edinburgh (with promises from Seamus practically written in blood that we would return to the city often) was a gift.

Seamus gave me a camera for my birthday that year, just a few months after that momentous camping trip. Previously I had used my mobile phone for photos and it wasn't very good. The camera unearthed a passion for photography I never knew I had. With that camera in my hand, I found I could make the Highlands come alive. I could see the interplay between light and shadow, between color and white space, that other people missed when they looked at a landscape.

So I started taking that camera with me wherever I went, and my favorite photos were the ones I took on our drives up to the Highlands. The craggy mountains capped with snow, the purple heather-covered moors, the dark peaty bogs, the deep blue lochs—I took pictures of everything. My cousin Eilidh convinced me to start selling my photos online and before I knew it I was making an income, however small, with my passion for photography. I had never had a job I loved: I had graduated from university with a degree in business and hopped from one boring office job to another for years until I discovered photography. Between Seamus's gift and the beauty of Scotland's breathtaking landscape, I had finally found more than a job—I had found a career that made working exhilarating and fun.

Seamus's feet didn't touch the ground for a week after I told him I was ready to make the move to the Highlands. He was thrilled and quite willing to do anything I asked in return.

So I made the one request I'd been mulling over: I told him I wanted to live in the tiny village where Eilidh and her husband, Callum, lived. Seamus agreed in the blink of an eye. Having lost his own parents in a house fire, Seamus heartily embraced my family—from Eilidh and Callum to Greer and Ellie to my mum, whom he loved as his own. He had been an only child, so having an extended family was new and wonderful to him. He loved the idea of living just a stone's throw from my cousin and Callum.

And that's how we came to live in Cauld Loch, a wee village clinging to a steep hill overlooking a loch of the same name, a small mountain lake with icy dark blue water. There was only one place for sale in the village, a house with a large attached shop, and we bought it. We named it Gorse Brae, after the gorse that grew in the front yard. We divided the shop into three parts: an antique art shop, a studio where both Seamus and I could work, and a gallery to display his paintings and my photos. We had been looking for a shop because just as I found a passion for photography, Seamus had found a passion for antique artwork. He had begun amassing his collection before we were married and finally decided he wanted to start selling it, too.

Seamus had invited Eilidh and Callum for dinner the night of Florian's visit, and the four of us pondered the mysterious stranger over our lamb stew.

"If he doesn't like the Highlands, why come all the way up here to find a painting? There are lots of places to find Highland art in London," Eilidh said.

"He didn't say," Seamus answered.

"How did he hear about the shop?" Callum asked.

"Saw one of my paintings in London and asked the gallery owner about me. I guess he likes the style of my paintings, but he wanted something old, something that had a previous life. And when the gallery owner told him I have an antique art shop up here, he took a chance that I sell the same types of artwork I paint, so he came up."

"He must be pretty serious about finding just the right painting," Eilidh noted.

Seamus nodded, his mouth full. Finally he swallowed. "Aye, and this one seems to be just what he's looking for. I've had nary a nibble on it in a long time."

"What's it called?" I asked.

"It's unnamed. I call it 'Old Kirk in the Field.'"

"So it's a picture of a church?"

"Yes, but there's an old woman stooped over in front of the kirk. It looks like she's picking flowers."

"I wonder why that reminds him of his awful childhood."

Seamus shrugged. "I've no idea."

"If William Whoever was such a famous painter, why do you have one of his works in your shop? Shouldn't it be in a museum somewhere?" Eilidh asked.

"It's William Leighton Leitch. When he died in the late eighteen hundreds, he left behind just a few paintings and drawings. Somehow this one ended up in a shop in Edinburgh. I bought it for a bargain because it's not in great shape."

"What's wrong with it?" Callum asked.

"There's a small tear in one corner and the paint is quite faded. Still, it's a steal. A famous painter, a painting that was lost after his death—it's all very exciting."

"It's too bad the painting isn't in good shape. If it was you could sell it to a museum instead of Florian and get a bundle for it," I said.

"Maybe," Seamus said, sitting back in his chair, "but I don't really have the time to restore it right now, and I don't want to pay for its restoration if I can get someone to buy it from me as is. Someone like Florian."

The phone rang in the gallery. We normally didn't answer the gallery phone after hours, but Seamus pushed his chair back from the table and hurried through the door into the gallery, saying over his shoulder, "Maybe that's Florian."

He was gone several minutes. I cleared away the dishes and was setting out bowls of berries and cream when Seamus came back in, shaking his head.

"Was that Florian?"

"You won't believe this," he said. "It was some guy wanting to look at the Leitch painting. The same one Florian is interested in."

"You're kidding."

"No," he said, rubbing his beard. He did that when he was thinking. "He said he heard I might have an old beat-up William Leighton Leitch painting in my shop, one with a stooped old lady at a church, and that he'd like to come up tomorrow to see it."

"What did you tell him?"

"I told him I might already have a buyer for it and that person gets first dibs." He turned to stare at me. "Can you believe it? I've tried to sell the thing for three years with no bites, and all of a sudden I have two potential buyers."

"What did he say when you told him he's second in line?"

"He didn't say anything about it. Just asked if he could come up tomorrow to see it. I'll have to call Florian and tell him about this. Maybe get him to make up his mind a wee bit faster."

"Do you think he will?"

"How do I know?" Seamus hates it when I ask unanswerable questions.

He drew Florian's business card out of his back pocket and punched some numbers into his mobile phone.

"Hi, Florian? It's Seamus Carmichael from Highland Treasures. I've received a call from a man who wants to have a look at the Leitch painting tomorrow. I told him you have first dibs on it, but you might want to make a decision soon."

Florian said something on the other end.

"Aye, great. It'll be ready."

Seamus ended the call and swooped me up in his arms, swinging me around the kitchen. "Florian'll take it! He's coming over tonight to pick it up! We finally sold it!"

I tilted my head back, laughing, already looking forward to my shopping trip in Edinburgh. Ignoring the berries, I cracked open a bottle of sparkling wine and the four of us raised our glasses to Florian. Seamus disappeared into the shop to wrap the painting, then joined the rest of us for dessert. After Eilidh and Callum went home Seamus waited by the shop door, watching for Florian's headlamps to sweep up the road.

"Sylvie, come here," he said after a few minutes.

"What?"

"Just come here."

I joined him at the shop door as he shut off the lights. "What are you doing that for? What if Florian can't find the shop?"

"Look," he said, pointing outside. A dark car crawled along the road just fifty meters from the shop, its lights off.

"Do you suppose that's Florian?"

"I don't know. I wonder why the driver doesn't have the headlamps on."

"Why did you turn off the shop lights?"

Seamus shrugged. "So whoever it is can't see us watching."

"It's a bit creepy, don't you think, standing here watching someone in the dark?"

He didn't answer.

The car slowed to a stop in front of our house. After just a moment, a slight figure stepped out of the car and stood looking up at the shop.

"That's Florian," Seamus said, his voice low. "Even in the dark I can tell him by his size and shape."

I nodded. Seamus took my elbow and we returned to the kitchen. "Why are we sneaking around our own house?" I complained.

"Something's a bit off about this whole thing," Seamus said, stroking his beard again. "Why would Florian drive around without his headlamps on?"

We stood in the kitchen, looking at each other, until the shop doorbell rang. Seamus returned to the shop, flipped on the light, and opened the door. I followed him, and together we watched as Florian skittered into the shop, checking over his shoulder.

"Is the painting ready?" he asked.

Seamus pointed to the large package on the shop counter. "Aye, it is. Say, Florian, did you realize your headlamps are out?"

Florian, who had been looking around the shop, jerked his head toward Seamus. "Is that so? That's funny. I didn't even realize it. I'll have to remember to switch them on when I go back."

"How far away is your bed and breakfast?"

"Just a few miles."

"It's dangerous to drive around here without headlamps. Lots of twists and turns in the roads. Be careful," Seamus cautioned.

"I will," Florian assured us. He pulled out a thick envelope. "How much do I owe you?"

Seamus quoted a high number and Florian opened the envelope. Rifling through its contents, he pulled out a wad of notes and handed them to Seamus, who watched him with wide eyes.

"Och, man, do you always carry that much cash wi' ye?"

Florian looked straight into Seamus's eyes with a boldness that seemed uncharacteristic. "Not usually." Seamus took the hint and looked away. Strange that such a meek little man could make Seamus feel self-conscious. Seamus had done time in prison, for heaven's sake, for injuring a man in self-defense. He wasn't afraid of anyone.

"Well, thank you for stopping by on such short notice," I said, hoping to hasten Florian's departure. "Good luck with your painting."

Florian gave me a long look and nodded, then left the store carrying the large painting with both hands.

"I'm glad he's gone," Seamus said as he locked the door and turned off the lights.

"Should you call the other man and tell him the painting is gone?"

"I can't. He hung up before I could get a mobile number from him."

"We really should get a caller ID service."

We stood by the door and watched Florian drive away, once again without the use of headlamps.

"He's going to get killed on these roads," Seamus muttered.

"He is a strange one, that's for sure."

CHAPTER 2

The next day dawned chilly, gray, and misty. The mountains outside the kitchen windows were hidden under a thick blanket of fog. I took my tea and wandered into the shop, where Seamus was turning on the lights and the heat to welcome the man who had called the night before, as well as any other customers who might venture out in the sodden weather.

"What time is that man coming? It's too bad you didn't get a number to call him back. Now he'll be coming for no reason."

"I don't know what time he's coming. Maybe there's something else he'd like to see whilst he's here, so his trip won't be for nothing."

It wasn't long before the bell jingled and a tall, burly man in a heavy parka came into the shop, bringing with him a cold, gusty wind. He rubbed his hands together.

"Is it always like this up here?" he asked in greeting, his accent hinting that he was English.

"It will be until spring," Seamus replied. He held out his hand. "I'm Seamus Carmichael. I own the shop. How can I help you?"

"I called last night about a Leitch painting."

"Aye. Unfortunately, the person who came to look at it yesterday returned last night and bought it. I didn't have your number or I would have called to tell you."

The man pursed his lips together and narrowed his eyes. "Who bought it?"

"Sorry. I can't give out that information," Seamus replied.

"Do you have any other Leitch paintings in the shop?"

Seamus shook his head. "No. They're hard to come by. If you want to leave me your name and number, I can give you a ring if I come across one."

"Maybe. Mind if I look around?"

"Of course not! Let me know if you have any questions." Seamus sat down at the desk, an antique roll-top, while I returned to the kitchen to clean up breakfast. I heard the man ask, "Where did you get the painting you sold last night?"

"Found it in an old junk shop. It wasn't even hanging up—I don't think the owner realized what he had."

"Where was the junk shop?"

"In Edinburgh. I don't remember the address offhand."

"Do you know if the owner had any more paintings by Leitch?"

"If he had, I would have bought them." I could tell from the tone of Seamus's voice that he was tiring of the man's questions. My husband needed to learn some patience.

The man's steps echoed on the stone floor of the shop. He was taking his time looking at the artwork. I peeked in to offer tea, but he shook his head. I glanced at Seamus, who raised his eyebrows and shrugged. Neither of us knew what to make of this stranger.

I went to the gallery to work on stretching some canvas photos over wooden frames. Tourists went wild for canvas prints. I heard the shop bell jingle again, and Seamus came in a moment later.

"He's gone. Another strange one," he said.

"What was he looking for?"

"Anything by William Leighton Leitch, apparently. Believe me, I'd like nothing more than to find more of his lost paintings."

"Do you think he was angry that Florian bought it?"

"I couldn't tell."

"Did he leave you his name and number?"

"Just his number. Wouldn't tell me his name, but he did say he just drove up here from London. Got in the car when he realized there was another buyer, he said. He must really have wanted the painting."

"I wonder why there's so much interest in that painting all of a sudden," I said.

"I've no clue."

"A weird coincidence, I guess."

"Hmm," Seamus replied.

Throughout that day there were several visitors to the gallery and the shop. If we sold just one of Seamus's paintings, it was a good week. Most of our income came from the shop and from my photography, but when Seamus sold a painting we always celebrated with champagne. At dinner that night Seamus pulled a bottle of bubbly from the fridge and twisted the cork with his beefy hands.

"When do we go to Edinburgh?" I asked.

"First things first," he replied with a wide smile. The cork popped out and landed in the living room. Seamus laughed and held the bottle over the sink as bubbles poured out. "Get those glasses, quick!"

We drank a toast to finding more lost art from the Scottish masters and sat down to dinner.

While we were eating, Seamus's mobile rang.

"Hello?" he answered, wiping his mouth. He listened, his eyebrows knit together, a frown forming.

"Yes, this is Seamus Carmichael." He listened for a moment. "You're kidding. I have no idea. Okay, thanks for letting me know. I'll be in touch if I hear anything." He hung up.

"Who was that?" I asked.

"Florian's wife. He's not home yet and he's not answering his phone. Before he came up here he left her a note with my name and number, told her if she couldn't reach him to call me."

"Well, maybe he stopped somewhere to break up the trip. It must take eight or nine hours to drive to London. He could have been exhausted. He left here late, after all."

"She said she's been trying to reach him on his mobile phone since the middle of the night. At first he just didn't answer, now it's going right to voicemail."

"Phone's probably off."

"Aye."

"Why did he leave her your number? Why not the bed and breakfast?"

"I have no idea." He turned back to his dinner, which was getting cold. We ate the rest of our meal in silence, both of us lost in thought.

The topic of Florian didn't come up again until the next morning, when there was a pre-dawn knock at the kitchen door.

"You get it," Seamus mumbled from his side of the bed.

"I'm not getting it. Who knows who's out there in the dark?" I hissed back at him.

He stumbled out of the bedroom first and I followed a short step behind. Before he turned on the kitchen light, he turned on the outdoor light. It flickered to life. A police constable was there. Seamus went to open the door while I turned on the light and the heater.

"Sorry to bother you so early, sir, but we have to ask you a few questions," the constable said.

My throat went dry. I had had dealings with the police in Edinburgh after my niece's abduction and they had always been helpful, thorough, and courteous. I had also dealt with them after a break-in—and assault—at Bide-A-Wee. Again they had been helpful and kind, but seeing them brought back bad memories, and ever since I learned about Seamus's criminal past I felt a cold prick of anxiety every time I saw a uniformed officer. It always seemed to me that Seamus would be a natural target if something went wrong in his vicinity. I know Seamus felt the same way, but he didn't show it.

He opened the door for the constable to enter. The man took off his coat and hat while Seamus motioned him over to the kitchen table and I started tea.

The two of them sat down while I busied myself setting out cups, saucers, milk, lemon, sugar, and honey. I had to do something to keep my hands busy because they were trembling.

Finally the constable spoke. "Ma'am, I'd like to talk to you, too. Could you join us?"

I didn't know whether to calm down or feel more edgy when I heard his words. Apparently he wasn't here to pester Seamus, but now it sounded like I was somehow in trouble, too.

I glanced at Seamus for reassurance, but he was looking at the constable. "How can we help you?" Seamus asked.

"There's been an accident involving a man you know," he said, glancing at his notes. "A Florian McDermott."

Seamus looked at me. "What kind of accident?" he asked the constable.

"An automobile accident. Mr. McDermott was involved in a fatal crash the night before last, on a road not far from here."

It took a moment for the information to sink in. Florian was dead? That explained the phone call from his wife. But how could Seamus know anything about it?

"How do you know Mr. McDermott?" the constable asked Seamus.

"He was a customer. I'd never met him until two days ago, when he came in looking for a painting."

"How did he come to find your shop?"

"He said he had seen my work in a gallery in London. It looked like the type of painting he was looking for, and the gallery owner told him I own an antique art shop, too. He figured I would sell the same type of art I paint, so he came up to see what I had for sale. Florian wanted to buy artwork that had a history."

"Do you know why?"

"He said he was looking for something that reminded him of his childhood."

"We've talked to his wife, and she said he gave her your name if she wasn't able to contact him."

"Yes," Seamus said, "I talked to her last night on the phone. She hadn't been able to reach him, so she called to ask if we knew where he was. Of course, we had no idea."

The constable turned his attention to me. "Did you talk to Mrs. McDermott last night?"

"No, she called Seamus's mobile. He talked to her."

"Did you speak with Mr. McDermott when he was here?"

"Yes."

"What did you two talk about?"

"I wondered about his childhood, since he wanted a painting that reminded him of it. I asked him what it had been like and said it was nice that he wanted to remember it with a painting."

"And what did he say?"

"That his childhood was awful."

"Did you ask him anything else?"

"No. I thought he was strange. I didn't really know what to say after that."

"Mr. Carmichael? What did you discuss with Mr. McDermott?"

"We discussed the history of the painting he wanted to buy. We talked about the price, the painting's condition, other works by the same artist, some of the other paintings I have in my shop, and why he wanted to buy that particular painting."

"Tell me about the painting he wanted to buy."

"It's an old painting by the Scottish master William Leighton Leitch. Normally you find Leitch's paintings in museums, but this particular one wasn't in great shape. It had a tear in the corner and it was faded. It obviously hadn't been taken care of over the years."

"Can I see the painting?"

"Florian bought it," Seamus replied, his eyebrows furrowing.

"He bought the painting you've been describing?"

"Aye, he did."

"Did he leave it here to be shipped?"

"No. He took it with him. It was wrapped in heavy brown paper. Wasn't it in Florian's car?"

The constable shook his head, scribbling something down and then flipping through his notes. "There was no painting in the car."

"Maybe it was in the boot."

"The officers on the scene checked the boot. It was empty."

"I don't know what to say," Seamus said.

"How much did Mr. McDermott pay for the painting?"

"Three thousand pounds."

The constable had been writing in his notebook again, but he jerked his head up at the price Seamus quoted. "Three *thousand* pounds?"

"Yes. I told you, it was painted by one of the old Scottish masters."

"But you said it wasn't in good condition."

"It was still by William Leighton Leitch. That makes it very valuable."

"Valuable enough to steal?"

"I suppose so."

"What else can you tell me about the painting?"

"Not much. Well, wait—there was another man who drove up from London once he found out I had another buyer."

"Who was this man?"

"I don't know his name. He left me his number, though."

"What's the number?"

Seamus looked at me. "Where did I leave that piece of paper?"

"Check the desk in the shop. It's probably there."

Seamus excused himself and was gone for just a moment. I offered the constable a cup of tea, but he declined. When Seamus returned he was holding a slip of paper. "Here it is," he said.

The constable wrote down the number. "Can I take this paper?" he asked.

"That would be fine. Just let me write down the number in case I need to get in touch with him again."

"Why would you need to get in touch with him?"

"I told him I'd call if I ever ran across another William Leighton Leitch painting."

"Oh." Seamus copied the number and slid the paper across the table. The constable placed it in a small plastic bag.

"Now," the constable continued, "tell me more about this man."

Seamus recounted his dealings with the second man from London, the constable writing the entire time. "Did this man seem angry that Mr. McDermott had left with the painting?"

"No, he didn't seem angry," Seamus answered.

"Tell me a little bit about yourself," the constable said. "I understand you're out of prison seven or eight years now. What were you in for?"

Here it comes, I thought.

"Assault. Self-defense. It was an accident. The guy came at me first, and I was just trying to defend myself."

The constable scratched his chin. "I see. Any other past trouble with the law?"

"I got in trouble for vandalism when I was a bairn, that's all."

"But you were never charged." It was a statement, not a question.

"No, sir."

"What did you vandalize?"

"A school."

"What happened exactly?"

"Me and a group of my friends splashed paint on the side of our school. We had to clean it off as punishment."

"How about robbery?"

Seamus cocked his head and looked at the constable. "No. Nothing like that."

"The painting you had in your store sounds valuable enough to steal."

Seamus studied the constable for a long moment, then said in a measured voice, "Perhaps, but I don't know who would have done that. Maybe Florian left the painting somewhere before continuing on his trip. If you're suggesting that I stole it, why would I? I had the painting before Florian did. I could have just kept it."

The constable gave Seamus a hard look, then turned to me. "Mrs. Carmichael, was your husband here last night?"

"Yes, every minute," I said. The words came out of my mouth in a rush, almost before he had finished the question. I didn't want this to become an investigation of Seamus. He had paid his debt to society and been perfectly behaved since then. There was no reason for anyone to suspect that Seamus had done something wrong.

"I'm sure I'll be back to talk to you both," the constable said, pushing his chair back and gathering his coat and hat from the table. "Don't go too far until I've had a chance to talk to you again." He left without a backward glance.

"Should we call the solicitor?" I asked as soon as the door was closed.

"What for? Neither one of us has done anything wrong. I'm an easy target, that's all," Seamus answered, smiling down at me. I knew what he was doing—trying to get me to believe he wasn't shaken up by the constable's words, that he was in full control of the situation. But I knew better. I saw him put too much sugar in his tea out of the corner of my eye, and later that morning I saw him pacing the floor in the shop. I saw him pick up his phone, then put it down again, as if undecided about something. He was nervous.

I was relieved when Callum rang up late in the afternoon and asked Seamus to go to the pub. Seamus closed the shop early, something he rarely did, and left. As soon as he did I phoned Mr. Howe, our solicitor, and told him the story. He told me he would demand to be notified the next time the constable wished to speak to either of us. The constable was probably just covering his bases, Mr. Howe said, but he advised me to let him know right away if I heard from him again.

Instead of waiting for Seamus to come home, I walked over to Eilidh's house. She put on the teakettle and we sat in her kitchen and discussed the same things I was sure Seamus and Callum were talking about—Florian's car crash, the second man from London, and the constable's visit.

"Too bad I couldn't meet this Florian—he sounds like a hoot," she said dryly, pouring me a second cup. I slowly drizzled honey into the tea, swirling it with my spoon.

"There was something about him that I just can't put my finger on," I said. "He was pale and scrawny, but he had big brown eyes that seemed out of place on his face. His handshake was limp and cold, but you should have seen the way he looked at Seamus when Seamus wondered if Florian always carried so much cash with him…." I trailed off, wondering if that was information we should have shared with the constable.

"He paid in cash?" Eilidh sounded surprised.

"Yes. The painting was three thousand pounds, and he just handed Seamus a huge wad of money. Most people pay for big purchases with a credit card."

"Sounds like Seamus ought to be more careful about who he does business with," Eilidh cautioned.

"It's not realistic for him to do a background check on everyone who comes through the door. Even if he could, he wouldn't. That would be bad for business, to say the least." I smiled at the thought of Seamus checking customers at the door, searching their names on the internet.

"But he knew this guy Florian was strange. Maybe he should have sold the painting to the man on the phone instead."

I was getting annoyed. I knew Eilidh was trying to help, but she was being unreasonable and, I thought, rather stupid.

"Seamus wouldn't refuse to sell someone a painting just because they're strange. He's not exactly qualified to judge others. He's been in jail, for God's sake." I knew I sounded testy, but I couldn't help it.

"It was just a thought," Eilidh said in a quiet voice. I was sorry I had spoken to her that way.

"Well, he sold the painting, so what's done is done," I said. "We'll have to be more aware next time."

The front door opened and we could hear loud voices from where we sat in the kitchen.

"We're out here!" Eilidh called.

"*Shh!* Don't tell them. Maybe they'll go back to the pub," I said with a smile. "It was so quiet until they came in." Eilidh laughed, her high voice tinkling.

Callum came into the kitchen, followed closely by Seamus. They both sat down at the kitchen table. "What are you ladies talking about?" Seamus asked.

"What else? Florian and the problems he left in his wake," I said.

"Seamus told me all about it," Callum said. "Want me to tell the constable to leave Seamus alone?" Callum was employed part-time in the historic preservation office of a nearby village. He knew all the local constables personally.

"No, but thanks anyway," I said. "We don't want to draw more attention to Seamus. He draws enough himself," I said, looking at him with a grin. My big, burly husband, with his fiery red hair and beard, his huge tattooed arms and his loud voice, tilted his head back and laughed a hearty laugh.

"Callum," he said, "I needed that trip to the pub. I feel much better." He turned to me. "Sylvie, I've decided we should call Mr. Howe."

"I'm glad to hear that, because I already did."

He looked at me in surprise. "You sneak! You already called? What did he say?"

"He said he would tell the constable to notify his office before visiting us again. He also said we're not to worry, but to let him know if the constable comes around asking more questions. He thinks he's just covering his bases."

"See, Callum? I told you I didn't need to worry." Seamus winked at Callum.

"Sylvie, your man here was being a nutter at the pub, wondering what to do about this whole thing."

"What is there to do?" I asked. "We don't know anything about it. We'll just have to wait to see if the constable comes back."

Seamus and I walked home in the dark. Spring wasn't far away, but the days were short this far north. Later, while Seamus was putting a pot pie in the oven, his phone rang. He answered it, and with a quick glance at me took the phone with him into the shop. I heard him raise the cover of the roll-top desk.

A few minutes later he came back into the kitchen. "Who was that?" I asked.

"A gallery owner in London. He had a question about one of my paintings."

We sat down to Seamus's delicious pot pie and spent a quiet evening together. The thought of the constable's return was never far from my mind, and I'm sure Seamus spent a good deal of time thinking about it, too.

We were getting ready for bed when Seamus asked, "What are your plans for tomorrow?"

"Nothing. Why?'

"I thought we'd take that shopping trip to Edinburgh."

My face must have lit up like Christmas, because Seamus laughed. "We'll leave early and make a full day of it."

I couldn't wait.

CHAPTER 3

The next morning we got in the car before the sun rose over the mountains. It promised to be a beautiful day. I hated to miss a gorgeous late-winter day in the Highlands because the shadows on the mountains would be perfect for photographing, but I was excited to go to Edinburgh. We drove for two hours until we hit traffic outside the city, then we slowed to a crawl. We used the time to discuss where we wanted to go during our few precious hours in Edinburgh. We decided on breakfast at a tiny café we'd loved when we lived in the city. Then we would go our separate ways for a few hours, then meet for lunch with Greer, Ellie, and James, Greer's almost-fiancé, or so I hoped. Then shopping in the afternoon, dinner, and back home after dark.

Breakfast was quick because I couldn't wait to get on my way. Seamus laughed as he ordered a refill of coffee. "Go on, then, be off. I'll see you at lunchtime. I can't enjoy my coffee with you being so antsy."

I kissed him goodbye and, slinging my camera bag over my shoulder, walked out of the café into the brilliant Edinburgh sunshine. As always, I looked for Edinburgh Castle to get my bearings. Just seeing it there in the distance, standing guard over the city the same way it had for centuries, gave me chills. Its gray and brown hulking mass was a symbol of strength and security for the entire British Isles. I took out my camera and got a few shots of the castle in the watery early morning light.

Then I headed straight for the Royal Mile. This area of Edinburgh could be kitschy and touristy, but I still loved it. The street was alive with people, even early in the morning. Everyone, it seemed, was walking with a cup of steaming coffee. I wandered down the street, taking photos of everything that caught my fancy, from shop fronts to wynds to the cobbles beneath my feet. It was a lovely way to spend two hours, and I wound up back at the magnificent St. Giles Cathedral just before it opened. It had been a long time since I visited the High Kirk—I hadn't been since before Greer was attacked in the nave several years ago.

I stood in line to go inside, but when it was my turn to enter the nave I found I couldn't go in. Images of Greer raced through my mind. She had gone inside the cathedral for a much-needed respite while searching for her little girl, my niece Ellie, when she'd been attacked. I don't know why my feet refused to take me into the nave, but I couldn't make them walk any farther. I turned around and left. As I made my way toward the exit my thoughts turned to the time I, too, had been attacked in Edinburgh. I had stopped at home for lunch one day when a man entered the flat. Thinking I was Greer, he attacked me viciously and left me unconscious. I suffered a concussion and several deep bruises, but most of the damage had been done to my psyche. Dreams of that attack still haunted me, and I had an irrational fear it might happen again.

After leaving St. Giles I stopped at the Scottish National Gallery, where I wandered through a fascinating exhibit on Renaissance clothing and beauty. I could have spent all day there, but I was excited to see Greer. I was meeting her before lunch so we could have time together without Seamus and James. James would bring Ellie when he met us. I had spoken to Greer early that morning—very early—and agreed to meet at a coffee shop not far from where the five of us were meeting for lunch. I got there a little early, but I didn't have to wait long for Greer. We hugged as if we hadn't seen each other in years.

"When were you last in Edinburgh?" Greer asked.

"About three months ago, I think."

"Seems longer, doesn't it?"

Greer gave me a calm smile. She was dressed in silk pants and a flowing blouse. She said she had given a lecture that morning at the University of Edinburgh, where she was a tenured professor in the art history department.

"How's everything with James?"

She sighed. "Great. The only thing is he's always talking about getting married."

"What's wrong with that? I thought you were ready for the next step."

"I'm not."

"Why is he pressuring you, then?"

"He's not exactly pressuring me," she said. "He just assumes we'll be married at some point."

"Do you want to get married?"

"I don't know."

"Why not?"

"What if he turns out like Neill?" She was referring to her deceased ex-husband, who became a gambling addict and went down a frightening path of violence and fear, taking Greer with him.

"Greer, an experience that horrible could only happen once in a lifetime," I told her.

"But I can't help it. I think I'm just scared to make that commitment only to learn that James has some dark secret he's keeping from me. I was in love with Neill once, too, don't forget."

"James doesn't have any secrets. Go ahead and marry the man." I gave her arm a playful shove. I felt sorry for my sister. Though she was older than I by fourteen months, since her arrival in Scotland I had felt the need to be her protector, the shoulder for her to lean on. Of course, much of that was due to the circumstances under which she had returned to Scotland: to search for her little girl. But I had a feeling she didn't need protection from James. He was a wonderful guy who thought the world of both Greer and Ellie.

I think she needed to hear the words "marry the man." She needed validation that James was perfect for her and nothing like Neill. She sat back and crossed her legs, visibly relaxing.

I asked her to go shopping after lunch, but she had to prepare for tomorrow's lecture. "Text me pictures of the stuff you get, though," she said. We sometimes shopped that way, even online, and it almost felt like we were shopping together.

We talked for a while, then walked over to the pub where we were supposed to meet the others. James and Ellie were already there. When James saw us he stood up and wrapped me in a smothering hug, then kissed Greer. Ellie hugged me, too, and held my hand so I would sit next to her. James held our chairs for us as we sat down.

"You're such a gentleman," I noted. "I don't think Seamus has ever held a chair for me. When it's time to sit down to a meal, it's eat or be eaten with him. He doesn't have time for the niceties."

James grinned. "That's part of his charm, huh?"

"Of course."

The three of us were looking at menus when Seamus sauntered up to the table. "Miss me?" he asked.

James stood up and shook hands with him, obviously happy to see his almost-brother-in-law. Seamus wrapped Greer and Ellie in giant bear hug, wrinkling Greer's silk outfit and making Ellie cry out that she couldn't breathe. I got a chuck under the chin.

"Where have you been?" I asked. "I thought you'd be early...and starving."

"Och, lost track of time, I guess," he said, glancing at his watch. He rubbed his hands together. "Got a menu for me?"

I handed him a menu as he sat down next to me. The five of us were silent as we made our choices, but after the server took our orders we all started talking at once. There weren't many things Seamus missed about living in Edinburgh, but seeing Ellie was one of them. He wanted a full update.

"How're you doing in your classes?" he asked.

Ellie beamed. "I love school. I love my teacher and my friends."

"And what are you doing in your free time?"

Ellie knew this was Seamus's favorite question because he wanted to hear how much she loved to paint.

"Painting! I use all the paintbrushes and paint you gave me for Christmas."

"I can't wait to see your work," Seamus gushed.

We talked about the weather, my photography, Seamus's work, new exhibits in the museum where James worked as a curator, and Greer's classes at the university. It was a comfortable and enjoyable meal, and it ended all too soon when James announced he had to get back to work. We took leave of each other outside the pub with promises to get together again soon, then Greer and Ellie headed back to Bide-A-Wee, James returned to the museum, and Seamus and I stood on the pavement.

"Are you going shopping with me?" I asked him.

"Och, no. You're better off without me in a shop, I think."

"I don't agree, but whatever you say. What are you going to do until dinner?" I asked.

"I don't know," he answered. "I might head over to the National Gallery for a wee bit."

"I was there this morning," I told him. "The Renaissance exhibit is wonderful." I kissed him and squeezed his hand. "Text me when you're ready and we can have dinner."

He walked off in the direction of the National Gallery and I headed straight for one of my favorite shops. I spent the next several hours trying on clothes and shoes, texting pictures of each ensemble to Greer for her feedback. Finally, laden with shopping bags, I browsed a camera shop while I waited for Seamus's text.

When we met a half hour later, he laughed as I lumbered up to him with all my bags. "Did you buy one of everything?" he asked, his face a wide smile.

"Almost!"

"Well, thank Florian. We wouldn't be here if he hadn't bought that painting."

Florian flitted across my mind like a ragged storm cloud, but I pushed him from my thoughts. "Let's not talk about Florian, however grateful I am to him," I suggested.

We had chosen to meet at a small romantic restaurant down a cobbled lane just a few blocks from Bide-A-Wee. The hostess took my bags and told me she would put them in the coat room until we finished our meal.

Seamus held my hand in his as he told me about his day. Besides the National Gallery, he had visited several tiny art galleries and two other museums dedicated to particular artists. He had clearly had a relaxing and thoroughly enjoyable day.

He didn't need to be told what I had done all afternoon—my shopping bags told the story. We chatted over a glass of wine and three courses of French food, savoring our final hours in Edinburgh.

"So what's happening with Greer and James?" Seamus asked. "I assume you girls talked about it before we all met for lunch."

"We did," I said, twisting the stem of my wine glass. "She doesn't know if she's ready to get married again. James is ready, and I think he's putting pressure on her without realizing it. He just assumes it's going to happen."

"What do you think?"

I thought for a moment. "I think they'll get married eventually, but James may have to wait a while. Greer has to feel totally comfortable with the idea first." I took a sip of wine. "She thinks that because her first husband was a scunner James will be, too."

"She knows better."

"I don't think she does. She's convinced herself it's true." I wiped a crumb off the table. "It must be hard for her, worrying that James is hiding secrets, that a second marriage will turn out like the first and end in total disaster."

"James is a good man. Anyone can see that," Seamus answered.

"But she's not seeing things clearly right now. At least not when it comes to love and marriage."

"Are you about ready to go?" Seamus asked, looking at his watch. "It's getting late."

I let out a long breath. "I guess. It's been such a nice day. The only thing that would have made it better is spending a little more time with Ellie."

"Aye, but we'll be back before long."

We drove home in the dark, each lost in our thoughts. Mine were all about Edinburgh, wondering how my photos would turn out. I didn't ask Seamus what he was thinking about, but looking back, I have a pretty good idea.

CHAPTER 4

We were exhausted when we got home, so we tumbled right into bed. I left my purchases on the kitchen table. In the morning I felt a little thrill going through them again, putting the clothes on hangers and taking the shoes out of their boxes. I had also bought a few items to decorate the gallery. I put the receipts in a little pile on the kitchen counter to remind myself to file them later.

Seamus and I ate breakfast quickly because we wanted to open the shop and the gallery early. He always did that after we closed for a day. Seamus whistled as he bustled around the shop, rearranging displays and welcoming visitors.

Time passed quickly in the gallery that day. I worked on a photo collage of Highland cows and entertained quite a few visitors who had come to see both Seamus's paintings and my photos. As soon as we locked the doors for the evening, Seamus started dinner and I threw the first of several loads of laundry into the washing machine, then readied the next pile. Seamus's jeans crackled when I picked them up—I grimaced. He had left something in one of his pockets. He did it all the time. My demands that he take everything out of his pockets before putting them in the laundry fell on deaf ears.

I reached into the back pocket and pulled out a slip of paper—a bank receipt for a deposit showing a modest balance at a bank where we didn't have an account.

"Seamus," I called, "what on earth is this receipt?"

There was no answer. I heaved the load of clothes onto my hip, carrying the receipt in one hand. I went through the kitchen to the washing machine and called for Seamus again.

"Seamus!"

He came in from the shop a moment later.

"What are you doing?" I asked.

"Just double-checking the lock," he answered.

"Oh." I waved the receipt at him. "What is this? I found a slip from Clydesdale Bank in your jeans. We don't have an account there."

Seamus looked at the paper and then at me. He shook his head. "I dinnae know."

"What do you mean you don't know? How did the receipt get in your pocket?" I could feel my cheeks getting flushed. Was he trying to hide something from me? How dare he!

"I must have picked it up from the ground thinking it was trash to throw away in a bin, then forgot about it."

I gave him a long look. "Are you sure about that?"

"Of course. Like you said, we don't have an account there."

He sounded sincere. I crumpled up the paper and threw it into our recycling bin. "I was afraid you were hiding something from me," I teased.

He smiled and I deposited the laundry in the basket near the washing machine.

Seamus surprised me after dinner by offering to do the dishes. We usually split the work at mealtimes—he made the meal and I cleaned it up. But I was tired and had other chores to do, so I pecked him on the cheek and left the room.

A few minutes later I went back into the kitchen to start another load of laundry. He was crouched near the recycling bin; I had clearly startled him.

"What're ye doing?" I asked.

"Nothing. Just taking the recycling outside."

"Why? The bin isn't full."

"I guess you're right. It can wait, then."

"No need to make more work for yourself," I said with a smile.

He laughed. "Certainly not."

He put the bin back where it was and joined me as I walked back to the bedroom to fold laundry. He stretched out on top of the bed, and we didn't talk much as I folded and put away clothes. I had some worrying thoughts running through my mind and he seemed exhausted and preoccupied.

It wasn't long before he was sound asleep, still in his clothes. I finally acted on my dark thoughts and went into the kitchen, quietly pulling the bedroom door closed behind me so I wouldn't wake him.

I pulled the recycling bin out from its spot under the sink. There were only a few pieces of paper at the bottom; the receipt was nowhere to be seen. Seamus had taken it out. My stomach sank.

Seamus was hiding something from me.

Why? What was so important about that slip of paper?

My first instinct was to barge into the bedroom, shake him awake, and demand he tell me why he was hiding a receipt from a bank where we didn't have an account. But I held back, vowing to think this through before making any wild accusations. I trusted Seamus. *Didn't I?* I wanted to give him the benefit of the doubt.

I needed to talk to someone about this. I needed another person's perspective. I didn't want Seamus to think I didn't trust him, but if the receipt belonged to him he didn't deserve my trust.

I was in a quandary. I picked up my mobile phone and texted Eilidh.

I need to talk to you. About Seamus. Can I come over?

Callum is wide awake. He'll hear anything we say. Can it wait until morning? He'll be at work.

I hadn't even thought about Callum. With his big mouth, he would repeat to Seamus anything I said. It was smarter to wait until morning.

Okay. I'll be over after 8.

I returned to the bedroom and woke up Seamus. He got on pajamas and crawled into bed. I faced away from him when I joined him.

"What's wrong?" he mumbled.

"Nothing. Just a slight headache."

I couldn't sleep. As if fulfilling the lie I had told, I soon developed a whopping headache. I dragged myself to the medicine chest and swallowed two aspirin, then turned on the television in the living room, hoping to find a boring program that would lull me to sleep on the couch.

I found a program, but it was anything but boring. It was a true crime show about a jilted wife. She had discovered her husband's infidelity and confronted him. In a rage, he killed her and dumped the body in a river. A family out for a picnic discovered it the next day floating downstream. My breath came in short bursts as I watched the drama unfold. As much as it horrified me, I couldn't tear myself away.

Thoughts of me confronting Seamus swirled around inside my head. He was brawny and much bigger than I—I would be no match for him. The entire pathetic scene played out in my mind. I pictured Eilidh, having searched for me for two days, forcing her way into my house and finding my body on the bathroom floor. I thought of my mother and how she would react when she got the phone call that I had been killed in my own home, probably by my husband, her beloved son-in-law. Greer would have to wait until Ellie was older to tell the dear child that her aunt had been the victim of a homicide committed by Uncle Seamus, an ex-convict who couldn't be trusted.

It wasn't long before I was in a full-blown panic. I shook my head to dislodge the ugly thoughts; it did nothing but intensify my headache. Headaches like this didn't strike me very often, but ever since I had suffered the concussion I got them whenever I was under a lot of stress or hadn't gotten enough sleep, both of which were happening now.

I opened the door leading to our small conservatory off the kitchen and lay down on the settee, closing my eyes in the darkness, willing my headache to disappear. About an hour later I was still lying there, rocking from side to side, when Seamus opened the door and turned on the light.

"Turn it off, please," I moaned.

"Sylvie, what's wrong? Why are you out here?" he asked as he switched off the light.

"My head is killing me," I said.

"Why aren't you in bed?"

My mind filled anew with pictures from the television show and my own vivid imagination. "I couldn't sleep and didn't want to wake you up." That was true, though a little misleading. My desire to let him sleep had nothing to do with my thoughtfulness and everything to do with my survival. Somehow I had convinced myself that Seamus was going to kill me when he found out I knew his secret. Damn that television show.

"Come to bed, Sylvie. You'll feel better if you sleep in your own bed." He reached for my hand and helped me back into the bedroom. I lay down on the bed, protesting that I didn't want to disturb him, but he was adamant that I try to sleep in there. "The sun will wake you up at dawn in that conservatory, love," he said. "You can have a lie-in tomorrow morning if you sleep in here. It'll be darker."

I couldn't argue any longer. The pain in my head was excruciating and all I wanted to do was sleep until the headache was gone. I heard him creep to his side of the bed and crawl under the covers carefully, trying not to disturb me. Eventually I fell asleep.

When I awoke the next morning the blinds were closed and I could hear birds singing outside. I moved gingerly in case my head still hurt, but my headache seemed to have disappeared. It took me just a moment to recall what had happened the previous night, and when I remembered my stomach lurched. I opened the blinds and looked out on a sunny day.

The gorse below our bedroom window was beginning to bloom, its bright yellow flowers mocking my sour mood.

I looked at the clock. Seamus would have opened the shop and gallery two hours ago and was probably manning both by himself. I checked my phone for texts—there had been none since the texts with Eilidh last night. I pulled on a pair of jeans and a sweatshirt and passed through the kitchen to the gallery, grabbing a cup of tea on my way.

Sure enough, Seamus was in the gallery, discussing one of his paintings with a prospective buyer. Once a customer showed a real interest Seamus's artwork, I usually called him in from the shop so he could talk to them about it. A conversation with the artist often tipped the customers' indecision and convinced them to buy a painting, and this customer was no exception. She bought one of Seamus's smaller paintings of a Highland snowstorm. He wrapped it for her and extended his hand in thanks. The high color in her cheeks told me she was delighted to meet the artist in person.

When the woman had left, clutching the painting under her arm, Seamus turned to me and kissed my cheek, giving me a concerned look. "How're ye feeling today, love?"

"A little better, I guess. Can you mind things here for a bit whilst I run over to Eilidh's? She has some herbal tea I'd like to try."

"Of course. Take your time." He gave me a long look through narrowed eyes. "Are you sure you're all right?"

I nodded. "Still a bit groggy, I guess." I hoped he wouldn't guess that I knew about the receipt before I could talk the whole thing over with Eilidh.

Her house was just up the road, and she was expecting me. Even before I was in the house she asked, "What's going on?"

I told her about finding the receipt in Seamus's pocket and his dubious story about picking it up to throw away later. Then I told her he had taken the receipt out of the bin after I left the room. She cocked her head. "Are ye sure of all this?"

"Positive. I searched that bin and the receipt isn't there. He's the only one who could have taken it out."

"I wonder what he's all about," she mused.

"Then you don't think I'm a nutter for doubting his story?"

She shook her head. "No. He's definitely up to something."

My lip twitched, which it did whenever I was concentrating on a problem. "Seamus isn't a secretive person, though. He's always been straightforward, even when he's talking about something that might hurt me."

"Maybe it's something different this time."

I thought about the dreadful television show I had watched and voiced the words we were probably both thinking. "Do you think there's another woman?"

The pitiful look Eilidh turned on me made my knees tremble. She didn't have to answer my question. She suspected another woman, too.

"I'll kill him," I said between clenched teeth.

"Let's not jump to conclusions, Sylvie," Eilidh warned. "It could be something entirely different."

"Such as?"

She fumbled her words. "Well, maybe...maybe he's...saving to get you a gift."

"There's an awful lot of money in that account, Eilidh," I said. "What gift could he possibly get me that's so expensive?"

"A new house?"

"No way. We love our house. Neither one of us wants to move." I paused, wondering if one of us would be moving out in the future. *What if the other woman moves in?* I shook my head to reassure myself. *If anyone is moving out, it's Seamus. Damn him.*

"A boat? Maybe a posh trip somewhere?"

"You know we're not the type to take posh trips," I said, rolling my eyes. So far Eilidh wasn't being much help. "What do you think I should do?"

"You want me to follow him?"

"What are you, a detective? Follow him where?"

"I don't know. Wherever he goes."

"The only place he goes without me is the pub, and then he goes with Callum."

"Want me to check his search history whilst you two are out?"

Should I ask her to do that? "Maybe," I replied. I was reluctant. I trusted Seamus. Or at least I used to. "Aye, that might be a good idea," I said after a moment.

Eilidh leaned forward, almost gleeful. "When should I do it?"

I hesitated. "Let me think about it. I don't know." I needed to talk to someone else. Greer.

I mumbled to Eilidh about forgetting something at the gallery and left in a hurry. She gave me a bewildered look as I bolted past her.

I ran back to my house, but stopped before I got to the gallery door. What would I say to Seamus when he asked where the tea was? Would he ask why I was out of breath? I didn't know where to turn. I had to find a private place to call Greer.

I had left my car keys on my bureau, so I went around to the back of the house, hoping Seamus hadn't seen me from inside the shop. I went in through the back door, stole through the kitchen, and tiptoed into the bedroom. I grabbed the car keys, scrawled a note for Seamus in the kitchen telling him I had to go for groceries, and left. I drove through two villages before I felt calm enough to stop by the side of the road and shut off the engine. I pulled out my phone, praying there was mobile service, and dialed Greer's number.

No answer. I should have expected that, given her busy schedule.

I sighed and slumped back against the driver's seat. What was I going to do? Part of me wanted to cry and scream and go home to my mother, part of me wanted to kill Seamus, and part of me just wanted information about the bank account.

I sat there for several minutes, wondering how I should behave when I got home. Should I give Seamus the cold shoulder? Should I pretend nothing was wrong? Should I light into him as soon as I got through the door, demanding to know more about that receipt?

I sat lost in thought until the mobile rang. It was Greer.

"Hi. Sorry I missed your call. What's new?"

I took a deep breath, suddenly feeling silly about everything.

"Sylvie? You all right? What's wrong?" *She sounds like Mum.*

"I think Seamus is cheating on me," I said in a rush.

"What?!" she exclaimed. "What makes you think that?"

I told her the story of the receipt. She listened without interrupting. When I had poured out all of my suspicions she asked, "Do you think you might be overreacting a bit?"

I leaned forward and put my head against the steering wheel. "I don't know. Maybe I am. That's why I called you, to get some perspective."

"Maybe you need to take a step back and think about this before you go jumping to conclusions."

"But don't you think the whole thing is weird?"

"I don't know. What if he took that receipt out of the recycling bin and shredded it to keep someone stranger's bank information private? It would be like him to try to protect someone else from identity theft. You shred receipts, don't you? We always shred any receipts we don't need."

I thought for a moment. "I guess he could have done that."

"It's the most likely explanation."

I leaned back against the headrest, feeling more relaxed. Greer had given me just what I needed—a reality check. Of course Seamus had shredded the receipt to protect the identity of whoever dropped it. The thought of him lying and cheating had filled me with sadness, rage, and self-pity. I smiled for the first time in hours.

"I feel so much better. Thanks."

"That's what I'm here for."

When I returned home, Seamus was looking for me. "Where'd ye go?"

"I had to run to the grocery store." Just one last lie, so he wouldn't know I had left in a panic to call Greer.

"Is everything all right?"

I smiled at him, relieved that Greer had talked some sense into me. "Fine."

"Headache gone?"

"Yes. I feel much better."

"Care to go to the pub for lunch?"

"Sure." The morning waned. We took care of a few more customers, then put out the "Be Back Soon" sign on the front door and walked hand-in-hand to the pub. I ordered the onion soup, Seamus had a giant burger and chips. We sat at a table for two in the back, and we were enjoying each other's company when Seamus's mobile phone rang.

It was our solicitor, Mr. Howe. Seamus covered the mouthpiece.

"The constable wants both of us to go to the station to give statements about the day Florian was in the shop." He spoke into the phone again. "Will you meet us there?"

He rang off a moment later. "He'll meet us there."

"Why does the constable need statements from us?" I asked.

"I don't know. There must be something they're not telling us."

The light mood had vanished, replaced by pensive thoughts and, in my case, anxiety over whether the constable would grill Seamus about his past.

After we closed the shop and the gallery for the evening we drove to the police station. Once we got there the police took us into separate rooms, probably so they could compare our stories about Florian. The detective questioned Seamus first, and then it was my turn. Mr. Howe sat in with both of us while we were questioned.

I wasn't able to give them much; Seamus had been the one dealing with Florian. I had only met him for a few moments. The police asked if I spoke to Florian's wife, Alice, and also if I had any other information. I told them that Florian drove to and from our home without headlamps, and that he had paid for his purchase with a large wad of cash. The officer seemed to find those revelations interesting, but I wasn't able to provide any further information.

Having cautioned the police to contact him again if they needed to conduct further questioning, Mr. Howe left. Seamus and I compared notes on the way home. Seamus had also mentioned to the police that Florian had arrived without his headlamps on, and he recalled cautioning Florian because the highland roads were twisty and narrow. I had forgotten Seamus's warning, and either Florian forgot, too, or he ignored it. I wondered if Florian's decision to drive without lights had cost him his life.

"I asked questions, but the police wouldn't tell me anything about the crash," Seamus said.

"I didn't even ask. I was so afraid that we were going to be charged with something that I wasn't even thinking about the way Florian died."

"I've been wondering about it ever since we heard."

"I assumed it was just a one-car accident."

We hadn't eaten dinner, so we sat down for a late meal when we got home. It was the first chance I'd had to look at the local paper, which had been delivered early in the morning, and I sat down to peruse it while Seamus fried eggs and potatoes in a skillet.

"Seamus, look at this. There's an article about Florian in here."

He came and stood behind me, reading over my shoulder.

The driver involved in Wednesday's fatal one-car crash outside Cauld Loch on the village road has been identified by police as 57-year-old Florian McDermott of London. It is unknown at this time what caused McDermott to drive his car into a tree by the side of the road, but the crash scene is under investigation. According to McDermott's wife, McDermott was visiting the Highlands in search of a piece of artwork.

I looked up at Seamus. "This doesn't shed too much light on what we already knew."

He shook his head. "Doesn't Callum know everyone in the village? I should ask him what's going on in the constable's office. It seems like they're doing a lot of investigating for a one-car accident. I mean, for us to be questioned separately is unusual."

"Call him up," I suggested. Seamus looked at his watch.

"I'll call him in the morning. Let's eat."

It had been a long day. I fell into bed, exhausted. Seamus put his arm around me as I drifted off.

There was another article about Florian in the paper the next morning. "Here, read this," I told Seamus as he brought two bowls of porridge to the table. He read the short paragraph aloud.

Police have determined that the one-car accident two days ago involving London resident Florian McDermott may have involved foul play. The circumstances of the crash continue to be investigated.

He put the paper down and looked at me. "Now we know why we've been questioned," he said.

"Do they think we actually had something to do with it?" I asked.

"I doubt it. It worries me, though. We're probably the last people who saw him alive."

I shivered. "I hadn't thought of it that way," I said in a quiet voice. I lapsed into silence, wondering about Florian's last moments. "I hope he didn't suffer," I said after a long pause.

"Me too," Seamus said.

"Why would someone have caused Florian's crash on purpose?"

"I don't know. We'll probably find out, though, either from the police or from the newspaper. It seems to be a more urgent story now that the police think it was more than just an accident."

"Someone must have known he was up here in the Highlands." I shivered again. "Whoever it was must have been following him. That means the person must have been right outside the night Florian died. Och, I can't stand thinking about it."

"It's possible, I suppose. But there are lots of things that could have happened. Maybe some drunk ran him down. Maybe Florian complained about a meal or miffed someone at his bed and breakfast and they decided to get back at him. It could have happened in a million ways and for a million different reasons. We shouldn't assume there was a killer lurking outside our home, waiting for Florian to leave." Seamus's voice was hard. I think he was trying to convince himself of his words, too.

"But the painting was gone. Doesn't that suggest that whoever was responsible for Florian's accident wanted the painting? What about the man who was in here the next morning? Maybe he wasn't in London, like he said when he called. Maybe he was already in Cauld Loch. Maybe he followed Florian to steal the painting."

Seamus shrugged. "The cop who questioned me mentioned that I knew the value of the painting. He implied that I might have sold the painting, pocketed the money, and then killed Florian to get the painting back because it was by one of the Scottish masters."

I couldn't believe what I was hearing. "And you didn't think to tell me this?" My voice was an octave higher than usual.

"Sylvie, calm down. It won't help to get all riled up. Mr. Howe made him stop that line of questioning. We have to stay calm." He spoke quietly, as if someone could hear us.

"And what did he say about it? Is he concerned?"

"Aye. I have a meeting with him this morning. I'll talk to him whilst you mind the shop, if that's okay with you."

He left an hour later. I didn't know what to do with myself afterwards. At first there were no customers, so I tried to stay busy working on my cow collage. But after I spilled the glue, ripped one of my prints, and tripped over the leg of my work table, I decided it was time to put the art supplies away and do something else.

I needed to move, to keep my whole body busy. I fetched cleaning supplies from the laundry room and attacked the floor of the shop with a mop and bucket. I was viciously scrubbing a particularly persistent spot of dirt when the bell jingled. I looked up, brushing a strand of hair from my face. A woman walked into the shop. She was dressed in dark green corduroy trousers and even darker green Wellies. A tan trench coat, too big, was cinched at her waist, and she wore a drab gray hat over elbow-length brown hair. She had thick glasses, behind which protruding eyes blinked once.

"Be careful!" I warned. "I just mopped over there." I stood up and leaned the mop against the wall, dragging the bucket behind me. "How can I help you?"

The woman looked around, then her bulging eyes came to rest on mine. "Is Mr. Carmichael here?" she asked in a cultured English accent.

"No, but I expect him back soon. Is there something I can show you?" I swept my arm around, taking in the entire shop and gallery.

"No, I just wanted to speak to him about something. I'll come back."

My mind was churning. What could this woman possibly want with Seamus that she couldn't share with me? "I'm Mrs. Carmichael," I offered. "I'd be happy to tell him you stopped by. What is your name?"

"You're Mrs. Carmichael? I guess I can talk to you. I'm Alice McDermott. Florian's wife."

"Oh, Mrs. McDermott, I'm verra sorry for your loss." I paused for a moment, not knowing what to say next. *This poor woman has been through so much.*

"I came to see if your husband has any information about the night Florian died. The police aren't sharing much with me."

"Seamus and I have both talked to the police, and they haven't told us very much, either. We've gotten more information from the local paper than the police."

"You probably don't know any more than I do, then. I drove all night to get here from London. I was hoping for more information," she said, her shoulders drooping. "I've read the newspaper accounts of the accident online."

My heart went out to her. She deserved to know what had happened during her husband's final moments. She deserved to know that something was being done to find the person who killed Florian.

"Won't you come into the kitchen and sit down, Mrs. McDermott? Can I get you some tea?"

"That would be nice, yes. And please call me Alice."

Alice was still there when Seamus came home an hour later. I introduced them and they chatted in the kitchen for a long time while I tended to customers in the store. We were starting to see a more steady flow of tourist traffic because the name of the shop had been on the television news, somehow connected with the death of a stranger from London. It didn't matter that we knew nothing about the "accident." Simply being in the news was enough to draw a crowd through our doors, and Seamus and I weren't complaining.

That afternoon Alice asked shyly if I would mind driving her to the scene of Florian's accident so she could see the place where her husband breathed his last. She was surprised by the narrowness of the road Florian was driving the night he died, by the twists and turns leading drivers past Cauld Loch on one side and thick woods on the other.

We spent a long time at the scene. The police had removed the yellow crime scene tape, so Alice was free to wander around without worrying about destroying any evidence. The trees, which had been broken in the accident, lay strewn in her path. She picked her way over them carefully, her long hair becoming tangled in the riotous green growth of the forest. I was self-conscious watching her, so I left her to her private grief while I waited in my car. She didn't say anything on the ride home, except to thank me for taking her.

Alice stayed for dinner that evening. Seamus cooked while the three of us talked about Florian.

"We didn't have any children," Alice told us. "And his parents and sister have all passed away."

I nodded solemnly, trying to imagine what it would be like to live through such a tragedy alone.

"I just wish you could go home with more information," I said, shaking my head.

"I suppose I didn't really expect to learn much," Alice said. Her eyes gleamed with the sheen of unshed tears. "I just wish I understood *why* he felt the need to come up here."

"He was looking for a painting that reminded him of his childhood," Seamus said, stirring the contents of a pan on the stove.

"Did he find one?" she asked.

"Aye, he did. A beauty by an old Scot named William Leighton Leitch."

"And he bought it?"

"Aye, but it wasn't among the wreckage," Seamus said.

"What do you think happened to it?"

Seamus pulled on his beard. "I've no idea. Looks like someone took it from the scene of the crash."

"Who would do such a thing?" Alice asked, her eyes wide.

"I don't know," Seamus answered. "The painting wasn't even in good shape."

"I wish I could have seen it. I would love to see what he chose to connect him to his childhood in the Highlands."

"I can tell you about it, and I can probably find a reproduction online, but I'm afraid you can't see the real thing until the police find it."

"Tell me about it."

"I don't know its real name, but I called it 'Old Kirk in the Field.' There's an old, crumbling stone church in a wood. An old woman is gathering flowers in front of the church. The painting had lots of yellows, greens, and browns. It wasn't in the best shape—it had a tear in one corner and the paint was rather faded, as happens over time when paintings aren't cared for properly."

"It sounds lovely," Alice said.

"It was," Seamus said.

"How did you come to have it?"

"I found it in a store in Edinburgh. Just happened to go in on a lark. Wasn't even hung up. It was on the floor, leaning against the wall. As I told the other man who was interested in buying it, I'm sure the shop owner didn't realize what a treasure he had there on the floor."

"There was someone else interested in buying it?" Alice asked.

"Aye, but I gave Florian first dibs, so the man left empty-handed the next morning."

"It was very kind of you to offer it to Florian. I'm sure he appreciated that." She gave us a tired smile, a faraway look in her eyes. Then she fixed her gaze on Seamus. "Do you suppose the other man had anything to do with Florian's death?"

"Don't see how he could have," Seamus answered. "He didn't find out that I had sold the painting to Florian until the next morning, and by then, according to the police, Florian had already been in the accident."

She grimaced. "Who would steal something from the scene of a fatal accident?"

Seamus came over to the table with a dish bearing three pieces of fish. "I'm sure the police will find the painting, Mrs. McDermott," he said in his most soothing voice. "It may take a wee bit of time, though." Alice merely shook her head.

"Alice, you must be exhausted. We've kept you here all day. Do you have a place to stay tonight?" I asked.

"No, I was going to drive back to London."

"That's an eight-hour drive! You'll be driving all night," I scolded. "You can stay here."

Alice demurred at first, but finally agreed to stay in the guest room. "I'll just go right to bed after dinner and be out of your hair first thing in the morning," she assured us.

"Och, don't worry about that," Seamus boomed, happy to be moving away from emotional territory and toward more practical matters. I smiled, knowing how much he hated being in the room when women were getting tired and teary. "I'll clean up dinner whilst you and Sylvie make sure you have everything you need."

Alice accompanied me to the guest room and I left her watching television after making sure she had blankets and towels. Seamus and I retired early, not wanting to be in the living room where our voices might bother our guest.

Once in bed, we talked about our visitor in low tones "Do you think she'll be all right driving to London by herself?" I asked. "It's such a long drive."

"She made the drive up here okay, love. I'm sure she'll be fine going back," Seamus answered in a loud whisper.

"I wonder if they'll ever recover that painting," I said.

"Who knows?" Seamus replied, turning over onto his side. "Don't exhaust yourself asking questions that have no answer, love."

CHAPTER 5

Alice left early the next morning after a quick breakfast of porridge and tea. Seamus hadn't even opened the shop when she pulled away from the house, giving us a limp wave as she drove out of sight.

"Poor thing," I said, shaking my head.

"You need to stay busy today, love," Seamus told me. "Why don't you finish your collage and we'll get it hung up?"

I was in a better frame of mind to finish my project that day, and it was hung up by mid-afternoon. Hairy Highland cows stared at me from the gallery wall, their huge brown eyes watching placidly as I greeted customers. I smiled every time I caught a glimpse of those wonderful cows.

Later that evening, Greer called. Seamus had joined Callum for a pint at the pub and I had the evening to myself.

"What's new?" she asked. I gave her all the details of Alice's sad visit.

"Sounds like she's lost. Looking for anything that could connect her to her husband in death. So sad," Greer said, her voice quiet.

"I felt awful for her," I said.

"Any fallout from that receipt?"

I was surprised by the question. I hadn't even thought about it since the night before Alice arrived. "You know, it completely left my mind."

"Good. Let it stay out of your mind. I'm sorry I brought it up."

"I think I would know if Seamus was up to no good. I mean, we live and work together, right? I'm bound to know everything he's doing." I laughed. It had been silly of me to suspect Seamus.

Greer laughed along with me, then we talked about our mum, who had told Greer that I never invited her to visit. That meant two things: First,

Mum and Greer had been talking about me, and second, it was time to invite Mum up to the Highlands.

Seamus called after I hung up with Greer. He wanted me to meet him and Callum at the pub. On the way I stopped at Eilidh's house and invited her to go with me.

"Sure!" she agreed. She pulled on her coat and locked the door, then turned and linked her arm through mine. "What's wrong, Sylvie?"

I told her all about Alice's visit, from her arrival to the minute she left almost twenty-four hours later. "I just can't seem to get her out of my head. The whole thing is so verra sad."

"Why would she want to see the place where her husband died?" Eilidh asked, giving an exaggerated shiver. "Seems morbid, if you ask me."

"Wouldn't you want to see where Callum died if he died far away from home?"

She slapped my upper arm lightly. "Bite yer tongue, Sylvie. It's bad luck to talk like that."

"Well, wouldn't you?" I persisted.

"Maybe," she relented. She bit her bottom lip. "But I wouldn't want to stay all day then spend the night with strangers, especially if they were the last ones to see him."

"I think she felt just the opposite. I think it was comforting for her to ask us about his last hours, since we knew what he was doing and where he was staying."

"Twisted."

"Och, Eilidh. You just can't put yourself in other people's shoes."

"I can, too. If there's one thing I have, it's sympathy."

"The word is *empathy*, and I don't know if you have any." Elidih's mother and my mother were sisters. We had grown up just down the road from each other and spent our childhoods together. That's why Eilidh and I could talk to each other—or bicker—like sisters.

An endearing frown appeared on her face. She looked at the ground and I knew I had been too harsh. "Sorry," I mumbled. "I just think it was good for Alice to spend some time with us."

"That's okay," she said, giving my arm a squeeze.

When we arrived at the pub Seamus and Callum were holding court in the back, laughing with a group of men over a game of darts. Seamus waved us over.

"What took ye so long?" he asked in a loud voice. He pecked my cheek. "Why the long face, love?" he asked.

"Alice." I didn't say any more. I wriggled out of my coat and motioned for the server to bring me a pint. Eilidh ordered a glass of wine. The game of darts ended and Seamus asked me if I wanted to join the next one.

"Sure," I told him. The men started to hoot, but Seamus shushed them. "She's better than most of you scunners," he said to a chorus of raucous laughter. I stepped forward, my toes touching the line on the floor. I stood still for a moment, judging where the dart needed to go, then I let it fly.

Bull's-eye.

The men, including Seamus and Callum, gave a collective shout of surprise. I had earned their respect with one flick of my wrist. Eilidh stood by, her hand over her mouth. "How did you do that?" she asked in wonder.

"Easy. Just takes practice," I answered. "Want to try?"

"Okay." She smiled and set her wineglass down on the closest table. Callum handed her a dart and she stepped up to the line. She drew back the dart and threw it hard toward the wall. It turned sideways and bounced off the dartboard, falling to the floor with a tinny thud. A sympathetic murmur rose from the group. Eilidh picked up her glass and took a sip of wine. "How did you get so good at this game?" she asked me once the next man was taking his turn.

"Seamus got me a dart set for Christmas one year and showed me how to use it. It was set up in our flat in Edinburgh. I'll have to get that out and put it up. Maybe on the patio. That would be fun," I mused.

"You'll have to show me how to play," Eilidh said, swirling the wine in her glass. "I stink at it."

"I'll teach you, and you'll be beating these fellows before you know it," I promised. I glanced at Seamus, who was tilting his head back, laughing at a joke one of his friends had told. Eilidh watched the men play darts with a thin-lipped smile, obviously wishing she could play well enough to be invited into the game again. Several times, Seamus or Callum or one of the others called me over to take my turn, but after each turn I went back to sit with her. We chatted about the things I'd bought in Edinburgh and how Greer and James were doing. Eilidh wanted to know all about Greer's reluctance to marry James. We also talked about the flowers she wanted to plant in the spring and where she should look for a job as a bookkeeper. She had been out of work for months, and her attempts to find a new job had met with no success. In addition to his part-time job, Callum worked for a construction firm, so he was often at work. Eilidh was getting bored at home, waiting for a job to open up.

At the end of the evening, after I had soundly defeated all the men at darts, Seamus flung his arm over my shoulders and kept it there the whole way home. Callum and Eilidh took their leave of us as we passed their cottage, both of them waving as they disappeared into their darkened living room.

"That Eilidh isn't much fun when she's out of the house, is she?" Seamus asked after we had walked a short distance from their house.

"She just doesn't know what to say or do around other people," I explained. "She's a bit of a homebody, and that's where she's happiest, around Callum and us."

"She's a wee wet blanket, if you ask me," Seamus said.

"She can't help it. She doesn't see much of Callum, she's bored at home, and she's discouraged because she can't find a job." The hills and valleys of my emotions over the last couple days were taking their toll, and my eyes glistened with tears as I looked up at his face.

"You're not crying now, love, are you?" he asked, a touch of hesitance in his voice. I laughed, knowing he was lost when women cried.

"No, just sniffling a bit," I answered, reaching up to hold the hand draped on my shoulder. "I'm just tired, that's all."

CHAPTER 6

Our lives went back to normal for about a week, with the exception of the welcome increase in visitors to our shop due to our recent mentions on the television news. Then came the chilly spring day when a man walked into the gallery and announced that he was there to see Seamus.

Seamus was in the shop tending to another customer, but as soon as he finished I called him into the gallery.

"Mr. Carmichael? My name is Felix Barnaby, and I own the Lundenburg Gallery in London. I'm on holiday, staying in Edinburgh, but I wanted to come up here to talk to you about showing your paintings in my gallery."

Seamus's mouth gaped. Even *I* had heard of the Lundenburg Gallery. It was known worldwide for its forward-looking artists and quality, eclectic exhibits.

"Aye, sir, I would be honored!" Seamus declared, pumping Felix's hand over and over.

"I saw some of your work in a shop in Edinburgh, and the owner of the place told me you're the type of person who has to be seen to be believed." He grinned. "I agree. At least physically, you're definitely not the type of artist I'm used to working with."

"Och, I expect not," Seamus said, his eyes squinting from his wide smile.

"That's exactly what I'm looking for. My gallery needs an infusion of new blood, and you seem to fit the bill perfectly. From what I've seen, your paintings are incomparable. Do you mind if I take a look around?"

"Not at all. Please," Seamus said with a sweep of his arm, "make yourself at home. Care for some tea? Or a dram?"

"I'll take tea, please. Black."

Seamus looked at me with pleading eyes, probably remembering all the times I'd told him that waitressing was not in my job description. But this time was different—I could see how excited Seamus was, how he longed to talk to Felix, how he wanted to be available to answer questions or offer commentary on his paintings. I gave him a quick wink and disappeared into the kitchen to put on the kettle.

When I returned with a tea tray, Seamus and Felix were in the studio, talking like old friends. Seamus had pulled up another stool and both men were perched on their seats at the counter. Seamus was talking about his techniques and his pricing and Felix had pulled out a phone and was searching for possible exhibition dates. I tended to the customers while Seamus and Felix chatted.

"We get a lot of collectors who are interested in the type of art you create," Felix was saying. "I've been promising them an exhibition soon, so when I stumbled upon some of your paintings last weekend, I knew your work was just what I've been looking for."

"I'd be happy to do a show any time you want," Seamus said.

"Normally it isn't done like this, as I'm sure you know. Usually there's a long lead time before an exhibit, but when I heard about you I just had to get the ball rolling. I'd like it to be as soon as possible. It looks like you have plenty of paintings in your inventory."

They talked awhile longer and Felix left after promising to have his assistant contact Seamus to set up a date for the exhibition. Of course it would require Seamus to stay in London for a couple weeks during the exhibit, and probably meant several shorter trips before then. Felix explained that he liked to get artists closely involved in the exhibition setup.

After Felix left, the shop and the gallery were empty for the first time all day. Seamus gave a whoop of excitement and drew me into his arms, swinging me around in a circle like a doll.

"This calls for a celebration!" he said with a laugh. "We're going out to dinner to the fanciest place we can find! Go get dressed!"

He waited in the studio until closing time, then he hurried to change into a suit and tie and we left for dinner. We ate at a seafood restaurant several villages away, one we'd heard of but had not had a chance to visit. We always said we'd wait for a special occasion, and this was a *very* special occasion—Seamus's paintings were going to be shown in one of the most well-regarded galleries in Europe.

Just two days later, Felix's assistant called with a few dates for Seamus to choose from. He chose the date closest to the summer solstice. That was less than three months away, so he needed to clear his schedule, have several new paintings ready to go to London, and have a solid idea of how he envisioned the exhibit's physical space. Felix invited Seamus down to London as his personal guest, to tour the gallery and "get a feel" for the place, as Felix put it. It was just a two-night stay, round-trip on the train, so we felt it would be best if I stayed to mind the shop and gallery while Seamus went to the big city. He left the following week.

I missed him while he was gone. Callum and Eilidh invited me for dinner the night he left, but the next night I ate a bowl of porridge by myself in front of the television after triple-checking that the door was locked. As I got ready for bed I wondered if Alice was spending every day in the same manner, missing her husband and being alone. She had certainly seemed forlorn and lost while she was in the Highlands.

Seamus was full of excitement and ideas when he returned. Felix had spent time with him each day, he said, and Felix's personal assistant, a man named Peter, had been exceptionally helpful by providing photos and ideas from past exhibits.

"Wait'll you see it, Sylvie. You'll be staggered at the gallery. It's huge. And the space for my exhibit is *three rooms*. One is going to be painted stark white, one in a blue the color of Cauld Loch, and one in a dark brown. Paintings will hang from the ceiling and the walls. Just wait until you see it," he repeated. His eyes gleamed with excitement.

I was thrilled for him, but I knew my wedding vows would be put to the test in the coming weeks—my job, my career, was going to take a back seat to Seamus's art. He would be spending countless hours in the studio, perfecting paintings he had already started, creating more, and getting still more ready to be shipped to the Lundenburg Gallery. He was in a constant state of high energy, and I must confess it started to get on my nerves.

The weeks went by without any further information about Florian's death. We had expected the police to come to a conclusion about the accident and, hopefully, to arrest someone for Florian's killing. Seamus and I seldom talked about it, but Alice was never far from my mind and I thought about the accident a great deal. One night I brought up the subject at dinner.

"Do you think it would be frowned upon if we rang up the police and asked them what happened to Florian's case?"

Seamus put his fork down long enough to stare at me. "After all we went through for the sake of that man, I would think you'd never want to hear his name again."

"But don't you wonder what happened? *Someone* was responsible for his death. Don't you worry that that person is still around?"

"No, but now that you put it that way, I suppose I'll have a hard time getting to sleep tonight," he replied with a smirk.

"Doesn't it bother you that the person who caused the accident has gotten away with murder?"

"If it would help you put Florian's death in the past, then I think you should ring up the constable and ask about the status of the case."

The next morning I did just as Seamus suggested. The constable didn't have much new information to report, except to say that the investigation was no longer being handled by the village police.

"Who's handling it now?" I asked.

"Scotland Yard."

"Scotland Yard?!" I repeated.

"Yes, ma'am. I'm afraid I can't help you any more than that."

After I hung up I went in search of Seamus. I found him in the studio, looking sideways at a painting he had done of the Cairngorms, a spectacular mountain range in the eastern Highlands and one of Scotland's natural treasures.

"That's one of my favorites," I said, walking into the room.

"I don't know," he mused. "I'm not sure if I should include it in the exhibit."

"You definitely should," I advised. "I talked to the constable. Florian's case has been taken over by Scotland Yard. Can you believe it?"

Seamus ran his hand down the length of his beard. I couldn't tell if he was paying attention to me or not.

"Mmm?"

"Would you listen to me?" I demanded, my voice rising in volume. "I said that Florian's case is being investigated by Scotland Yard."

He looked at me and blinked once. "Why?"

"The constable couldn't give me any more information."

"That's odd," Seamus remarked.

"Do you think I should contact someone at Scotland Yard?" Now I had his full attention.

"Absolutely not!" he roared. "Leave it well enough alone! It's none of our business, so just let it go," he added belligerently.

I poked my index finger into his chest. "Don't talk to me that way again, Seamus. I'm warning you."

"You asked for my opinion."

"I didn't ask you to yell your opinion. I'm trying to have a discussion with you and all you're interested in is your work. I'm getting tired of it."

"Sylvie, you know this is very important to me. To both of us. Can you just let me work in peace for a bit and we can talk later?"

I spun on my heel and stalked out of the room, fuming. *How dare he talk to me like that?*

I sat down at the desk in the shop, waiting for the first customers of the day to arrive. My fingers tapped on the desk relentlessly, a staccato non-rhythm. I was furious, and a headache had started to spread behind my eyes. *That selfish, pig-headed scunner. I can't wait until he's in London for two weeks.*

One hour and a dozen customers later, the pain in my head was so bad I was having a hard time keeping my eyes open. The overhead lights seared into my vision, making it difficult to help anyone who came through the door. Reluctantly, I asked Seamus to mind the shop while I went to lie down. He took over for me, but not happily. I didn't care.

Several hours later I woke up in my darkened bedroom, wondering what time it was. My headache seemed to have lessened, so I stood up slowly and checked outside. Still daylight. I went to the kitchen and made myself a cup of tea, hoping the caffeine would help dispel the remainder of the pain in my head. I peeked into the studio, where Seamus was painting. I opened the door quietly. "No customers?" I asked.

He spun around. I had surprised him. "Och, I put up the closed sign so I could get some work done."

"I'm feeling a bit better, so I'll open up again and stay until dinner."

"You don't have to do that." He looked down at the paintbrush in his hands. "Sylvie, I'm sorry about earlier. I'm just nervous about this gallery exhibit, that's all. I don't mean to take it out on you."

I walked over to him and put my hand on his arm. "I know you're nervous. I want to help you, not be a hindrance. But I just wanted your opinion about something that's important to me, and I didn't expect you to blow up like that."

"I'm sorry," he mumbled.

"I can't quite hear you," I said with a smile.

"Yes, you can. Now you're just being a pest," he said, using his free arm to pull me into a hug. "Am I forgiven?"

"Yes. But don't ever talk to me that way again," I warned, wagging a finger at him.

"I won't. Did I cause that headache?"

"Yes. But it's getting better, and now that you've apologized properly, it'll probably get better even faster." I went to the shop and turned the closed sign to "open." "Now get back to work so you can take the evening off," I called to him.

That night at dinner he opened a bottle of wine for us to share. My headache was gone and he was in a conciliatory mood after our argument. He poured me a glass and clinked his against mine. "What do you want to do whilst we're in London?"

I pondered for a moment. "I don't know. I'll only have a day or two, so I'll have to choose carefully."

Seamus looked at me in surprise. "What do you mean, you'll only have a day or two? You'll be there the whole time."

"What?! How can we leave the shop and gallery for two weeks?"

"We'll put Eilidh in charge. She can tend to things whilst we're gone. I need you with me in London, Sylvie."

"Why?"

"For moral support. And because you're my wife and I want you to be where I am." He reached out and ran his finger down my cheek.

"But putting Eilidh in charge? She's not the brightest bunny in the forest, if you know what I mean. She might just give away everything whilst we're gone."

"We'll check on her every day. We can call her anytime and she can call us anytime if she has any problems or questions. And we'll pay her, of course. That's got to be a help to them."

"You have this all figured out, don't you?"

"I do, love. I want you to come to London with me. For the whole time."

So I was headed to one of Europe's most glamorous cities with Seamus. As much as I loved the Highlands, I couldn't wait to see what London had in store for the Carmichaels.

CHAPTER 7

As the date of the exhibit grew closer, Seamus and I were busy getting things ready for the show and getting our business in order. I spent extra time framing photos, making canvas prints, and ordering extra business cards so Eilidh could hand them out to customers.

Seamus was a firecracker of nerves, easy to anger and quick to forget it as he prepared for the exhibit. He traveled twice more to London before we left for the opening, both quick overnights to assess the progress of the exhibit plans and speak in person with Peter, who was handling arrangements very capably. Eilidh came to the shop several times to learn how to use the cash register, how to handle credit cards, and what to do when an online order came in. I showed her where inventory was kept so she could keep the walls covered in art if anything was sold.

When the day arrived to leave for London, Seamus and I were ready. Eilidh came over early in the morning to take her place behind the counter and bid us goodbye.

Seamus and I had argued, of course, over how to travel down to London. I suggested we drive and take two days to enjoy the sights between the Highlands and the south of England. Seamus disagreed, saying he couldn't stand to wait. In the end we took the train to London in one long day. I was thankful Seamus won the argument—I couldn't have borne his edginess another minute, and a second day on the road would have sent me straight 'round the bend.

We arrived in London before twilight. It was two nights before the solstice, so fingers of sunlight cast lingering rays of pink and orange warmth along the streets of London until after nine o'clock. I wanted something to eat as soon as we put our bags in the hotel, but Seamus insisted upon visiting Lundenburg Gallery first.

The gallery was closed to customers when we knocked on the glass door, but Felix let us in and greeted us warmly. He introduced me to Peter, who was busy snapping photos of Seamus's work. The paintings, he said, would be prominently displayed on the Lundenburg website. The paintings we had shipped hung from the walls and the ceiling across three rooms, and I walked through the spaces by myself while Seamus and Felix talked in Felix's office. The rooms were cold and quiet. Peter had gone to the front desk to pull up his photos on the computer.

I tried to gaze at the paintings through the eyes of a guest. They *were* striking and beautiful, there was no doubt. I felt a swell of pride for my husband and his talent for sharing his vision with a paintbrush and canvas.

He came looking for me just a bit later. "Well? What do you think?"

I walked over to him and put my arms around his chest. "I think it's perfect. I'm so proud of you." He kissed the top of my head and took my hand. "Ready for dinner? Felix wants to take us out."

The conversation at dinner, as I should have known, was focused on the work that needed to be done before the show and the clients that Seamus would be expected to coddle at the opening. There were more such clients than paintings.

The following morning, Seamus helped at the gallery while I took a walk. I had only been to London a couple times. It was a long distance from my childhood home in Dumfries, and we didn't have the money for holidays when I was young. This trip was an experience that I might never repeat, so I wanted to explore every cranny before it was time to return to the Highlands.

I started out not in search of Big Ben or Westminster Abbey, but of the Getty Images Gallery. I could see the more well-known tourist attractions over the next two weeks. As a photographer, I was interested in seeing what one of the world's largest photography galleries was like on the inside. It was renowned for its collection of photos dating back to the mid-eighteen hundreds and for its five-story industrial space. Armed with my mobile phone's GPS, I took the Tube to Oxford Circus and walked up Oxford Street until I came to Winsley. From there I turned left onto Eastcastle Street and found the gallery on an unassuming corner, looking like any other glass-front establishment in an old redbrick building.

But when I went inside, I was greeted with a soaring, gorgeous space filled with pictures displayed in creative and unique ways. Whatever other plans I had for the day evaporated as I wandered through the rooms of photographs, in awe of the camera's abilities and of each photographer's vision and imagination. I forgot to eat lunch, I was so engrossed in the exhibits. It wasn't until Seamus texted me that I remembered I was supposed to meet him for an early dinner.

We met near the Lundenburg at a small restaurant, where we swapped stories about our days and where, Seamus said, Felix would be meeting us for coffee after dinner. I knew I wouldn't have much time alone with Seamus over the next two weeks, so I enjoyed our dinner together. I promised to take him to the Getty Gallery before we left for home.

Felix arrived as we were finishing a dessert of fruit and cream. He kissed my hand before he sat down, apologizing for taking up so much of Seamus's time. Then he turned to Seamus. "My friend, I've received a rather disturbing visit from Scotland Yard."

I was immediately on alert. Scotland Yard? What did they want with Felix? And why was he mentioning it to Seamus?

Seamus set his fork down, fixing Felix with a wondering stare. "Care to share with us?" he asked.

"I rather think so," Felix replied. "It was about you."

"Me?!" Seamus asked, his eyes bulging. "What about me?"

"It seems Scotland Yard heard about your exhibit at the Lundenburg and had some questions for me about my dealings with you."

"What did they want to know?"

"They asked if I was familiar with a certain painting by William Leighton Leitch. They wanted to know if I had seen that particular painting when I was in your shop."

"Obviously not, since I sold it before I met you," Seamus replied. "Was there something peculiar about the painting?"

Seamus shrugged. "I didn't think so, besides the fact that it was painted by a Scottish master. It wasn't even in good shape when I sold it. Torn, faded. I got a nice price for it because of the identity of the artist."

"So why is Scotland Yard asking me about it?"

Seamus recounted the story of Florian's purchase and all the mysterious events that followed. "Sylvie and I have been interviewed by the local police, but we don't know anything. They suspected that I arranged to steal the painting back so I could sell it again upon Florian's death."

I could do nothing but gape, still astonished by the news that Scotland Yard knew of Seamus's whereabouts and wanted information about him.

"Did they have any other questions about Seamus or the painting?" I asked Felix.

"They wanted to know where Seamus is staying, and so of course I had to tell them."

"They probably knew it already, since I've used my credit card at the hotel," Seamus told him.

Felix nodded. "I'm sure you're right. I don't know how any of this might affect the opening at the Lundenburg, but it just may be good for business. Who knows?" He grinned, albeit with a worried look in his eyes. "There's no such thing as bad publicity, right?"

Seamus gave an unsure smile. "I hope so."

"Is it common knowledge that Scotland Yard is asking questions about Seamus?" I asked.

"Probably not, but it's pretty easy to search for a particular person online. If anyone planning to come to the opening looks up Seamus, it might be there."

I whipped out my mobile phone and punched the internet app. I did a search for "Seamus Carmichael" and his web page, along with several pages of mentions and information, popped up. "Nothing about Scotland Yard, as far as I can tell," I said, "but there's no telling what might be there by morning."

"Well, there's nothing we can do about any of it," Felix said with a sigh. He signaled to the waiter. "We'd like three coffees, please."

I didn't want coffee and the last thing Seamus needed was caffeine, but neither of us spoke up. I didn't touch mine, but Seamus drank his dutifully. Felix and Seamus talked while I sat in silence, wondering what Scotland Yard had learned about Florian and his accident.

Should I call Scotland Yard? No. What could I possibly tell them? I rubbed my temples. Seamus noticed.

"Are you getting a headache, love?"

"I think so," I replied in a tired voice.

"Go on back to the hotel and lie down. I'll get you a cab. I'll be along later, after Felix and I have talked." He excused himself and left to hail a taxi while I gathered my jacket and handbag.

"Feel better, Sylvie," Felix said. I managed a wan smile.

"Thanks, Felix. See you at the opening tomorrow."

Seamus managed to hail a cab. He paid the driver in advance and directed him to take me to our hotel straightaway. I was grateful.

When Seamus climbed into bed several hours later, my headache was in full force. I moaned as he lay down.

"What did Felix say?" I mumbled.

"Just more about the opening," he said quietly. "You need to sleep. Stop talking."

I didn't need the advice repeated. I turned over and slept, waking up without a headache and in good spirits. How I wish Seamus had been able to do the same. He told me the next morning that the coffee had done its work and he was restless all night long. He was in a foul mood, and I told him so before he left for the gallery.

"You'd better practice being charming before you get to Lundenburg," I told him. "You've been nothing but cross since you got up."

"It's because of that coffee," he snarled. But I suspected it was more than that—he was unnerved that Scotland Yard had been asking about him.

As Seamus was preparing to leave for the gallery there was a knock at the door. He yanked it open and gave a start when he saw that both men standing in the doorway held badges from Scotland Yard. I looked at them in surprise. I didn't even have time to get nervous about their visit before Seamus invited them in. They sat on the couch and motioned for Seamus and me to sit opposite them on the foot of our bed, then they proceeded to ask us questions about Florian, the events on the night he had died, and the painting he had bought. They didn't seem interested in Seamus or me as suspects in Florian's death, and their visit ended cordially and quickly.

After Seamus had closed the door behind them he turned to stare at me. "What do you make of that?" he asked.

"It seems like they're just gathering information. I felt strangely at ease whilst we talked to them," I answered.

"So did I. I've been wondering when they would show up, and now that they've been and gone I feel much better."

"Good. Now maybe you won't be so grouchy."

He smiled, his good humor restored, and left for the gallery.

Left to myself, I formed a plan of action for the day. I was to meet Seamus, Felix, and the rest of the gallery's employees at Lundenburg early in the evening. Felix thought it would be a good idea for me to attend the opening cocktail party with the important, wealthy clients so I could regale them with stories about Seamus.

But that was hours away; I had plenty of time to put my plan into action. First, I searched online for Seamus's name again. There it was—a brief mention in a gossip column that said that officers from Scotland Yard had visited Lundenburg Gallery. There was no speculation about the reason for the officers' visit, just a tantalizing item that was sure to invite juicy gossip about their presence.

Next, I placed a call to Scotland Yard. I had no idea how to find the people in charge of the investigation, so I was put on hold again and again until I was finally connected with one of the detectives who had visited Lundenburg Gallery the previous day. As I had feared, he was "not at liberty to divulge any details of the investigation."

So I was stuck. But all the discussion and worry about the investigation had made me start wondering again about Florian's wife. I was concerned about Alice and hoped she was beginning to recover from the shock of her husband's death. I pictured her back in our Highlands shop, lethargic, her big eyes confused and unbelieving.

She had given me her address when she visited. I scanned my list of contacts until I found her, then put her address into the GPS on my mobile phone. Her house was in Highgate, over three miles from our hotel. I decided to walk—that would use up some of my nervous energy.

It was a beautiful day. Summer solstice, the longest day of the year. A warm breeze bore me gently along the bustling streets as I made my way from King's Cross toward Highgate. Not having spent much time in London, I was unfamiliar with its various sections and neighborhoods. The actual city of London, I had learned, was a one-square-mile area in the center of a much larger metropolitan area. I passed through lovely neighborhoods with homes behind trees coming into full leaf, run-down areas with flats stacked one on top of another like children's blocks, and areas with expanses of parks and gardens.

I stopped for a cup of tea at one quaint shop. As I sat at a tiny sidewalk table I decided I would ring up Alice and let her know I was coming. She seemed glad to hear from me and suggested that we meet for lunch at a café in Highgate rather than at her house. I continued on my way, looking forward to lunch at the end of this walk.

As I moved closer to Highgate, the streets became less crowded. People living this far from the city center, I presumed, would take the Tube or other public transportation. The detached homes were spaced a wee bit farther apart, and the buildings of flats were larger and surrounded by more trees.

The village of Highgate sat atop a hill. Walking up the incline, I almost didn't notice my breath coming faster as I gazed at the beautiful buildings, the churches, and the lovely shops and cafés I passed.

I found the café easily. It was a small restaurant, with al fresco dining in a shaded English garden behind the stone walls of the building. It was charming, with dappled sunlight glowing among shrubs and groupings of plants covered in tiny pastel blooms. Alice had asked me to meet her in the garden. She wasn't there when I arrived, so I chose a table by a tinkling fountain and took several photos with my mobile phone while I waited for her.

She arrived shortly, stepping out of the café and onto the flagstones of the garden in black trousers that were a tad too short, a white peasant blouse, and black brogues. Her long brown hair hung loosely down her back as it had when she visited our shop. I thought she would look much nicer if she cut her hair and wore it in a more modern style, then felt ashamed for silently criticizing her appearance. Her huge eyes blinked behind thick glasses as she walked toward me. I stood and shook her hand, feeling that a hug would be too familiar and unwanted, then motioned for her to take the seat opposite mine.

"I hope it's okay to sit here," I began. "It's such a pretty spot, and we can hear the water from the fountain."

"That's fine," she said. "It's my favorite table."

We sat in silence for several moments, both of us looking around the garden. I suddenly felt awkward—maybe this hadn't been such a good idea. I shifted my gaze back to the table and found her looking at me.

"I...I just thought you might like to have a bit of company. I'm in London for a couple weeks, so I had the idea to ring you up and see how you're doing."

"Thank you. I'm doing all right, all things considered."

"Have you gotten out much?"

She nodded. "A little bit."

"Have you heard any more about the accident?" I wanted to ask her if she knew Scotland Yard was investigating Florian's death, but I didn't want to upset her.

"Not really. Scotland Yard has taken it over. They don't share details of their investigations."

"So you know about Scotland Yard. I didn't want to mention it for fear it would upset you."

She waved a hand limply, as if to shoo the idea away. "I know about it. I was probably the first person they interviewed. They wanted to know how well we got on, if we ever had rows, that kind of thing."

"I can't believe it! Did they actually think you had something to do with his accident?"

She gave a half-hearted shrug. "I suppose when someone dies under suspicious circumstances, the spouse is always the one they look to first."

"But you're obviously grieving. How can they be so insensitive?"

"It's really all right. I expected it," she said with a touch of annoyance. "Anyway, I suppose they're done with me and have moved on to other people."

I could see my questions had upset her, so I vowed not to mention Florian again. A server brought us menus and we looked at our lunch choices, the falling water and the birds for accompaniment.

When the server returned, I ordered a glass of lavender lemonade, a selection of finger sandwiches, and a small salad. Alice ordered a glass of iced tea and fish and chips. We chatted about the weather while we waited for our food, and as we ate Alice told me her favorite places in London and suggested I visit as many of them as time allowed during my visit. She showed a polite interest in Seamus's show, but I got the feeling she didn't want to talk about art. She wrote down a few restaurant names for me and told me I *must* visit them before going home. I was surprised—Alice didn't strike me as a foodie, but she was well acquainted with several restaurants I had read about in travel and food magazines.

Alice was an enigma. She looked dowdy and simple, but she spoke in posh tones and was clearly knowledgeable about the finer points of London culture.

We took leave of each other after our leisurely chat. She suggested a couple shops I might enjoy in Highgate, and she pointed me in the direction of the Tube in case I didn't feel like walking all the way back to the hotel.

I took my time browsing in the shops she suggested. Highgate was indeed a lovely, upscale village. I longed to explore some of the streets leading away from the village center, but time was growing short. I still had to return to the hotel, shower and change my clothes, and meet Seamus and Felix for a glass of wine before the opening. I hopped on the Tube and was back in King's Cross in just under twenty minutes.

I put on one of the two fancy dresses I had brought to London, secretly hoping I would need to buy one or two more before returning home. It was a striking black evening dress with a square neckline, tiny cap sleeves, and a flared skirt. I wore it with simple black high heels and my hair in a chignon. Seamus had become so used to seeing me in jeans and a long-sleeved t-shirt that he probably wouldn't recognize me.

When I walked into the restaurant, carrying my beaded clutch and a filmy black wrap, he was waiting at the bar, talking to Felix, a highball glass raised to his lips. He saw me and did a double-take. He put his glass down and came over to me, beaming. "I can't believe you married the likes of me!" he exclaimed with a laugh. I looked him up and down. He was resplendent in a traditional Scottish tartan kilt, complete with belt, sporran, sgian-dubh, kilt pin, hose, and ghillie brogues.

"You look wonderful, my laird!" I said with a laugh.

He led me over to Felix, who kissed my hand and bowed. I felt like a princess.

"My wife is meeting us for dinner after the opening, but I asked her to come for a glass of wine beforehand," he said. "Let's give her a few more minutes, then we'll head over to the gallery. Everything is ready. It's going to be a wonderful evening."

I glanced at Seamus, whose hand was shaking almost imperceptibly as he lifted his glass to his lips. He had had plenty of gallery shows in the past, but this one was different. This was the *Lundenburg*. He was understandably nervous—this was a huge step forward, and his future as an artist hinged on the opening's success.

I ordered a glass of mineral water. I could feel Seamus's anxiety seeping into my tingling hands and couldn't stomach anything stronger. As the bartender handed me my drink, Felix said, "Ah, there she is," and turned to look at a woman walking toward us.

"Sylvie, Seamus, I'd like you to meet my wife, Chloe," he said with pride in his voice. He introduced us and we all shook hands. Chloe was a petite woman, with purple-red hair cropped close to her head. She wore an ivory dress embroidered with gold accents around the neckline and the hem. Her gold high-heeled sandals added three inches to her height, but she was still several inches shorter than I. The four of us found a tall table where we could stand and talk. Felix and Chloe, accustomed to these openings, appeared at ease. Seamus and I probably looked like nervous schoolchildren.

Chloe made a valiant attempt to calm our nerves. She wanted to know where I had been sightseeing and offered some of her own favorites. She gave us a list of restaurants and pubs near our hotel, and she asked about Cauld Loch and where we had lived before that. She even wanted to know how we met. Seamus told her how he happened to be visiting Dumfries in search of Morton Castle, a nearby ruin that was almost impossible to find without very specific directions. He was standing on a corner in town, scratching his beard and wondering where he could buy a map, when I walked by. I assumed he was a vagrant and I handed him a one-pound note.

"I gave the money back to her, we got talking, and the rest is history," Seamus said with a laugh. He loved to tell that story. "We dated for a few years and then we got married. Best thing that ever happened to me," he added with a smile, placing his hand over mine. Chloe grinned. She had done her job in getting Seamus to relax. "Shall we get back to the gallery?" Felix asked, glancing at his watch. "We want you to get settled in before people start arriving," he said to Seamus. We left the restaurant, and the men walked ahead of Chloe and me on the way back to the Lundenburg. "Don't worry about anything," she said quietly. "Felix likes Seamus. He's not going to let anything go wrong tonight. Seamus is going to be a hit. You'll play a big part, though. I'll introduce you to some of the clients, and your job is simply to converse with them and be charming."

When we arrived, Felix knocked on the window lightly and one of his assistants unlocked the door. Apparently the gallery had closed early in preparation for the opening. I stepped into the cool, soaring space. A bar was set up on an exquisitely carved wooden table near the entrance. Bottles of all shapes and sizes, filled with liquids of all colors, sparkled under the bright white lights. Silver ice buckets held bottles of white wine and an array of glasses was displayed behind the bar. The exhibit space was dotted with small tables, each with twinkling votive candles.

I accepted a glass of white wine from the bartender, just to give my hands something to hold. I had no intention of drinking it—my nerves were causing my stomach to do flip-flops. Seamus was talking to a few of Felix's employees over on one side of the gallery and I was by myself. I wandered over to the first room of Seamus's paintings and walked slowly through it, admiring his work and marveling at how I had seen all these paintings come to life from blank canvases. So many people would see these paintings tonight for the first time, but I had lived with them for months, and in several cases, years.

The exhibit space was quiet. The murmurs coming from the main gallery subsided into the background as I walked deeper into the room, mostly looking up at pictures of places I recognized—John o' Groats, Moray Firth, the Cairngorms, Corrieshalloch Gorge, the Isle of Skye, Ben Nevis, Loch Torridon, and so many others. The pictures represented all the seasons in the Highlands, but especially spring, Seamus's favorite.

I turned when I heard heels clicking across the gallery floor. It was Chloe. "Sylvie, people are starting to arrive. Come with me and I'll start introducing you to some of the collectors." She offered me her arm and I linked mine in hers. She patted my arm and offered me the same reassuring words she had said at the pub.

"Don't worry about a thing. Just be yourself. Seamus is going to be a hit." She led me over to two men standing near the bar.

Chloe whisked me from one group of collectors to another, always making sure the conversation moved along, always keeping a discreet eye on people milling around the exhibit. She was more valuable than any of Felix's employees. And she was charming—the collectors all seemed to know and like her. In spite of my rattling nerves, I began to relax and enjoy the opening. I caught Seamus's eyes several times and he would grin and wink at me. I could hear him laughing throughout the exhibit. He was obviously having the time of his life.

I was talking about one of Seamus's paintings to a couple interested in purchasing it when I noticed out of the corner of my eye a small group of people standing nearby. Chloe was with them. Without even looking, I could see the color of her hair.

I promised to introduce the couple to Seamus before the evening was over. When they moved on to another painting, with pledges to buy at least one of Seamus's works, I turned to Chloe and her companions, a tall, solid man with dark hair and a hint of scruff on his face and a woman of medium height and blond hair, with a generous mouth and large blue eyes.

It was the man who visited our shop the morning after Florian died—the one who was interested in buying the William Leighton Leitch painting. I wondered if Seamus knew he was here.

My eyes must have betrayed my surprise, because Chloe raised her eyebrows and motioned to the couple with her.

"Do you know each other?"

I recovered myself quickly and said, "Good evening." The man responded with a smile and a nod of his head, and the woman shook my hand with long, graceful fingers.

"Sylvie, I'd like you to meet Dr. Hagen Ridley, one of my coworkers." Dr. Ridley gave me a look—was it a warning?—that stopped me from relating the story of how we had met. Chloe continued. "This is Thea, Hagen's date for the evening." She winked and smiled at the two of them.

Chloe and Dr. Ridley were coworkers? I realized I didn't know where Chloe worked or what she did for a living. I would ask her at dinner. It seemed rude to ask her now.

Dr. Ridley was interested in Seamus's paintings because, he said, they reminded him of a more contemporary version of William Leighton Leitch. That was odd. Why hadn't he shown any interest in Seamus's artwork when he visited the studio? That had been the perfect opportunity to speak to Seamus about his paintings without the distraction of highfalutin collectors milling about.

"Is there a particular painting I can tell you about, Dr. Ridley?" I asked.

"Please, call me Hagen. I'm just taking my first reconnaissance around the gallery," he said.

Chloe responded for him. "Hagen studies Scottish art, so he's always interested when there's a Scot artist in the gallery."

"Scot artists have a rugged way of expressing themselves on canvas. I find it fascinating to meet Scot painters, to find what makes them different than painters from, say, France or Spain," Hagen said, gesturing widely with his hands to encompass the paintings in the gallery. I merely nodded, not versed in the differences among painters from different countries.

Hagen moved away, gently taking Thea's arm and gliding along on his wing-tip shoes, which were much more cosmopolitan than the boots he wore when he visited the Highlands. I wanted to follow him to ask him more about his trip to our studio, but I had a hunch that was something he didn't want to discuss.

I didn't see him again that night. I tried to get Seamus's attention to ask him if he had seen Hagen, but he was busy talking to people for the rest of the evening.

We all heaved a sigh of relief when the last few collectors left and the gallery doors were locked. Seamus was buzzing around, his eyes bright. He held a glass of mineral water, which had been in his hand so long it had lost its fizz.

"How are you feeling?" I asked him.

"I feel great!" he answered. "What did you think? How do you think it went? Did you meet people? They were braw!"

I laughed. I hadn't seen him so excited in a long time. He was in his element—the evening had been perfect for him. He had met new people and talked about art for hours. Felix, who had been talking to two of his assistants by the bar, came over and put his hand on Seamus's arm.

"Seamus, the evening was a huge success, both for the gallery and for you. The collectors loved you and your art." He nodded toward me. "Having such a pretty woman helping you didn't hurt, either." He winked.

Seamus let out a whoop, probably the first one ever heard in this hallowed gallery. Felix and Chloe laughed. I smiled and shook my head, grateful that the night was over and we could decompress with some dinner and a stiff drink.

"Where should we go for dinner?" Felix asked. "Seamus, the choice is yours. Anywhere you want. Though it's late, so your options might be limited to pubs at this point."

"A pub sounds like just the thing," Seamus said, rubbing his hands together. "I'm starving."

Felix left his assistants in charge of closing up while he and Chloe and Seamus and I left to find a pub. We found one that was dark and quiet, an upscale place, where we didn't feel outrageous in our fancy clothes. Several of the patrons, dressed conservatively in suits and loosened ties, smiled and stared at Seamus as he walked in looking every inch like an ancient Highlander.

We sat at a round table in the back and ordered a round of whisky. We looked at menus until the drinks came, then we drank to Seamus's success and started down the road to relaxation. Another round of drinks, and we drank to the success of the Lundenburg. By the time our meals arrived, we were old friends. Felix and Chloe, though dressed to the nines and clearly at home among the rich and famous, reminded me of James and Greer. They were easy to talk to and laughed often. I was comfortable with them.

"So tell us what you do, Chloe," I said during a pause in the conversation.

She sat back in her chair with a contented sigh. "I am an archaeologist for the University of London, as well as a consultant for two preservation societies. I usually work in a lab or in an office, not out in the field."

"That sounds fascinating. What sorts of things do you work on?" Seamus asked.

"Right now I'm working on putting together a grant proposal for the preservation of a building up in the Cotswolds. There's so much to do to preserve old buildings, and in this particular case it has to be done quickly, because developers are looking to tear down the place. It's ancient. They can't do that."

"Chloe, my dear, don't get all worked up about it. This is supposed to be the relaxing part of the evening," Felix said, putting his hand over hers.

She smiled at him. "I can't help getting worked up about it. You know that."

"Do I," he responded, laughing and rolling his eyes.

"Tell us about Hagen," I urged her, in part to change the subject.

"Who?" Seamus asked.

"Dr. Hagen Ridley. Chloe introduced him to me, but I've met him before." I waited for Seamus to respond.

"The name doesn't sound familiar. Where did you meet him?"

"At our shop. He was the one who came in to see the William Leighton Leitch painting that Florian bought.."

Seamus stared at me. "You're kidding. Really? He was at the gallery? I wonder why he didn't introduce himself."

Chloe had been watching our conversation like a tennis match. "I knew you had met Hagen before," she said to me. "I could tell from the expression in your eyes."

"We never learned his name. He just left us with a phone number to call in case we got in any more paintings by William Leighton Leitch."

"He studies Scot artists," Chloe added.

"What was he doing at the opening?" Seamus asked.

"He always comes when there's an artist from Scotland being featured," Felix replied. "But I don't know why he didn't introduce himself to you. I'm sure he'd love to talk to you sometime. Would you like us to set up a time for you two to meet?"

"Let me ask him when I see him at work," Chloe said. "I'll find out why he didn't talk to Seamus himself. He's not exactly shy."

"Is Thea his wife? I noticed you gave a wink when you introduced her," I said.

Chloe smiled. "It's a sweet story, really. Hagen and Thea used to be married, but they divorced because he wasn't ready for children and she was. Neither of them found anyone else, though, and as Thea got older she gradually changed her mind. Now they're dating again, and I expect to hear wedding bells again someday."

We ate in silence, then Chloe spoke again. "You know, I remember Hagen saying a while back that he was taking a quick trip up to the Highlands. I'll bet that was to see you, Seamus."

"I'm sorry to say it was an unsuccessful trip," Seamus said. "He had driven all the way from London in a hurry because he heard the William Leighton Leitch painting was in our antique shop. But someone else had expressed interest in the painting, so I gave that person first dibs on buying it."

Chloe gave the table a light smack with her hand. "That's right. Hagen told me about it. Then the poor man who bought the painting was killed in a car crash. Did they ever recover it during their investigation?"

"Not that we know of," Seamus said. "As a matter of fact, that's why the detectives from Scotland Yard called on Felix and paid us a visit at our hotel."

Chloe looked at him in surprise. "Felix didn't tell me that. What did they want?"

"They asked questions about Seamus and how I met him," Felix answered. "Seamus, what did they talk to you about?"

"Just more questions about how I knew Florian—he's the man who bought the painting—and what happened the night he died."

"Why have they taken over the investigation from the local police?" Chloe asked.

Seamus shrugged. "Who knows. I assume because Florian was from London and the police up in Cauld Loch exhausted all their leads."

I debated whether to tell Seamus that I had been to see Alice earlier in the day. I didn't think he'd be very happy to hear that, so I opted to keep it to myself for a while. I certainly didn't want to mention it in front of Felix and Chloe.

Chloe shook her head. "Poor man," she said again.

Felix left the table to take a call from one of his assistants. He came back smiling, and told us that the evening had been even more successful than he first realized. Quite a few of Seamus's paintings had been either sold or spoken for by the collectors at the opening.

"And this was just the first night," Felix told Seamus. "You've got almost two more weeks here. What do you say we set up a makeshift studio in the gallery and you can work whilst you're here?"

Seamus looked at me, his eyes twinkling. "Sounds braw, man!"

Life couldn't get any better for Seamus.

CHAPTER 8

I explored London like a tourist for the next several days. I saw Covent Garden, Westminster Abbey, Parliament, Buckingham Palace, and countless other sites. My feet ached from walking so much.

I didn't see much of Seamus, as he was busy going back and forth between the hotel and the gallery, painting by day and meeting with collectors and customers by night. We would usually meet for dinner quite late, after the gallery had closed, but I lunched alone. A couple times I called Eilidh while I ate, to check on things and chat. Things back at the shop seemed to be going well.

One morning I was walking through Harrods, gawking at the department store known the world over for quality, service, and history, when my mobile rang. It was Chloe.

"I called to see if you'd like to meet me for lunch," she said.

"I'd love that!" I exclaimed. Eating lunch alone was getting tiresome. We agreed to meet in a few hours and I continued my exploration of Harrods.

When we met, at a café near Covent Garden, Chloe kissed me on both cheeks. I smiled, remembering what Mum always said: "That's how the beautiful people greet each other."

We found a table outside and sat down. Chloe wanted to know where I'd visited and what I wanted to see, then she offered her own suggestions for not-to-miss destinations.

After we ordered, she leaned forward in her chair. "Sylvie, I talked to Hagen. He told me something absolutely fascinating. Have you ever heard of Christian Fletcher?"

I thought for a moment. "I don't think so. The name doesn't sound familiar."

"I didn't think so. She lived almost four hundred years ago."

"No wonder I don't know her," I said with a laugh.

"Christian Fletcher was born in the early sixteen hundreds," Chloe began. "She was married to a man of the cloth, a Reverend Grainger. The reverend was the leader of the Kinneff Church in the village of Kinneff, Scotland. Christian and her husband lived in a house next to the church—like a vicarage.

"During the mid-sixteen hundreds, as you may recall from your history books, Oliver Cromwell was mounting an invasion of England's neighbor to the north. One of the places he was keen to secure was the Castle Dunnottar. This happened to be the place where the Honours of Scotland, or the Scottish crown jewels, were kept. The Scottish crown jewels consist of three pieces: the crown, the Sceptre of Scotland, and the Sword of Scotland.

"Christian was a friend of the lady of the castle, and together they devised a plan to save the Honours from the invading army. Christian would spirit the Honours away from the castle in bags of flax. She would drop the Honours from a high window in the castle to her maid, Elizabeth, who would wait below, out of sight of any soldiers who might be approaching.

"When Christian and Elizabeth had buried the Honours in bags of flax, they lugged the bags through the woods and across the fields and woods to Reverend Grainger, who was waiting for them with a coach. Elizabeth never returned to Kinneff Church. It's believed she knew too much, so Christian and the Reverend gave her money to leave the area for her own protection.

"Christian then hid the Honours in cloths, under a floorboard in Kinneff Church, where they remained for several years. No one ever discovered their whereabouts and Christian is considered a national hero—or heroine, I suppose—for her role in saving the Crown jewels."

"That's fascinating. I don't recall learning about that in school. So what does all of this have to do with Hagen?"

"It seems that when Christian threw the Honours—wrapped in cloths, of course— to Elizabeth, Elizabeth either caught the Honours or retrieved them where they fell. She then buried them deep in the bags of flax and waited until Christian could escape the castle and join her on the beach.

"But in the confusion that followed, some of the stones from the Crown of Scotland, which contained twenty-two gemstones and twenty precious stones, went missing. It's believed Elizabeth stole the gems before taking her leave of Christian and Reverend Fletcher."

"So is the story true?" I asked.

"It seems likely. When Christian and her husband returned to Kinneff Church, they realized the jewels were gone, but by then Elizabeth had disappeared, too, and they never found her. At some later time, new gemstones were put in the crown in place of the lost ones.

"Here's where the story becomes even more extraordinary. After Elizabeth's death, in England, a map was found among her belongings. She died whilst giving birth to her third child, leaving behind the infant and two older children. Their father eventually sent them to live in an almshouse, and the authorities ended up in possession of the map."

"So what was on the map?"

"No one knows whether anyone ever followed the map to see where it led, but it's believed that Elizabeth drew it herself, to document the place where the original Crown of Scotland jewels were buried."

"You're kidding."

"There's more: Though no one ever figured out how it happened, the authorities misplaced the map and somehow, several hundred years later, it ended up in the hands of a man who was a descendant of Elizabeth.

"That descendant happened to be friends with the artist William Leighton Leitch. Before the start of the Great War, he hid the map behind a painting Leitch had given him as a gift so that it wouldn't be found and destroyed by enemies of England. Hagen told me the whole story."

She waited as the information sunk in.

"Wait. That can't be the painting we had in our shop. Can it? Is there a map hidden behind the Leitch painting?"

"That's exactly what Hagen believes. He thinks the painting and the map were either forgotten or never retrieved after the war."

"No wonder there was a sudden interest in the painting!"

"It surprises me that there wasn't *more* interest in it," Chloe said.

"Why didn't Hagen say something to Seamus?"

"Because he wanted to study it, and the painting was suddenly going to be a lot more valuable if Seamus knew what was behind it."

"That doesn't seem ethical," I said.

"How did Seamus get the painting?" Chloe asked.

"He bought it for a song from someone who didn't know its value," I answered ruefully. Chloe nodded and I realized Seamus had done exactly what Hagen had tried to do—buy the painting for a low price, knowing it was worth more than its owner suspected.

"I wonder if Florian knew about the map," I mused.

"I assume he did," Chloe said. "Otherwise, why would he come to get it in the middle of the night?"

"It's possible he thought he was just buying a painting by an old Scottish master and felt a connection to it because it reminded him of his childhood,"

I noted. "Maybe he thought he was getting a good deal and didn't want someone else to buy it out from under him."

"It's possible, I guess," Chloe said with a grimace. It was clear she didn't believe that.

"We'll never know what Florian knew," I said. "He took that information to his grave, just like Elizabeth."

"I guess it doesn't really matter what Florian knew," Chloe pointed out. "What matters is who has the painting now."

She was right. Was the accident caused by someone who wanted that painting? Or, more specifically, someone who wanted the map that might be hidden behind it?

"I wondered why the interest in Leitch's painting was so sudden. Seamus had it in his shop for three years before anyone showed interest, and then *two* people wanted it."

"Hagen said that after the owner hid the painting, he fought in the war and moved to France. He left behind two sons, both of whom grew up hearing the story of the map. Apparently the man always believed he would someday return to England to retrieve the painting and map from their hiding spot, but he died before he could ever make the trip. So the sons went in search of them."

"And did they find them?"

"No. They followed their father's instructions, but the painting and map were gone. Hagen thinks someone found the painting at some point, didn't realize its value, and sold it to the junk shop in Edinburgh where Seamus bought it."

"But how did Hagen—and Florian, apparently—realize it was in the shop in Edinburgh?"

"Apparently there had been a picture of the painting on the junk shop's website. Anyway, by the time the sons went looking for the painting, there were whispers about its hidden secret in the art department at my university. I guess one of the sons told an old professor about it, and he told Hagen. He knew Hagen would be interested in the story."

Interested enough to kill Florian for the painting?

"Do you think a lot of people know about it?" I asked.

"Probably not. Otherwise you would have been getting far more people in the shop."

"True." I thought for a moment. Something didn't seem right. "Does Seamus know about this?" I asked her.

"I haven't told him, if that's what you mean. Hagen just told me about it this morning, and you're the first person I've told since. Do you want me to tell Seamus?"

"No. I can tell him. So what now? Is Hagen looking for the painting?"

"I doubt it. He's busy editing an anthology." I couldn't wait to tell Seamus what I had learned.

* * * *

That evening, he and I were walking back to the hotel when I told him about Hagen's story. Seamus had been spending more evenings with me since the opening. Every couple days he would stay late at the gallery to meet collectors, but most of the time we met for dinner and then went back to the hotel to relax and watch television.

"You're kidding," he said, coming to a stop on the pavement. A couple walking behind us had to quickly skirt around to avoid a collision.

"Chloe seemed to think it was true."

"Can you believe it? If I had only known, we could have made a fortune off that painting!"

I slapped his shoulder. "That's not the point. The point is that the painting went missing after Florian's accident, and whoever took it probably knows its true value."

We resumed walking. Seamus asked the question I had wanted to ask Chloe, but was afraid to: "Do you think Hagen had anything to do with Florian's accident?"

"I don't know. I didn't say anything to Chloe because I don't know how friendly she is with Hagen, but the thought certainly crossed my mind."

"He came to the shop after Florian left with the painting, but he didn't seem at all upset about missing his chance to buy it. Did he say he was heading right back to London?"

"I don't remember," I said.

"What if he was already in Cauld Loch? What if he tinkered with Florian's car whilst he was in the shop? He could have followed him up the road until the accident occurred, then stolen the painting before the police even had a chance to get there. Or maybe he followed Florian from the shop and ran him off the road."

"So you think he wasn't upset about missing his chance to buy the painting because he already had it in possession by the time he came in the next morning?" I asked.

"Aye."

"But why would he bother visiting the shop?"

"Maybe he wanted to see if we had anything else of value. I didn't know the value of the Leitch painting, maybe he thought I was stupid enough to be selling off other national treasures, too."

"I don't know, Seamus. There must have been other people who knew how much the painting was worth."

"What about Alice?" he asked.

"What about her?"

"Do you think she knew?"

"I doubt it. Florian said he was looking for a painting that reminded him of his childhood, remember? We don't know if he knew the real value of it. And if his story was true, that he wanted the painting for sentimental reasons, there's no reason Alice should know about it."

"But he wanted it badly enough to come to the shop late at night because he knew there was someone else interested."

"You, of all people, ought to know that a person can feel a sense of connection with a particular piece of art. He wanted something that connected him to his childhood, and when he found it, he would do anything to keep it."

"Then why didn't he buy the painting when he was in the shop the first time?"

"Sometimes a painting's value increases because there are lots of people who are interested in it. You know that. So when Florian heard that there was someone else who wanted it, that spurred him to action."

"Aye. Maybe he thought he could get me to lower the price, but he knew I wouldn't once there was another potential buyer." Seamus didn't often show his cynical side, but it was laid bare now.

"I suppose that's a possibility, too. The point is that Florian may have known absolutely nothing about the painting except that he liked it," I said.

Seamus ran his hand down his beard. "What do you suppose Scotland Yard is doing about all of this? Do you think they know about the map?"

"I don't know. How could they? Chloe indicated not too many people knew of the map's existence. I'm sure Scotland Yard is just investigating Florian's death."

"I wonder if there's another reason someone would have wanted him dead."

"Surely the detectives have asked Alice about that."

"Aye, but I wonder what she told them."

"I could just ask her," I suggested, forgetting Seamus didn't know I had met Alice for lunch.

"What're ye talking about?" he asked.

"I met Alice one day for lunch. You know, just to talk. I thought she might like some company after her husband's death."

"Why didn't you tell me?" Seamus asked.

"Because I knew you wouldn't have wanted me to go. If I didn't tell you, you couldn't demand that I stay away from her. Not that I would have," I added.

He sighed. "I don't think we should have anything to do with her. The less contact we have with the wife of a man who was murdered, the better."

"But she's lonely. I wasn't about to leave her alone in her grief if I could help her. I think you're being very unkind."

"How did you know she was lonely? She could have had a dozen kids at home to boost her spirits."

"She and Florian didn't have any kids, remember? I just assumed she was lonely. I would be, if you were killed, God forbid. I reached out to her because I kept thinking about how sad she must be. I would want someone to do the same for me. I would hope you'd want that, too."

"Why are you even bringing that up?" Seamus roared. "Why do we have to talk about what you would do if I was killed?"

"All right, all right. I'm sorry I mentioned it. Now please just leave me alone about Alice. I intend to visit her again before we leave, and I don't care if you try to lock me in the hotel room. I'm going."

We walked the rest of the way in silence. I could practically feel the angry heat rising from him. I had known he would be mad if he found out I visited Alice, but I didn't think he would be *that* mad.

We were almost to the hotel when he turned to me on the pavement. "Do you understand why I'm upset?" he asked.

"Not really."

"I just don't want us to be in the sight lines of the police. I would think you'd realize that. The last thing I need is to be involved in a murder investigation. I'm sorry Alice is lonely, and I'm verra sorry she's lost her husband, but I have to think about us and our future—which doesn't include me going to prison again."

I squeezed his hand. "You're right. It was thoughtless of me to visit her when I knew Scotland Yard was investigating Florian's death. Am I forgiven?"

He put his arm around my shoulder. "Of course."

CHAPTER 9

The next time Alice and I met for lunch it was completely by accident. I just happened to be visiting the shops in Highgate when I decided to have lunch in the delightful garden of the restaurant where she and I had met previously.

She was sitting alone at the same table as before. A large straw hat covered her eyes, and she was looking down at a book in her lap. I walked up and bent down so I could see her face.

"Alice? How funny that we should meet here! I was just doing some shopping and I thought I would stop in for some of those wonderful finger sandwiches. May I join you?"

She nodded and closed her book, indicating the other chair with her hand.

"How have you been, Alice? I've been thinking about you."

"Getting along, I suppose."

"Have you been staying busy?"

"I've been trying. Rearranging the furniture and household decor, you know. Changing it up a bit."

It sounded like she was grasping at anything to stay busy. "Do you have a job?" I asked.

She looked at me as if horns were growing from my head. "No," she answered. Her tone suggested I should have known better than to ask such a silly question.

"Oh."

"My family has always been involved in philanthropy," she explained. "I suppose I help by choosing charities to receive various gifts throughout the year, but other than that I have no interest in attempting to earn a paycheck." She shuddered, as if the thought was repugnant.

I was surprised. Alice hadn't struck me as the snooty type, or as someone whose days were spent counting the family money. Her choice in clothing and hairstyle indicated a person unconcerned with worldly things. She didn't seem to be the type who would disparage the idea of working for a living. I wondered if Florian had been employed before his death.

I changed the subject quickly. "Have you eaten yet?" I asked brightly.

"I've ordered, but only just a moment ago." She signaled to the server, who came over to our table right away.

"What can I get for you, Mrs. McDermott?" she asked. So Alice was a regular. I hadn't gotten that sense the first time.

"Please bring my friend a menu, Susan," Alice replied.

"Actually, Susan, could you just bring me an order of the finger sandwiches? They're wonderful. And a lemonade, please."

Susan nodded and disappeared. I looked around the garden while Alice put her book in a cloth bag that lay on the ground beside her chair.

"What are you reading?" I asked.

"A book about investing. It was written by a friend, and she asked me to read it and review it."

"What do you think of it?"

"I'm not sure I like it. I'm not learning anything I didn't already know."

"Is that what you're going to put in the review?"

"Naturally not. I'll write a glowing review."

Alice seemed to be a different person from the woman I had met before. She seemed stronger, more forthright, more sure of herself. I wasn't so sure I liked the new Alice.

"So what have you been up to since we last spoke?" I asked her.

"I appreciate what you're trying to do, Sylvie, but I can't keep up this charade any longer."

"What do you mean?" I asked in surprise.

"I mean I can't go on pretending like I am a grieving widow. The truth is that I am glad the bastard's dead. I would have killed him myself if someone hadn't done it for me."

My mouth gaped. I could do nothing but stare at her.

"You're surprised?" she asked with a sneer. "Are you learning something new about the dearly departed Mr. McDermott?"

"I am surprised, yes," I said, swallowing hard. "I just assumed..." My voice trailed off.

She finished my sentence for me. "You just assumed I had lost the love of my life. If you were in the same position, you would feel devastated. Am I right?"

I nodded mutely.

"Well, don't think we're in the same position. Does your husband cheat on you? Does he tell people he married you for money? That it was all for business?"

I could feel my eyes getting wider and wider. Finally I blinked in amazement. "Alice, I'm so sorry to hear it. I had no idea." Uncomfortable memories of the movie I watched the night I found the receipt in our house back in Scotland came rushing to my mind, but I pushed them away.

"Of course you didn't. Why should you? He kept it all very discreet."

"How did you find out?" It was a nosy question, but she seemed to be in the mood for disclosures.

"The other woman confronted me. In my own home, if you can believe it. It happened about a week before Florian died."

I shook my head. "You must have been devastated."

"Well, I admit it took me by surprise," she answered.

"Did Florian know that you knew?"

"Yes. He was there when she told me. They told me together, but she did the talking. Cozy, huh?"

"It must have been horrible."

"You've no idea." She lit a cigarette and took a long drag, closing her eyes. "I took up smoking again. I had given that up years ago."

"I think you're entitled to a vice now and then."

"You're right—I am. You know what's amazing, though? I was embarrassed—not hurt or sad. Florian and I were more like roommates than spouses. Our relationship was really quite business-like."

I didn't know what to do with that information. She didn't seem the sort who wanted people to feel sorry for her. And there was no way I could really put myself in her shoes. Maybe I didn't need to offer anything except an ear.

She continued. "We were married because my mother wanted the 'union,' as she would always say. I'm old money, he was new money. The family name needed contemporary marketing. Florian lent his name to many of my family's investments, and people started to notice. Before long those investments were worth more than ever."

"Florian didn't strike me as the high-power financial type," I told her.

"Well, he made mistakes, too. He lost a lot of money right before he died," she said with a harsh laugh. "Investments went bad."

Alice had given me much to ponder.

* * * *

Throughout the rest of the afternoon I wondered how I was going to break the news to Seamus. When he and I had dinner in our favorite pub after he was done for the day, I decided to tell him the truth—most of it.

"I was shopping today, and you'll never guess who I ran into," I began.

"Hmm?" He was studying the menu as if he had never seen it before, barely listening as I spoke. I put my hand on top of it and pulled it down so he could see me.

"Who was it you saw?" he asked.

"Alice."

"Alice, as in Florian's wife?" His eyes narrowed in a skeptical look. "And what did dear Alice have to say?"

"You won't believe it. She told me that Florian was having an affair before he died. Alice knew about it—the *other woman* told her."

"You're kiddin' me."

"It's true. She's not the person we thought she was. She's much more posh than we imagined. She doesn't have a job except for helping distribute her family's money—can you believe that?"

"She certainly doesn't look the part."

"No, but neither did Florian and apparently he had oodles of money, too. Alice said their marriage was a 'union' and that her mother wanted it to happen because Alice's family needed some fresh blood...." Seamus raised one eyebrow pointedly.

"So to speak. You know what I mean. Anyway, when he added his name and his money, the value of Alice's family's investments went way up. Apparently, though, he lost a lot of money right before he died in investments that went bad. He told his girlfriend he married Alice for business reasons. Unbelievable." I shook my head.

"Alice must be furious," Seamus said.

"She seems more angry than sad, that's for sure. She said she'd have killed Florian herself if someone didn't do it for her."

"Do you believe her?"

"I guess so. I'd want to kill you if you were having an affair." We were approaching a topic I didn't want to discuss.

"No—you missed my meaning. Do you think it's possible Alice killed him?"

I hadn't thought about that. "You mean because he was having an affair?" Seamus nodded.

"I don't know. Maybe. But she called looking for him."

"If she called from a mobile phone, she could have been calling from anywhere, including the pub right down the street. Or the scene of the accident."

I didn't know what to think. Alice didn't seem the type to kill, but would I really recognize a killer if I saw one? I had misjudged her once—she wasn't the person I thought she was. I had taken her for a grieving widow, but she had fooled me. Was she fooling me about Florian's death, too?

"I suppose you're right. Should we tell Scotland Yard?"

"Absolutely not," Seamus answered, jabbing a finger in my direction. "We leave the whole thing well enough alone. Didn't we talk about this? I don't want to be involved with Scotland Yard again for any reason, at any time."

"First of all, never point at me like that. And second, there's no need to get huffy. I was merely asking."

"All right then. Please, no more talk about Scotland Yard."

We ordered our food, then sat in silence waiting for our meals. Seamus read something on his phone, I texted Greer. I hated to see us fall into the same trap that so many other people had—texting and scrolling instead of talking face-to-face, but we both knew we needed to wait for the tension to dissipate before we could carry on a conversation.

When the food came it was time to talk again. I avoided any touchy subject.

"How were things at the gallery today?"

"Braw. I met some collectors who want to visit the studio at home. Not too many people have been interested in making the trip to the Highlands, but these two seemed verra keen on the idea."

"Why do they want to go all the way up there?"

He shrugged. "They want to see me work in my natural environment. Makes me sound like an otter. But that probably sells well—you know, portrait of an artist at work in his humble studio. That sort of thing."

"Has Felix talked to you about sales since the opening?"

Seamus grinned. "We went to lunch today, as a matter of fact. He told me the opening and the exhibit have done *incredibly* well. I don't know exact numbers, but I think they'll be verra high."

I smiled. "That's wonderful. I'm so proud of you." He clinked his glass of mineral water against mine and grinned back at me.

"I see another trip to Edinburgh in your future, lass."

"I don't need a trip to Edinburgh—I've just spent almost two weeks in London, for heaven's sake. It'll be enough for me just to get home."

I was missing the Highlands more with every passing day. We only had a couple more days and it would be time to go home. As much as I had looked forward to our stay in London, I couldn't wait to be in my little house again, with the mountains out my kitchen window and Cauld Loch only a few meters away. I longed for the quiet of the tiny village where Seamus and I had chosen our home. I even missed the tinkling of the bell above the shop door whenever a customer came in.

I had been checking in with Eilidh daily to see if she was having any problems in the shop or the gallery, and she had done surprisingly well. No botched credit card transactions, no forgetting to lock up at night, no irate customers to placate. She had been depositing the sales proceeds in the bank every day—I was checking.

On our last full day in London, after Seamus left for the Lundenburg, I packed our bags to leave. When I finished I looked around the room, wondering what to do next. On impulse, I picked up my mobile phone and dialed Alice. She answered on the first ring.

"Hi Alice, it's Sylvie."

"Oh. I didn't expect to hear from you again."

"We're heading home in the morning and I wanted to say goodbye."

"Well, goodbye. I am really very busy, so if that's all you wanted..." It was a patronizing brush-off. Alice clearly did not want to be on the phone with me. I wondered why. It could be something completely innocent, but my conversation with Seamus the night before was nudging me. What if she did have something to do with Florian's death? Was she trying to get me off the phone because her conscience was bothering her? Should I try to find out? Should I share my suspicions with Scotland Yard? I got off the phone quickly.

With effort I thrust away the thought of Scotland Yard. If I contacted them, I'd have a very hard time explaining it to Seamus.

I took up my backpack from where it lay on the bed, flung it over my shoulder, then grabbed my aviator sunglasses and a big floppy hat. I could practically hear Greer's voice saying, "Don't go to Highgate, Sylvie. It's a mistake. Enjoy your last day in London and quit thinking about Alice."

But I couldn't listen to Greer's voice in my head this time. Since my last lunch with Alice I had been unsure of her. I wanted to see for myself the neighborhood where she and Florian had lived as husband and wife. I wanted to see what kind of car she drove and if she always dressed like a bohemian. She had managed to shake my confidence in my ability to judge people and their moods, and that had unnerved me. Seamus would say I was becoming obsessed, and I feared he'd be right.

I went to the closest Tube station and stepped off the train not far from the café where Alice and I had eaten lunch. I had looked up her address online and typed it into the GPS on my phone, giving me walking directions to her house.

Before I set off I fished around in my backpack for the sunglasses and hat so that if Alice was home she wouldn't recognize me. I felt like Mata Hari. I walked uphill and down, through magnificent neighborhoods where I gawked at the homes lining the streets. My GPS was telling me I was very close.

When I saw Alice's house, I was awestruck. Three stories tall, its brick walls clad in dark green ivy, it was the nicest home on a block of beautiful homes. I slowed my pace, trying to get a good look at the house without being too obvious. I hoped my disguise was working.

The house exuded a feeling of emptiness. There was no car in the driveway, and two newspapers lay on the grass near the steps leading to the front door. I pushed on the wrought iron gate, which swung open without a sound. Looking around to see if any of the neighbors were watching me, I ascended the front steps and peered through the sidelight next to the front door.

The inside of the house, at least what I could see, was exquisite. Gleaming antiques graced the foyer under a huge crystal chandelier that must look magical at night. A huge vase of flowers sat on top of a gorgeous round wooden table inlaid with swirling patterns in lighter wood.

But what surprised me the most were the walls. Every inch of them was covered with framed paintings. I could barely make out their color, which seemed to be a light, buttery yellow. The paintings were of various subjects and by different artists—I could tell just by looking at them. The paintings gave the foyer a jarring, disconcerting appearance. It was a shame; a lighter touch could have resulted in a beautiful display.

I turned away, wishing I could see more of the inside of the house. The ground-floor windows were just a few feet away. Did I dare peek inside to see more?

When my mobile phone rang I jumped straight up in the air and gasped. It was Seamus. "What's going on?" he asked.

"Nothing," I answered, trying to regain my composure.

"Can you meet us for lunch?"

"Who's 'us'?"

"Me and Felix and Chloe. We're leaving in about an hour for that nice pub right up the block."

My heart was still pounding. I looked up the block with a start, then realized he meant the block where the Lundenburg was.

"Ah, sure. I'll meet you there. In an hour?"

"Aye. Are you all right?"

"Yes. Why?"

"You don't sound like yourself."

"Oh, it's nothing. I just had a coughing fit."

"All right. You'll meet us, then?"

"I'll be there."

I didn't have time to wonder about trying to peek through the windows. I needed to get back to the hotel to change my clothes. Leaving the house behind, I walked back through the village to the Tube station.

I was surprised every time I learned something new about Alice. First I had taken her for a grieving widow, but that turned out to be wrong. Then, though I knew she and Florian were wealthy, I had not pictured her house to be as elegant as it was, although I found the display of paintings in the foyer bizarre and unnerving. I wondered if the rest of the house was decorated the same way. I sighed. I would probably never know.

And what of the paintings? Were any by William Leighton Leitch? I wasn't familiar with his work except for the one Florian bought, so I wouldn't recognize any if they were hanging in the foyer.

I changed my clothes at the hotel, then quickly left to join the others. I was the last one to arrive.

"What have you been up to?" Seamus asked. Did I look guilty? Could he tell I had something to hide? I studied his face before deciding he had just asked me to be polite.

"I went for a walk."

"Oh? Where?"

"Just around," I said.

"Around where?"

"Just around," I snapped. Seamus looked surprised, as did Felix and Chloe.

"I'm sorry," I said. "I didn't sleep well last night and my temper is a wee bit short this morning."

"Och, that's all right, love," Seamus said, patting my hand. "I understand."

Why did he have to be so nice? I was being miserable and evasive—I didn't deserve such a wonderful man.

Chloe spoke up. "Tell us what has been your favorite part of London." Dear Chloe. So good of her to change the subject and smooth over the obvious strain between me and Seamus.

"You go first," I told him.

He didn't even have to think, "The gallery opening," he said with a grin.

Felix laughed. "I should think so, man! It was a huge success for both of us!" He turned to face me with a broad smile. "Your husband is going to be right famous before you know it. He's on his way, Sylvie."

"That's wonderful," I said. I was still waiting to hear exactly how much money Seamus had earned at the Lundenburg, but no one said anything. They were all looking at me expectantly, waiting to hear about my favorite part of our trip.

"Making new friends," I said, lifting my water glass to salute Felix and Chloe. They returned the gesture and Seamus joined in.

"Sylvie's right," Seamus declared. "We've been very lucky to meet you two. To good friends," he exclaimed, holding up his glass again. We all clinked our glasses and settled back to chat while we waited for our food to arrive.

Felix and Chloe were eager to come up to the Highlands for a visit, and Seamus pressed them to pick a date. "You should come up before the summer ends," he said. "The beautiful weather doesn't last long up there."

By the time lunch was over we had made plans for our new friends to come in August. We had enjoyed every minute we spent with them in London and already looked forward to seeing them again.

I took my leave of Felix and Chloe after lunch. I was sorry to say goodbye, but I only had one afternoon left in London and I would see them again soon. I thought briefly about going back to Alice's house in Highgate and trying to peer through her windows, but I decided against it. I banished all thoughts of Alice from my mind and concentrated on picking one final tourist spot.

I chose the Churchill War Rooms, where the larger-than-life wartime leader of England had led his country through the darkest days of World War II from an underground bunker in the city of London. It was a fascinating look into the lives of the people who made decisions and executed orders in the war-weary city, both above and below ground.

I took my time at the War Rooms and left when they closed for the day. Suddenly I wanted a few more days in London. It was such an exciting, beautiful, sophisticated place to be—I felt like I was part of something much bigger when I wandered the streets. I picked up a few more souvenirs for Ellie before heading back to the hotel to finish packing.

Seamus was waiting for me when I got back. We went to dinner and I told him all about the Churchill War Rooms. He was fascinated. I was sorry we hadn't had a chance to explore London together—we had never made it back to the Getty Images Gallery—but I knew he was happy with the way our trip had turned out. After I told him about my afternoon, carefully leaving out any mention of my activities before we met for lunch, he gushed about how much he loved the Lundenburg and how he couldn't wait to return.

"Felix is thinking about instituting an artist-in-residence program, and he wants me to be the first guest painter!" he said, his eyes bright.

"That's wonderful!" I cried. "When is that going to happen?"

"He doesn't know. We're going to talk about it when he and Chloe visit us in August."

"So we might be able to come back to London?"

He nodded, piercing a piece of fish from his huge platter of fish and chips and putting it in his mouth.

I was already looking forward to our next trip.

CHAPTER 10

We went home on the train the next day. As the rolling hills and quaint villages of England gave way to the rugged mountains and lochs of Scotland, I could feel myself getting more excited to be home. As much as I loved London and as much as I wish we had more time to spend there, I was thrilled to be back in Scotland.

We arrived in Cauld Loch in the early evening, after Eilidh had closed up the shop for the day. After we unpacked the artwork and supplies that belonged in the studio, we invited Eilidh and Callum to dinner at the pub.

We were thrilled to see them. We hadn't seen them much when we lived in Edinburgh, but since moving to the Highlands we spent time with them often. Two weeks away from them had seemed more like a month.

Eilidh couldn't wait to tell us all about the sales she had made in our absence. I already knew about each one, having checked the inventory and the bank balances every day we were in London, but I listened to her with intense interest because she was so proud of the job she had done.

The rest of us ate while Eilidh regaled us with stories of her salesmanship and persuasive abilities. I hadn't seen her so animated in a long time.

"Eilidh, you should get a job in a shop or a gallery. You're a wonderful salesperson," I said.

"You think so? I've been looking for a position as a bookkeeper."

"I think you should broaden your search. We'd hire you if we needed one more person, but we're not at that point yet."

Seamus nodded his agreement. "Aye, I wish we could take you on, Eilidh, but maybe someday soon. If we ever need someone else, the job is yours."

Eilidh beamed. "Thank you! Callum, what d'ye think?"

Callum leaned back in his chair. "I think that would be braw. Seamus, did the opening go well enough that you think you could hire some help?"

"Aye, that's what I'm hoping. We haven't seen the actual numbers yet, but Felix assures us the opening and the gallery appearances went very well."

"We'd be grateful if Eilidh could work in your shop," Callum said.

"Well, you'll be the first to know," Seamus said with a grin.

The rest of dinner was talkative, noisy, and comfortable. We told Eilidh and Callum all about Felix and Chloe. My cousin couldn't wait to meet our new friends from London.

"When are they visiting?" she asked eagerly.

"In August," Seamus replied.

"A real gallery owner? How exciting!" Eilidh exclaimed.

"What am I, then?" Seamus asked, his expression one of mock hurt.

"Oh, you ken what I mean," Eilidh said, slapping his arm. "I mean an important gallery owner!"

"You're making it worse," Seamus said with a wicked grin. Callum and I laughed.

"I mean a *London* gallery," Eilidh spluttered. "Och, Seamus, leave me alone!"

Seamus tilted his head back with a hearty laugh. "Aye, I know what you're trying to say, Eilidh. Felix *is* an important person in the art world. We're lucky to know him."

"We're lucky he likes you," I put in.

We shared stories of our time in London. I glossed over any discussion of Alice and Florian, but they were never far from my mind. Seamus looked at me once or twice with a question in his eyes, probably wondering if I would say anything. He still didn't know I had visited Alice's house. I would have to tell him sooner or later; I didn't like keeping secrets. Talk eventually turned to Florian, though. Eilidh and Callum were eager to know if the police had made any progress with their investigation. We told them Scotland Yard had taken over the case and there were no new developments. We also told them what we had learned about the possibility of a map being hidden behind the Leitch painting. They were stunned.

The four of us walked home together after dark. Seamus and I still had to unpack, and Callum had to be at work early the next morning. I invited Eilidh to the shop in the morning because I knew she would miss it keenly. She pounced on the invitation with glee.

"I hoped you would ask. Maybe I can help put stuff away from your trip."

"We put away most of the artwork and supplies before dinner, but if you want to come over and help rearrange displays, you could do that. I'm afraid we can't pay you now that we're home, though," I said.

"Och, that's all right. I just want to come over and chat. It's nice to be with other people."

Poor Eilidh. I hated that we couldn't pay her now that we were around to take care of the shop, and that we would have to wait awhile before we knew if we would have the resources to hire her. She really needed a job, if only to get out and talk to people more often. Minding our shop and gallery had been good for her.

The next morning brought sunshine, cool temperatures, and a beautiful breeze. I threw open the windows in the house and in the shop before Seamus was even awake. I was full of energy. I couldn't wait to get back to my photography. I had taken hundreds of pictures in London and I wanted to start going through them, deciding which might make good prints, which would be good on canvas, and which could be deleted.

I sipped coffee in the studio as I browsed through the photos on my laptop. I was so engrossed that when I heard a knock at the door, it startled me. It was Eilidh.

I knew something was wrong before I opened the door. Her face, normally flawless, the color of porcelain, was red and blotchy. Damp streaks lined her cheeks where tears had fallen.

"Eilidh! What's wrong?" I asked, drawing her into the shop by her arm.

She hiccupped before answering. "I had a fight with Callum. He had to get up early for work, so I got up and made him a nice breakfast. But he started in on me, asking why I wasn't trying harder to get a job. He says we shouldn't be relying on you and Seamus to hire me. He's embarrassed." She let out a small sob.

"He shouldn't be embarrassed! We would love for you to work here. And you're family. Who better to work with us than family?" I asked, giving her a hug. "Now dry your tears and let me get you a cup of tea. Or coffee. Which do you prefer?"

"Coffee, please. I need the extra jolt this morning."

I went to the kitchen and returned with a steaming cup of coffee, fixed just the way Eilidh liked it, with two sugars and lots of cream.

"You're so good to me. I can never repay you," she said with a sniffle.

"Who said you have to repay us? I wish we could have paid *you* more for minding the shop and the studio whilst we were gone. Especially since you sold more of Seamus's paintings in two weeks than I think I ever have!" It wasn't true, but she needed the encouragement, and it worked. A smile broke through her sad countenance and she looked at me gratefully. "Thank you," she said.

She followed me into the studio, where I turned my computer around so she could see some of the photos I took in London. I gave her some context to each one, explaining where it was taken, what time of day, and what else I had been able to see outside the frame of the photo. She perused the photos slowly, exclaiming over each one.

"This one is gorgeous!" she said. I looked over her shoulder.

"I took that on the grounds of Westminster Abbey. It was raining hard that day, but I couldn't stay inside with limited time in London. I had toured the Abbey and was walking to my next destination when I turned around to look at the Abbey behind me. And it was so strikingly beautiful that I had to take one more picture. I forget to turn around or look up sometimes, and often the best shots are behind or above."

"Will you put this one on canvas?"

"I don't think so. The detail is too intricate for canvas. I'll make prints of this one. Maybe I'll dry-mount the prints and sell them here in the studio."

"Great idea."

Eilidh raised her finger to slide the screen to the next photo when something caught my eye.

"Wait a second. Can I see that?"

"Sure." Eilidh slid off the stool and waved her hand toward it. "Sit down there."

I sat and peered closely at the screen. Was that who I thought it was?

Alice's face stared back at me from the entrance of the Abbey. So she had been inside the building while I was in there. How had I missed her?

"What d'ye see?" Eilidh asked.

I pointed to Alice. "That's Florian's wife. I recognize her because she's got that distinctive long hair and a very thin face. She also wears those huge sunglasses. And those boots—I recognize those boots from when we met for lunch one day. I thought they were hideous. Why do you suppose she was at Westminster Abbey?"

Eilidh shrugged. "Maybe she was sightseeing, like you."

I shook my head slowly. "When I asked her about places I should visit before leaving London, I distinctly remember her saying that Westminster Abbey was overrated. Why would she visit after advising me not to?"

"Was it overrated?"

"Are you kidding? Absolutely not! It was one of the most stunning places I've ever seen."

"Maybe she was following you," Eilidh suggested.

"Why would she follow me?"

"Maybe you should ask her."

"I'm not sure I want to." I hesitated, wondering if I should tell Eilidh about my encounters with Alice, but finally I spoke. "Alice isn't exactly the person I thought she was. I met up with her a couple times in London and each time she said or did something that was unsettling."

"Like what?"

"When she first visited us here at Gorse Brae, she seemed meek and timid. I got the same impression of her when we met for lunch the first time in Highgate, where she lives. But the next time we met, she seemed stronger and more assertive. Strong and assertive are good qualities, don't get me wrong, but it was unnerving because she hadn't seemed that way when I first met her. And she dressed differently, too. Normally that wouldn't be a big deal, but I felt like she was trying to confuse me, to tilt my perception of her."

"I'm sure she was still in shock over Florian's death when she came here. She must not have cared how she was dressed or how she talked or anything like that."

"I'm sure she was in shock, too. There was just something about her that seemed off when I met her that second time. I can't really put my finger on it. And she told me that Florian had cheated on her. She found out about it shortly before he was killed."

"That must have been awful for her," Eilidh murmured.

"I'm sure it was. But I got the sense that their marriage was more a matter of economics than love."

Eilidh shook her head. "That's sad. What made you think that?"

I repeated what Alice had told me about her family's investment portfolio increasing in value after her marriage to Florian, and his recent financial losses. Eilidh looked at me with wide eyes.

"I can't believe people really marry for money. I mean, I've seen it on television, but I never knew it happened in real life. Thank goodness Callum and I don't feel that way." Her mention of Callum brought on another bout of sadness. "What do you think I should do about getting a job?" she asked after a long silence.

"I wish I had an answer for you," I said with a sigh. "We'd love it if you could work here, but we have to make sure we can afford it before we bring you on. It would be terrible if we hired you and then had to let you go because we couldn't pay you. Maybe you should look for something temporary whilst we're waiting for Felix to give us some definite numbers from the gallery show and whilst we're waiting to see if there's an influx of work for Seamus."

"Maybe there's a shop around here that could use some temporary help for the rest of the summer," she said.

"That's a good idea. Why don't you start looking today?"

"Are you trying to get rid of me?" Eilidh asked with a grin.

I rolled my eyes. "Of course not. But I know you, Eilidh. You're happier when you're busy. The sooner you find something, the sooner you'll cheer up and Callum won't have to worry about you."

"You're right, as usual," she said, standing up and giving me a hug.

"Now, shoo. I need to get to work and so do you," I said with a grin. She left just as Seamus was coming into the gallery from the kitchen. He stood behind me and put his big hands on my shoulders, massaging them. I tilted my head back to look at him.

"Good morning, sleepyhead. What's your plan for today?"

"I want to paint today. Do you mind looking after the store?"

"No, but I'm going to work on some photo projects, too."

"That's fine. If we get lots of people, come get me and I'll give you a hand."

"Are we expecting lots of people?"

He shrugged. "I dinnae know. I hope so. The more word gets out about my work, the more visitors we should have."

"Do you want to talk to people who come in to look at your paintings, or do you want me to deal with them?"

"You can deal with them first; if they seem serious about buying, you can call me."

"Okay." I swatted his backside with a magazine from the worktable. "Now be off wi' ye. I've got stuff to do."

He chucked me on the chin and returned to the house.

It wasn't long before customers started to arrive. Between talking to some of them about Seamus's paintings and talking to others about the antique artwork for sale, I began to ask customers how they had heard of the shop and the gallery. If people were hearing about Seamus through word-of-mouth, or through one of the many articles written about him during his stay in London, then his name was traveling far and wide from the exposure he enjoyed at the Lundenburg.

Just as we had hoped, several customers stopped in because they had read about Seamus online, or in newspapers, blogs, or magazines. Most of those customers were visiting from London, keeping in touch with the London art scene even while on holiday. Whenever someone mentioned reading about him, I called him in to introduce himself. Customers seemed thrilled to meet him, and his personable conversation made them all feel welcome. We sold more paintings, antique art, and photographs that day than we had since leaving for London. Some of the articles had noted when he would be returning to the Highlands, and several customers told us they had waited to visit the gallery until they knew he would be there.

Seamus was exhausted but beaming by the time we closed the shop. "Can you believe it?" he asked me during dinner. "All those people. If this keeps up we'll be able to hire Eilidh sooner than we thought."

"Any word from Felix about the Lundenburg profits?"

"As a matter of fact, I did hear from him." He grinned.

"And? What did he say?" I asked impatiently.

"We made fifteen *thousand* pounds!"

I cocked my head, thinking I heard him wrong. "Really? Fifteen thousand? That's how much you made after the Lundenburg took its share off the top?"

"Aye. What's the matter?"

"I—I don't know. Somehow I thought it would be more than that."

"Fifteen thousand pounds is a lot of money, love."

"I know. I'm sorry. I just—I just figured the profit would be higher. I mean, after all the things Felix said..."

"He never actually told us how much we made."

"I know. I'm being silly. I'm sorry. Fifteen thousand is great. It's incredible, really."

"You don't sound convinced," he said, looking at me through narrowed eyes. "You wanted *more*?"

I was mortified. Even to my own ears my greed sounded insatiable. "It's not that," I said, struggling to explain myself. "I just had visions of the amount being much higher." My attempt to explain was failing miserably.

"Sylvie, I'm not Salvador Dalí. I'm not Claude Monet. What do you want from me?"

"Forget I said anything."

"I think I will," he said, his eyebrows raised in reproach. "I work hard. I can't work any harder."

I walked around the table and put my arms around his shoulders. He didn't return my hug and I knew I had hurt him. "I'll do the dishes," I said in a low voice.

"Thank you." He pushed his chair back and went back into the studio. Was he going back to work to avoid me? Because he couldn't believe my selfishness? I hated myself for saying anything.

And yet—there had been something in Felix's words, in his tone, in his smiles whenever he spoke about the profits from Seamus's exhibition that prompted me to think Seamus had made money beyond our grandest imaginings. We hadn't dreamed of making anywhere near fifteen thousand pounds, and that amount was a true blessing, but somehow I thought Felix had a higher number in mind.

I carried a heavy weight of embarrassment and selfishness that night. I went to bed alone and though I was still awake hours later when Seamus crawled into bed, he didn't touch me or even face me and I knew he was still angry. I didn't sleep at all.

I was cranky and weepy in the morning. I made tea and drank it alone in the kitchen while I waited for Seamus to wake up, but I didn't feel like eating anything. I was wiping a stray tear from my eye when he came in the room.

"Morning, love," he said, pecking my cheek as he poured himself a cup of tea. "Have you been awake long?"

"Aye," I replied. "Seamus, I—"

He held up his hand to stop me. "You don't have to explain, Sylvie. I'm sorry I was angry last night. I got thinking about what you said and I realized you were right. Felix *did* give the impression that we had witnessed a miracle. But the fifteen thousand is more than I dared to hope for, so I'm happy with that amount."

"I am, too. I swear. I know how selfish I seemed last night and I never meant for my words to sound that way."

"So you won't leave me because I'm a pauper?" He grinned, and I knew my foolishness was forgiven.

"You know I would never do that," I said, returning his bear hug.

"Let's get to work," he said, holding me at arm's length. "I got two emails last night, each commissioning a painting of the Cairngorms. From people who live and work in London. They heard about me in one of the art magazines." He was wearing the widest smile I'd ever seen.

"Why didn't you tell me sooner?" I cried. "That's wonderful news!"

"We had to clear the air first. And last night I didn't want to wake you up just to tell you that."

"I wasn't sleeping. And even if I was, you should have gotten me up for that." I gave him a mock grimace. "Wake me up next time."

"I will. Promise."

We each went to work in the studio that morning, taking turns helping customers. Seamus was studying physical and virtual maps of the Cairngorms, making plans to camp up in the mountains for several days to work on his paintings. I worked on my photo projects, wondering all the while whether I should show Seamus the photo of Alice in front of Westminster Abbey.

I decided against it. Seamus was over the moon about his commissions and busy making plans for a camping trip—I didn't want to spoil his anticipation.

"Are you going to come with me?" he asked that night at dinner.

"Come where?"

"To the Cairngorms. When I go camping. I don't want to go by myself."

"Who's going to stay behind and watch the shop?"

"We can ask Eilidh to do it."

"I don't know, Seamus. Maybe you should go solo this time and I'll go next time."

"Please?" he whined.

"Oh, all right. I'll call her after dinner. When are you leaving?"

"Friday morning. Early."

"Okay."

But when I talked to Eilidh later that evening, she surprised me by telling me she had already found a job in the village pottery shop. "It's just for the summer, mind you, but I can't wait to start," she said.

"That's great!" I was so happy for my cousin. "When's your first day?"

"Tomorrow." That answered the question of whether or not she could mind the shop.

"I'm so happy for you, Eilidh. By the time your job at the potter's ends, maybe we'll be able to take you on here."

I was thrilled for her. I could hear excitement and happiness in her voice. And I wasn't disappointed about being left behind while Seamus went camping. I loved to camp, but I felt the shop needed my attention and I needed to get more of my photographs framed, hung, and placed online for sale.

Seamus was disappointed, though. "Let's just close up for a couple days. I want you to go with me."

"We can't close now, Seamus. Not with all the customers we've been getting. If this is the only time some of them are going to be up in the Highlands, we need to be open so they can come in and take a look around."

He sighed. "I suppose you're right. I'll miss you, though."

"I'll miss you, too. But maybe I can go next time."

"I'm considering that a promise."

"That's fine with me," I said with a grin.

The rest of the week sped by. Seamus was busy answering customers' queries, trying to paint, and packing for his camping trip. I helped him when I could, but I was busy, too. We checked inventory, rearranged items in the shop to make room for extra stock, and hired a webmaster to update our website and keep track of online traffic.

Two hours before dawn on Friday, Seamus bounded out of bed, ready to get on his way. I staggered behind him, made tea, and wrapped up a few buttered scones while he finished packing last-minute items in the car. It was chilly and dark outside, but a million stars lit up the darkness just enough to see the smile on his face. He was ready for this trip. A couple days in the wilderness of the Cairngorms would do him good.

He kissed me goodbye and promised to be home in time for dinner on Sunday. I watched him drive away until the darkness swallowed his car, then I went back to bed and fell asleep almost instantly.

The customers in the shop that day kept me from thinking too much about how much I missed Seamus. But when evening fell I couldn't dispel the loneliness that settled around me. I called Eilidh and Callum and they invited me to join them at the pub for dinner.

They knew I missed Seamus, so they tried to entertain me throughout dinner. I heard stories about Callum's family, about Eilidh's new job, about a camping trip that had gone awry before they were married, and countless other stories calculated to make me smile. I laughed dutifully, but I didn't feel the happiness. I wished I had gone camping with Seamus. I couldn't even talk to him—he wouldn't get a mobile phone signal on his trek in the Cairngorms.

I left Eilidh and Callum at their cottage after dinner, then continued walking home by myself. It was quite dark, quiet, and peaceful. The little houses I passed were snug behind closed curtains, dim lamplight shining out of upstairs bedrooms.

Gorse Brae was completely dark. I thought I remembered leaving a small lamp burning in the shop. *I'll have to check that bulb in the morning.* I unlocked the kitchen door and flipped on the light switch as I entered the room.

It was the laptop on the kitchen table that caught my attention first. I had been using it before I left for dinner, but something wasn't right. I had closed it, as I always did to protect the screen. It was open. I took a tentative step toward the table, pausing for a moment to listen to the silence, which was complete. I felt a rush of dread, wishing more than anything that Seamus was home, in the kitchen with me. Nothing happened in the silence, so I reached for the laptop cover and closed it. As I did so I noticed that the machine was warm. I had been at the pub long enough for the computer to cool.

"Seamus?" I called. No answer.

I was afraid. I wheeled around to run out the kitchen door when the room was plunged into darkness with the soft *click* of the light switch.

I froze, not knowing which way to turn. I couldn't see anything. The light switch was next to the kitchen door, so the person who had turned the light off was between me and safety outdoors.

"Who's there?" I asked in a strangled whisper, my voice stuck in my throat. No answer.

I spun back around to face the living room and took off running, moving from side to side where I knew furniture stood in the darkness. I didn't even stop to turn on the lights. In my terror, my brain was somehow working logically enough to remind me that I knew the inside of the house better than whoever was running after me. If I turned on the light I would lose my advantage.

But the person was close on my heels. Twice a hand reached out from the blackness to grab my sleeve, but I shook it off and raced for the front door. I had to get outside—somehow I knew safety lay outside the walls of my cottage. But my hands were trembling too much to turn the lock on the front door—and I couldn't open it. I knew I had lost.

A rough shove, and I was on my back inside the front door. I hit my head on the door handle as I fell. And though I was listening for the other person's voice, I heard nothing but my own grunt as I fell to the floor, dazed and hurt. In contrast to the distant, twinkly stars I had seen from the driveway just nineteen hours before, when I'd kissed Seamus goodbye, the stars I saw lying on the floor were exploding from pain and terror.

It had all happened so quickly—it probably took less than a minute.

I recoiled in shock when a flashlight rent the darkness with its beam of blinding light. My assailant shone it into my eyes, making it impossible for me to see his—or her—identity.

"What do you want?" I managed to ask, my voice slurred and slow.

"You know what I want," the person said in a hoarse whisper. I still couldn't tell if I was at the mercy of a man or a woman, though the strength with which the person had shoved me to the ground indicated it was probably a man. I wished I could reach up and turn on the light, but I was paralyzed with panic and pain.

"I don't know," I said, suppressing a sob. I hated the weakness in my voice. "Tell me what it is and I'll give it to you." Why did Seamus have to be so far away?

"The painting," the voice growled. The low tones of the person's voice also led me to believe I was dealing with a man.

"What painting?"

He landed a fierce kick in my abdomen. "The one with the map! I'll find it myself." Lying on my side, I curled up to prevent any more damage to my midsection. He yanked me into a seated position, then I heard the sound of ripping duct tape. The assailant bound my hands together in front of me. There was no way I would be able to escape the binding even if I had all my faculties.

When he pulled me to my feet, he steered me toward the coat closet next to the front door and shoved me inside. I could hear him dragging one of the living room chairs in front of the door to prevent me from escaping. I sank to my knees on the floor of the closet and tried yelling, but the throbbing in my head was too crippling. I couldn't manage any but the faintest noises.

Under the door I could see he had turned on the lights in the living room. I strained to hear what was happening. The banging and crashing were, no doubt, my attacker's attempts to find the painting he was looking for.

As the minutes crept by, the fog in my mind started to lift. I realized with a gasp that the painting he was looking for had to be the William Leighton Leitch that Florian had bought just before his tragic death. The person, whoever he was, must have known the painting's centuries-old secret.

But who was it? The only people who knew about the painting were Felix and Chloe and Hagen, plus the old professor who had told Hagen the story. While I sat in the dark I wondered again whether Alice knew of the existence of the map.

I wished I had asked her when I had the chance. But knowing now that she had followed me as I toured London, would her answer be trustworthy? There was no way for me to know.

The invader was returning to the closet. I shrank back in fear, wondering wildly what would happen when he opened the door. He obviously would not have found the painting anywhere in the house, the shop, or the studio, because we didn't have it. I was terrified of what he would do to me out of frustration and desperation.

But I was shocked by what happened next. I saw nothing but darkness again under the closet door—he had turned off the lights. There were more bumps and jostling noises as the living room chair was dragged away from the closet, then I heard the front door open and slam. In a matter of seconds, silence had descended upon the cottage once more.

I was sure the person had left. I yearned to open the closet door and check for myself, but fear kept me rooted to the floor. I stayed there for several minutes, until the pain behind my eyes went screaming through my head and overcame the need to stay hidden and safe. I needed to see a doctor.

I pushed open the door with my foot. Slowly its familiar creak echoed through the silence and I peered around the edge of the door into the darkened living room.

I was alone—I was sure of it. I stood up by bracing myself against the closet door, then walked over to the front door, where I used my shoulder to flip the light switch. Soft lamplight flooded the room, and I was met with the unwelcome sight of overturned furniture and desk drawers lying on the floor, their contents spilled about the room. The front lock was broken—that must have been how the person got in while I was at the pub.

I hurried through the kitchen, ignoring the damage, and went straight into the shop. My stomach lurched when I saw what my attacker had wrought. Dozens of pieces of antique art lay on the floor, shredded and smashed. Seamus's original paintings lay scattered around the floor, scuffed, torn, ruined.

My first thought was to cry, but that would only hurt my head more. My next thought was to call Eilidh and get help.

My wrists were still bound in duct tape and my mobile phone was in my back pocket. For one fleeting moment I thought of running to Eilidh's house for help, but a crippling fear that the person might be waiting for me outside prevented me from leaving. Instead I dragged myself to the kitchen drawer, where I kept a pair of scissors. Holding the scissors open, I used them to pierce a hole in the duct tape. I wrenched my hands this way and that until the duct tape tore and eventually ripped completely, allowing me to break free. My wrists were bruised and raw where I'd ripped off the tape.

In an instant I was on the phone with Eilidh. "Please come over, and bring Callum," I pleaded in a choked sob. "And please phone the police and ask them to come, too."

"What's the matter? What happened?" The alarm in her voice was palpable.

"Someone attacked me in the house. My head is killing me. I need to get to a doctor."

Without a word Eilidh rang off, and only a minute or two later she and Callum ran up the path to the kitchen door. I was standing in the shadows of the kitchen, waiting for them. I unlocked the door as soon as they arrived, then quickly locked it again once they were inside. I limped to the table and slumped into a chair.

"What on earth happened?" Eilidh asked, glancing around and taking in the disarray.

"Someone was waiting for me when I came in from dinner. The lights were out and I knew I had left a light on in the shop. I should have known something wasn't right," I chided myself, "but I came inside and as soon as I turned on the kitchen light the person—whoever it was—switched off the light and came after me. He must have been hiding in the laundry room."

"You don't know who it was?" Callum asked.

I shook my head, forgetting how much it would hurt. I winced.

"We need to get her to hospital," Eilidh told her husband.

Just then we heard the siren of a police car. Looking through the kitchen window I could see a car jerking to a stop in the drive. Within minutes, two police officers had made sure there was no one still in the house or on our property. They had called an ambulance, which was on its way. They asked very basic questions about the break-in and my injuries, but my head hurt too much to talk to them for very long, so they said they would have an officer meet me at hospital.

"Have you called Seamus?" Eilidh asked.

"No. I doubt he'll have a signal." I said with a grimace. "That's part of the appeal of being in the mountains."

"We need to try, though," Eilidh replied. She dialed his number on her mobile phone and listened for a moment. Then she turned off the phone, shaking her head. "You're right—no service."

"I'll just have to wait until he comes home on Sunday," I said.

"Maybe Callum can drive up and look for him," she suggested.

"It's nice of you to offer, but he'd never be able to find Seamus. He likes to go completely off the grid when he's camping. I'll just wait."

When the ambulance arrived a few short moments later, Eilidh grabbed my handbag and my set of keys from the kitchen floor, where I had dropped them when the intruder turned off the kitchen light. Callum stayed at the house, since the police said they would like to have a look around and begin gathering possible clues as to the intruder's identity. Callum could answer some of their questions about the house and the attached shop. He also offered to make any necessary arrangements to have the locks replaced. I was so grateful to him. I didn't relish the thought of returning home after seeing a doctor; I was too afraid.

I refused to be strapped to a stretcher, so the paramedics supported me while I walked to the ambulance, and Eilidh made sure she could ride with me. I was still trembling from my ordeal and from the pain in my head.

When the officer arrived at hospital to talk to me I was awake, but groggy. I had no idea what time it was. Eilidh left the room at the officer's request, then I told him everything that had happened since I finished dinner at the pub. I answered his questions as best I could, but the pain in my head was becoming too great for me to concentrate. He left after talking briefly with Eilidh, promising me we would talk when I felt better. The doctor ordered several tests on my head. The sun was rising when I was finally assigned a room and allowed to sleep. Eilidh promised to stay with me until Callum could come to relieve her. She also said she would call Greer and Mum.

When I awoke a few hours later Callum and Eilidh were in my room, along with Greer and James. I opened my eyes and looked around, then squeezed them shut again.

"Where's Ellie?" I asked, alarmed at her absence.

"*Shh*," Greer said, rubbing her fingers lightly across my forehead. "She's with a neighbor. I didn't want to bring her here until we found out how you're doing."

"How do you feel?" James asked.

"My head hurts," I mumbled.

The lights in my room were off and someone had closed the blinds. It was as dark as possible, but it wasn't enough. I couldn't open my eyes without a searing pain.

Everyone except Greer left when the doctor came in.

"It seems you've suffered another concussion," he told me in a quiet voice. "I had a look at the records from your last hospital stay, just over three years ago. That makes two concussions in about three years—not a good record, as I'm sure you know."

"What can we do for her?" Greer asked. I was content to let her do all the talking.

"She needs lots of rest, quiet, no visual or mental stimulation, and as little stress as possible. The effects of this brain injury are likely to be more severe and last longer than her first concussion. That's normal."

"When can I go home?" I murmured.

"Probably tomorrow," the doctor said. "I want to keep you today for observation."

"Okay."

"Is she married?" the doctor asked Greer.

"Yes, but her husband is camping in the Cairngorms and can't be reached by mobile phone. He's expected home tomorrow." I was embarrassed when I felt a tear slipping from my eye onto the pillow.

I still didn't want to open my eyes, but I could feel Greer's hand on my arm. "I've left him a message, and I know Eilidh and Callum have both left messages, so his mobile will buzz as soon as he comes back into range. He'll be here before you know it," she said.

I sniffled. "Thanks."

The doctor and Greer left the room to continue talking, but I didn't care. I didn't want to listen; I just wanted quiet. I heard someone come in and I could smell food, so I knew there was a tray of breakfast for me, but I couldn't bear the thought of food.

The police officer paid me a visit later in the day to explain that detectives had found numerous fingerprints in the shop, the gallery, and the house. Eilidh, Callum, James, and Greer were all in the room.

"Will you be able to analyze all of them?" asked James.

"Yes, but it's going to take some time," the officer answered.

"There would naturally be a lot of prints from people coming in and out of the shop and the studio," Greer said.

I could hear the rising alarm in Eilidh's voice when she spoke. "My prints will be everywhere, because I worked in the shop for those weeks Sylvie and Seamus were in London, and Callum's prints will be in there, too, because he was there last night."

Greer must have sensed the conversation was becoming stressful for me, because she suggested they all go talk in the hallway or a waiting room. I was left alone in the blissful silence, trying not to think about all that had happened and all that awaited me on my return home.

All I cared about was seeing Seamus's face and getting rid of the headache and nausea I was feeling.

I started crying when Mum showed up later in the day, having driven up from Dumfries as soon as she heard about my injury. I had been sleeping, but I heard a voice through the fog of exhaustion and knew Mum had come.

"My little girl," she murmured into my hair as she bent down to kiss my head. "How are you feeling?"

"I've been better," I said, trying to smile for her.

"I don't want you to worry about a single thing," she said in a quiet voice. "I've come to stay until you're better."

The relief I felt at hearing Mum's words washed over me like a gentle wave on Cauld Loch. I squeezed her hand and opened my eyes.

"Thank you," I said. "I'm sure Seamus will be happy to hear it. I know he'll be worried when he gets home."

And he was. When he swept into my room the next morning, tears in his eyes, he could only stare at me and hold my hand.

"Say something," I said with a smile.

He shook his head. He didn't want to cry in front of me. My big burly husband, the ex-con, couldn't stand to see me in the hospital bed. Mum put her hand on his arm and led him away for a moment.

"It's okay to cry, Seamus dear," I heard her say. "Sylvie's all right. I know those are tears of relief."

She crept from the room and Seamus and I were left alone. The tears rolled down his cheeks as he looked at me.

"I'll never forgive myself for being gone and completely out of reach when this happened," he finally said.

"You couldn't have known someone would break in," I told him.

The doctor came in to discharge me and Seamus stood to shake his hand. The doctor reminded him to keep me quiet, keep my stress to a minimum, and keep me from doing anything that would be visually or mentally taxing.

"How long will she be like this?" Seamus asked.

"It's hard to know, but probably longer than the last time," the doctor replied. "How long did her symptoms last back then?"

"A little over a week," Seamus said.

"Then I would expect her to be house-bound for two weeks, at least," the doctor cautioned. "You can't risk her getting hurt again, because it can be dangerous when a head injury occurs before a concussion heals." Seamus nodded.

I kept my eyes closed on the drive home. The sunlight was too much for me to bear comfortably.

CHAPTER 11

Back at the cottage, a cold fear swept over me, covering me in a thin layer of sweat. Seamus took my hand when he noticed my hesitation to go inside.

"Dinnae worry about the locks, love. Callum had them changed. No one is getting in here."

"But the intruder broke the lock. He could do it again," I worried.

"*Shh*. You let me worry about it. We'll simply check each lock every time we come into the house. No one is going to break in again, anyway. Whoever it was saw that we didn't have what he was looking for, so he has no reason to come back."

He led me to the bedroom. Mum followed, carrying my bag. They worked, each on one side of the bed, to make sure I was as comfortable as possible, then left the room after closing the blinds and turning off my mobile phone. I slept for hours.

When I awoke Mum was sitting in an armchair next to the bed.

"This is one way to get you to come up to the Highlands, isn't it?" I asked with a sleepy smile.

"I would have come even if you didn't get hurt. I was just waiting for an invitation."

"You know you don't need an invitation to visit. Seamus and I love having you here."

Mum and I talked quietly about my trip to London for a few minutes, then I settled back against the pillow. The talking had made me tired, so remembering a trick that used to make me relax as a child, Mum rubbed the back of my hand with her fingers until I fell asleep again.

I woke up to the smell of dinner. Seamus had made my favorite: fish and chips. We didn't eat fried foods very often, but when we did it was a treat to savor. I helped Mum clean up after dinner. Both Mum and Seamus objected, but I was wide awake and feeling like I needed to do something useful. I couldn't read or watch television or do anything on the computer, but I could help with the housework. I had a feeling we would have the cleanest cottage in the Highlands after a few weeks of recovery.

That night, Seamus and I talked quietly in bed.

"Who do you think broke in?" I asked.

"I dinnae know, but you're not supposed to be worrying about that. Let me worry about it."

"Do you suppose he was looking for the painting you sold Florian?" I asked, ignoring his advice.

"Probably. What else would someone go to such great lengths to find?"

"Nothing, I suppose," I replied with a sigh. "I thought the whole search for the painting, and the investigation into Florian's death, had died down because we hadn't heard anything in a while. But I guess not."

"I dinnae think so," Seamus agreed. "The police may not have been around here lately, but there's clearly someone who thinks we have the painting."

"There are only a few people who know about it," I pointed out. "The list of people who could have broken in here looking for it is pretty short."

"Let's see. Felix and Chloe both know about it, because Hagen knew and told them," Seamus said, counting on three fingers.

"Plus the professor in London who told Hagen," I added.

He nodded. "Then possibly Alice." He gave me a dark look. "Did you by any chance ask her about it during your little get-together?"

"Of course not," I said, remembering I hadn't told him about seeing her in the Westminster Abbey photo, or about our last meeting in London. *Should I tell him now?* I decided to wait. Bedtime was never a good time to have a discussion that was likely to make someone angry.

I fell into a fitful sleep. My head hurt from thinking so hard about the break-in and trying to figure out who did it. I had a bad dream that night. Alice was at the kitchen door, rattling the handle, trying to get in. I was watching her from inside the laundry room, unable to move or utter a sound. Hagen was in there with me, urging me to let her in. I searched the kitchen for Felix and Chloe, but they were nowhere to be seen. I tried calling out for Seamus to help me, but no sound would come out. Alice was growing angrier with each attempt to open the door. Her eyes, black and flashing, were huge. Like the eyes of a bug.

I woke up panting and sweaty. I must have thrashed around, because Seamus woke up at the same time. He sat up and I felt his hand on my arm in the dark.

"Sylvie," he whispered, "calm down. You were having a nightmare. Calm down, love. You'll make your head hurt."

"Too late," I moaned. "It hurts so much." I felt his cool hand on my forehead, caressing my skin and smoothing my hair. I settled back under the sheet, but sleep would not come after the dream. Eventually he turned over and went back to sleep; I could hear him snoring after only a few minutes. My head was pounding. After an hour of trying to find a comfortable position, I got up and made a pot of tea. I didn't think it would hurt too much to look through the photos of London I had printed out, so I sat at the kitchen table and perused the pictures. I wanted to get more from the studio, but I was afraid to go in there at night by myself. I hated to be scared, but I knew the feeling would go away someday.

Mum was always a light sleeper—I should have known I would wake her up if I went into the kitchen. She padded in and sat down across from me.

"Can't sleep?" she asked.

"No. I'm sorry if I woke you," I replied.

"You didn't wake me," she said. I knew she was lying. "I've been restless."

"Why?"

"Oh, I suppose I worry about Greer and James. And now you and Seamus, too."

"I know why you're worried about me and Seamus, but don't be. Seamus won't go away again and he'll make sure nothing happens to us. Why are you worried about Greer and James?" I asked.

"Greer can't decide if they should get married."

"I think they should. They're perfect for each other," I said.

"I agree, but she's worried she'll make another mistake," Mum said with a sigh.

"She won't," I said with certainty.

"You know that and I know that, and even James knows that, but Greer has to know it for herself before she makes a decision. James will wait as long as it takes."

"There can never be another Neill," I pointed out. "He broke the mold."

Mum chuckled. "He really did. That man was daft." She paused for a moment. "Greer is afraid that James has some secret he's keeping from her. But I'm convinced he doesn't. They've known each other for several years—if he had a secret she'd know about it by now."

I was silent, thinking back to that receipt. I knew what it was like to think your mate has a secret, even though I trusted Seamus.

"I can understand how she feels," I said. "She just wants to be sure. But I wish she would hurry and come to her senses. I feel like going to a wedding."

Mum smiled. "You get better, then you can dance at your sister's wedding without getting a headache," she advised. She pushed herself away from the table. "I'm going to try going back to sleep. What about you?"

"I may as well clean out the fridge since I can't sleep," I said. "I'll nap later. What else is there to do?" I laughed.

She gave me a hug and went back to the guest room. I started cleaning the refrigerator, possibly my least favorite household chore. It was hard trying not to think about anything in particular.

Just as the sun was rising I heard Seamus moving around in the bedroom. He came into the kitchen scratching his beard. "What're ye doin' out here? I was worried when I woke up and you weren't in bed," he said, wrapping me in a big hug.

"I couldn't sleep, so I figured I might as well clean," I said, smiling up at him. "Tea's ready. Want some?"

He sipped his tea while I finished wiping down the walls inside the refrigerator. "What are you doing today?" I asked.

"I'll be in the shop and the studio, working and finishing the clean-up from the break-in. Then I have to submit photos and documents to the insurance company."

"I wish I could help," I said.

"You just concentrate on getting better. That'll help me more than anything else," he said.

Mum came in while Seamus was in the shower, then the three of us had breakfast together before Seamus opened the shop for business. He had already enlisted Mum's help in getting the shop and gallery ready for customers—he had spent some time cleaning up the mess while I was in hospital, but most of it remained to be done.

I was taking a break from mopping the kitchen floor when the phone rang. It was Peter, Felix's assistant from the Lundenburg.

"I'll see if Seamus is busy," I answered when Peter asked to speak to him. I peeked into the studio, where he was deep in conversation with a young couple.

"Can I have him ring you back?" I asked.

"Actually, I can probably just ask you," he answered. "Seamus was going to get us the deposit information for the sixty thousand pounds from the gallery opening. Do you happen to have the account number handy?"

I stared at the phone in my hand, dumbstruck.

"Hullo?" he asked. "Are you there, Mrs. Carmichael?"

"Aye." I was struggling to understand what he had said.

"And do you have the account number?"

"Um, no. I'll have Seamus call you back." I was fumbling for words in the face of this news. *Sixty thousand pounds? And he told me he only made fifteen thousand? What's going on here?*

My head was starting to hurt.

Forgetting about the mopping, I went into the bedroom to fetch Seamus's laptop. I didn't know what I was looking for—I just felt compelled to check his email, his spreadsheets, anything I could think of to attempt to figure out what was going on.

I knew all his passwords. Typing quickly, I accessed his email and scrolled through his inbox and folders. There was nothing out of the ordinary. Orders, updates from galleries that sold his work on consignment, advertisements, and spam. I accessed his spreadsheets next—he kept records of earnings from different galleries, museums, gift shops, and cultural centers. There were no entries from the Lundenburg. *That's odd.*

Seamus would never leave financial records from such a huge gallery opening to memory. They had to be somewhere. I had to find them.

I closed his emails and spreadsheets and started scrolling through other files. But it quickly became obvious that there were too many files for me to search, so I shut down the laptop before he came looking for me.

I didn't know what to do or where to look for more information about his earnings. Should I confront him? There was a forty-five thousand pound difference between what he claimed he made and what Peter told me he made. Surely he knew about it. Perhaps he had been mistaken. But why wouldn't the amount be on the spreadsheet with all his other earnings?

Something wasn't right.

I felt that familiar need to talk to someone. Mum was just a few meters away in the shop, but I wasn't sure I wanted her to know there was a problem, as I didn't want her to worry. I rang up Greer. She answered on the first ring.

"How are you feeling?" she asked.

"Not great," I answered, then launched into an explanation.

"That's a bit different from finding a random receipt, Sylvie. You need to talk to him about this. That's a huge discrepancy."

"But why would he do something like that?"

"I honestly don't know. He could have accounts you don't know about, but I think you're entitled to know how much he's making."

"I hate to approach him about this."

"I know. But I think you need to this time. It could be nothing," she said in a hopeful voice. "Maybe it's nothing more than a misunderstanding."

"That's a pretty big misunderstanding."

"It is," she agreed.

After we ended our call I went back into the kitchen, where Seamus was eating a scone over the sink.

"How're ye feeling, love?" he asked.

I shrugged. "All right, I suppose."

He arched his eyebrows at me. "Are ye overdoin' it? The kitchen floor's clean already. You don't have to mop. Why don't you have a lie down?"

"Seamus, I—" I began.

"Hmm?" he asked, turning back to the sink.

"I think you're right. I think I will lie down for a bit."

He pecked me on the cheek before going back to the shop, then Mum came in. She ate a container of yogurt at the table. There had been a lot of customers throughout the morning, she told me, and she hadn't had time to do much tidying up in the studio. She stood up to discard the yogurt cup and looked at me with a critical eye.

"You're not looking verra good, Sylvie. I think you need to rest this afternoon. No more cleaning. Mum's orders. Seamus would agree, I'm sure."

I nodded. I desperately wanted to tell her about the money, but I just couldn't bring myself to say anything.

Though I tried resting during the afternoon, I knew I wouldn't be able to quiet my mind. My thoughts were a vicious cycle of worry about my concussion, about Seamus, and about my concussion getting worse because of my worrying.

I was in a ragged state by dinnertime. Seamus came into the bedroom to let me know that dinner was ready and found me curled into a ball on the bed, my head in my hands.

"Sylvie! What's the matter?" He hurried to my side and sat down.

I couldn't stand the wondering any longer. "Seamus, I need to talk to you."

"What is it, love?"

"Peter, from the Lundenburg, phoned earlier. He wanted to know if I knew your account number, because he wanted to deposit the sixty thousand pounds you made at the gallery." I stopped, waiting for his reaction.

None came. He didn't blink, didn't frown, didn't do any of the things I thought he might. Instead he simply said, "I'll call him back."

"But Seamus, you told me you made fifteen thousand pounds. Which is it?"

"I have to look into it," he said vaguely. He looked away.

"Seamus? Is there something we have to discuss?"

"Nay. It's time for dinner."

He was lying. I was sure of it. I could tell by his short, clipped sentences and the way he wouldn't look me in the eye.

"I'm not hungry. I want to know what's going on."

"Nothin's goin' on, Sylvie."

"I know when you're lying to me."

"It's nothing!" he roared. I was stunned into silence. He walked out the bedroom door, slamming it behind him. He didn't speak to me the rest of the evening, and Mum went to bed early, exhausted from her long day. Seamus left our room early the next morning, clearly not wishing to talk to me again about the discrepancy I had brought to his attention. I got up once I knew he was in the shop. After my shower and breakfast, I wondered again how I was going to spend a day that stretched for so many hours in front of me. I couldn't visit Eilidh, since she was working at the potter's. I could talk to Mum, but she was needed in the shop where Seamus would be nearby, and I didn't want to talk to him. I could call Greer, but I knew she had a class to teach.

I could call Chloe. She might be able to shed some light on whatever was happening with Seamus. She might be at work, too, but I took the chance that she would be available to chat for a few minutes.

She did, indeed, have some time to talk.

"What's new, Sylvie?" she asked. I didn't know if Seamus had spoken to Felix about the break-in, so I gave her a brief summary of the attack. It seemed so long ago.

She gasped. "Are you all right? Would you like Felix and me to come up there to help?"

"That's verra kind, but you don't need to do that. My mum is here visiting, so she's helping Seamus in the shop and in the gallery whilst I'm not able to work."

"I can come up just to keep you company," she suggested.

"That's lovely of you, but if you and Felix are still planning to visit at the end of the month, there's no need to come before that. It's a long drive. Hopefully I'll be fully recovered by then and I'll be able to show you around and hike the Highlands with you both."

"If you're sure..." she said.

"I'm sure. I actually didn't ring you up to tell you about my injuries. I phoned to ask you about something else." I hesitated.

"I'll help if I can," she said.

"I was wondering if Seamus ever spoke to Felix about the money he made during the time he was working at the Lundenburg."

"I don't know. Felix hasn't mentioned it. Want me to ask him?"

"No, no," I said hurriedly. "If he hasn't said anything, I don't want to draw his attention to it."

"Can I ask why you need to know?"

I sighed. I had asked her an unusual question, and I felt it was only fair that I tell her why. "He told me he only made fifteen thousand pounds from his time at the gallery. But Peter called here yesterday and said the amount was sixty thousand pounds."

"You know, Felix did mention that Seamus had done very well at the gallery. He wouldn't have said that if Seamus had made only fifteen thousand pounds. Not that fifteen thousand isn't good," she hurried to add, "but I know what Felix considers 'very well,' and it's more than fifteen thousand."

"That was my initial reaction, too," I said. "Seamus told me I should be grateful, because it's a lot of money."

"And he's right, but it's not sixty thousand pounds. Tell you what. Let me try to get the information out of Felix without actually asking him. I'll get back to you."

I didn't know what to do after Chloe rang off. I tried cleaning, but my efforts were half-hearted and sloppy. I was bored, and the feeling made me tired. I was frustrated because there were so many things I wasn't allowed to do.

But I could go for a walk. After telling Mum where I was going, I slipped out the front door, making sure it was locked behind me. I wasn't afraid to be outside in the daylight, though I wondered if I would ever be able to go out at night again.

I wandered up and down the lanes of the village until I arrived at the potter's shop. The heavy bell above the door jangled when I walked in. Eilidh, who had been standing with her back to the door, turned around.

"Hi! What are you doing out of the house?"

"I was so bored. I had to get out before I went mad. How are things going here?"

"Great! I'm glad you came by."

I wandered around the shop, admiring all the pieces of pottery. Eilidh followed me, chatting, since there were no other customers.

"I love working here," she said. "My boss is great, and the people who come in love to talk," she said with a laugh.

"Hmm," I answered, picking up a serving bowl and examining it.

"What's up, Sylvie? You're barely listening to me. I can tell your mind is somewhere else."

I put the bowl back on the shelf and let my hands fall to my sides. "I think Seamus is hiding something from me. Remember the receipt that had me all upset? Well, it's more serious this time. I think he lied about how much money he made in London."

"What did he tell you?"

"I found out yesterday that he actually made four times the amount he told me."

"You're joking."

"I wish I was joking. I'd be much happier right now."

"Have you talked to him about it?"

"I tried, but he yelled at me and said he would look into it."

"That doesn't sound like him."

"I know. That's what has me so worried."

"I don't blame you," she said. I was hoping she would have some helpful advice, but she didn't. After a few minutes of browsing I left and continued walking.

As I walked my thoughts kept returning to Hagen. He knew about the map hidden behind the Leitch painting. He had shown an interest in the painting—so much so that he had driven all the way from London to see it. He held a position of prominence in the art world. He probably knew the value of a painting by an old Scottish master, even if it was impossible to put a value on the map behind it and the discovery of the ancient jewels from the Honours of Scotland.

And he was tall. And brawny. He could easily have been the one who broke into our cottage and attacked me.

It had been Hagen. I was sure of it now.

I turned on my heel and walked briskly back to the cottage. Oddly, the realization that I knew who had been in my home rattled me enough to send me scurrying back for safety. I unlocked the kitchen door and charged into the room breathlessly.

Mum was standing over the sink, eating a banana. "What's the matter, Sylvie?"

"Where's Seamus?" I asked, ignoring her question and forgetting temporarily my anger and confusion toward him.

"He's in the shop. Are you all right?" she asked, walking toward me.

"I'm fine. I think I know who broke into the house."

"Who?"

"A man you haven't met. His name is Hagen, and he's a professor at the University of London."

"How do you know it's him?"

I held up my hand and walked to the shop doorway. "Seamus?" I called.

"Aye?" he answered. His voice was coming from the studio. I glanced around the shop. It was empty.

"Come here!" I called. "I'm in the kitchen." I turned back to Mum and in just a moment Seamus came into the room.

"What's going on?"

"I went for a walk, and whilst I was out I realized something. I think Hagen is the one who broke in."

"Hagen?!" Seamus repeated.

"Aye. It had to have been him," I insisted. "He was one of the few people who knew about the painting, he came all the way from London to see it, and he's part of the art world, so he probably knows its value." I sat down, exhausted from walking and thinking and speaking.

"Sylvie, I think you need to rest," Mum said.

Seamus nodded. "Sylvie, you're not going to recover from your concussion if you tire yourself out trying to solve crimes."

"But don't you want to know who did it?"

"Of course I do, love, but I want you to get well. Let's leave the investigating to the police."

"But I'm not investigating anything—I'm just thinking," I insisted.

"And that's the problem. You're supposed to be relaxing."

"It's so boring," I whined.

Seamus grinned. "I know, love. I'm sorry. I'll go for a walk with you as soon as the shop closes, if you'd like."

"Okay," I said with a small smile. If he could make an attempt to get out of the doghouse and back into my good graces, the least I could do was go for a walk with him.

That afternoon I sat at my work table in the studio and leafed through photos. I still wasn't allowed to look at them on my computer, but I figured it couldn't do any harm to look through physical photos. I made lists of photos that I wanted to group together for collages and photos I would make into larger prints to sell on consignment at various gift shops around the Highlands. That was a good way, I had found, to make some extra income.

Seamus and I took our walk later that evening, after making sure Mum was locked safely inside and promising to be back before dark. We didn't even talk while we walked—we just savored the cool summer evening and the soft lamplight coming from inside the cottages of our tiny village.

But something was nagging at me. As much as I wished I could enjoy the time I was spending with my husband, I couldn't get the questions about money out of my head. I chose not to ruin the evening by trying to discuss it again, but more than anything I just wanted some straight answers.

Instead, I ended up with more questions.

The next morning I was tidying up the kitchen when I heard Seamus's mobile phone ring. I stood still, listening for his voice coming from the shop. But as soon as he answered, he must have moved farther away, into the studio.

Tiptoeing, I stole through the shop and stood outside the studio door, straining to hear what he was saying. I hated eavesdropping, but I didn't have a choice. I wasn't getting any answers directly from my husband. Though I couldn't make out most of the words, there were a few I heard clearly: "Clydesdale," "forty-five thousand," and "private."

When I could no longer hear him speaking, I turned and went back to the kitchen as quietly as I had come. But I had no more interest in cleaning up from breakfast. I was lost. I couldn't bear to think that Seamus was hiding something from me, but now I had confirmation that he did, in fact, know something about Clydesdale Bank. That receipt I had found hadn't belonged to someone else, after all.

And that wasn't all. He had quite clearly named the amount of money in question—the difference between what the Lundenburg said he made and what he said he made.

Why was he keeping forty-five thousand pounds private, in a bank with which he claimed not to have an account?

Without realizing what my fingers were doing, I rang up Greer. I was surprised when James answered.

"Hullo, Sylvie. Good to hear your voice. How have you been feeling?"

"Fine," I answered in a flat voice.

"Greer isn't here. She left her phone behind when she went to work this morning. Can I help you with something?"

I hesitated. I didn't want to unburden myself to James.

As if reading my thoughts he said, "If this is about Seamus and the money, Greer already told me."

"Oh." I wished Greer had asked if she could share what I had told her, but at least maybe James could give me some good advice.

I told him about the phone call I had overheard. There was a momentary silence on the other end after I finished talking.

"It certainly sounds like you're not wrong to think there's something he's keeping from you," James said. "But I know Seamus, and I just can't believe it's anything too serious. Want me to talk to him?"

"No!" I almost shouted. "Thanks anyway. I think this is something I should handle myself. Any advice?"

"You know me, Sylvie. I'm always one for being up front and honest. I would just talk to him and ask him outright about the money and the phone call."

"But he yells when I try to talk to him about it. It's obviously something he doesn't want to discuss. And if I tell him about the phone call, I'll have to admit I was eavesdropping."

"But you don't want your marriage to be tainted by secrets. So what if he yells? It sounds like you're entitled to an explanation. And so what if you eavesdropped? His refusal to answer your questions necessitated it. At least that's what I'd say if he accuses you of listening in on his conversation."

I sighed. There *had* to be another way to find out what Seamus was doing. But the more people I discussed it with, the more I was hearing to confront him directly.

And I knew what Mum would say—she would advise me to talk to him about it.

But I couldn't. Though we had declared a silent truce, I preferred its distrustful peace to the anger and tension I knew would erupt if I broached the subject of money with Seamus again.

Just then Chloe texted me. She and Felix were beginning to wind things down for their holiday to the Highlands, she said, and she wanted to make sure everything was okay between Seamus and me and that she and Felix could still visit.

I welcomed the thought of having Felix and Chloe at our cottage. Without even knowing it, they could be the buffer Seamus and I needed right now. They wouldn't come for a couple more weeks, but hopefully I would be recovered from my concussion and I could get out of the house and show them around.

Seamus was pleased when I told him Felix and Chloe were making their plans to visit. We talked at dinner about the places they should see, along with the possibility of introducing them to Callum and Eilidh.

Though Seamus would not be able to spend as much time with our friends as he would like, he would be able to leave the shop and gallery in Mum's capable hands while they visited. He and Mum prepared for visitors, tourists, and clients who might be looking for Seamus while he was touring with Felix and Chloe. As the days passed, I was able to help them in the shop, cataloguing inventory and making sure Mum understood how to use the register, how to run credit cards, and how to make bank deposits. Though she had been in the shop since the attack on me, she had insisted on helping by keeping the spaces tidy, interacting with customers, and helping to clean up the damage wrought by my attacker. She hadn't wanted to learn about the money side of the business, so Seamus handled all the money during my convalescence. But when Mum learned that Felix and Chloe were visiting, she insisted upon learning how to complete transactions so we could be out for an entire day and not worry about the shop.

Seamus planned meals, too. He knew Felix and Chloe were familiar with all the latest food trends in London and visited restaurants frequented by the rich and famous, but he wanted to show them how outstanding Scottish food could be in the hands of the right chef. He planned menus with everything from salmon to fish and chips to cullen skink to haggis. He wanted our big-city friends to go home with a new appreciation for Scottish cuisine.

The days until Felix and Chloe arrived passed quickly. I was able to spend time each day helping Mum and Seamus in the shop and the gallery. I shopped for the pantry staples Seamus would need to cook, and I even found some time to sneak in some work on my photography. I worried a bit about having them stay at our house—they had such a magnificent flat in London that staying in a cottage in Cauld Loch might seem dowdy. But Seamus assured me that they lived the high life in London because it was expected of them. They longed for simplicity, and he was sure they would enjoy our hospitality.

Nothing happened to mar the uneasy peace that had settled between me and Seamus, and I didn't want to disturb it by asking questions about money. As the summer drew to a close, though, we would have to decide whether we could hire Eilidh. I would need more information about our financial situation in order to make a decision. And as I was feeling better and beginning to work more on photography, Seamus was realizing how much he appreciated Mum's help in the shop. I suspected Seamus would miss having an assistant when she returned to Dumfries.

It was a perfect day in the Highlands when Felix and Chloe arrived. It was late August; the weather had started to get cooler and it felt delightful. Our friends had taken an early morning train from London, so they were in Cauld Loch before evening. Seamus and I went outside to greet them when we saw their hired car coming up the drive. We were thrilled to see them.

Chloe stepped out of the car in an outfit worthy of a Highland life magazine, complete with dainty—but useless—boots, a plaid button-down shirt over a silk t-shirt, and perfectly clean, creased denim trousers. Her aviator sunglasses were perched on top of her head.

Felix looked much the same as he slid from behind the wheel. He could have just come from a photo shoot, with Doc Martens, denim trousers, a shirt similar to Chloe's, and a light leather jacket.

Seamus laughed when he saw them. After shaking hands with Felix and hugging Chloe, he said, "You know those posh clothes are going to get dirty up here, right?"

"Oh, yes," Chloe hastened to assure him. "We just wanted to look the part for our trip today."

Seamus shook his head, still chuckling, and helped Felix take their bags from the boot of the car. Chloe tucked her arm through mine and we made our way into the house ahead of the men.

"I'm so happy to finally be here!" she squealed. "I've missed you."

"We've missed you, too," I replied. "We've got all sorts of things planned for the next two weeks, so I hope you're ready to spend some time outdoors with us."

She spread her arms wide. "It's just gorgeous up here! I can't wait to get outside and explore."

I laughed. "Good. We'll start in the morning. I hope you still feel the same way after a few days in the Highlands."

We introduced Mum to Felix and Chloe and the five of us sat down to one of Seamus's specialties—fish chowder.

Over big bowls of chowder and lots of bread, we chatted about everything from the weather to Scottish food to United Kingdom politics and back to lighter topics like shopping and tourist attractions. After dinner Mum went to her bedroom to watch television and the rest of us sat in the living room having coffee.

"So what's new in London?" Seamus asked.

Felix warmed to the subject quickly. He talked about the gallery, the artists who had been in recently, and some new ideas he had for exhibits. Chloe and I listened, but didn't contribute much.

Finally, during a lull in the conversation, Chloe turned to me. "Remember Hagen?"

"Of course," I replied, thinking back to the night I was attacked.

"He's taken a leave of absence from the university. No one knows where he is."

Seamus and I exchanged glances. His eyes warned me not to say anything about my suspicions that Hagen had been the intruder, but I wouldn't have. I knew Chloe and Hagen were colleagues, perhaps even friends.

"He didn't tell anyone where he was going?" I asked in surprise.

"No. No one, including Thea—remember Thea, his ex-wife?—has been able to reach him at home or on his mobile."

"Where could he be?" I wondered aloud.

Chloe shrugged. "I have no idea. He seemed very keen to find more information about that painting we talked about in London—the one with the map hidden behind it."

I looked over at Seamus, who was studiously avoiding my gaze. "Do you suppose he came up here to look for it? The painting, I mean?" I asked.

"I suppose it's possible," Chloe conceded. "He seemed to think it hadn't made its way to London after it went missing from the scene of that horrible accident."

"Why does he think that?" I asked.

"I guess because he hasn't heard anything about it, and a rumor like that would make its way around the art world very quickly. I'm surprised we haven't heard about it in the mainstream news. It seems to be a mystery that very few people know about."

I had nothing else to say. I wanted more than anything to ask Chloe if she thought Hagen was capable of violence, of taking drastic steps to obtain the painting he sought, but I knew Seamus would be furious if I said anything.

But he and I discussed it at length after we'd gone to bed. Felix and Chloe were sleeping in our room—our bedroom for two weeks was a small office off the living room. We had set up an air mattress and let Felix and Chloe think we were sleeping in a second guest room.

"Do you think it was Hagen?" I whispered to Seamus.

"I suppose it could have been him," he said. "You're pretty sure it was a man?"

"No," I admitted. "I just assumed it was a man because he knocked me down so hard and because the voice sounded low."

"It seems like reckless behavior for someone with a big-deal job in London."

"It does," I agreed. "But maybe he doesn't care about the job as long as he finds the painting. Maybe the painting and the map would make him so much money that he would never have to work anyway."

"And just live off the profits from the sale of the painting?" Seamus sounded skeptical.

"Why not?" I asked. "Just because you want to paint until the day you die doesn't mean that everyone feels the same way about their job."

"But he's important in the art scene," Seamus insisted. "I can't imagine that he would risk his position by committing a crime."

"If he found it, he would become important in different circles of people," I pointed out.

Seamus sighed. "You're right. I guess it's impossible to know what Hagen's motives are. We barely know the man."

I felt like we were banging our heads against a wall. We weren't getting anywhere in figuring out who had broken into our house, and we hadn't heard a word from the police.

"Do you suppose the police have learned anything?" I asked after a long moment.

"Seems like they would have told us if they had a suspect," Seamus answered. I sighed. My head was starting to ache from going around and around with the same questions. Seamus leaned over and kissed me goodnight. "Please try to get some sleep, love," he said sleepily. "We've got a long hike tomorrow and I want you to be rested. I don't want your head to hurt from exertion."

"Do you ever worry he'll come back?" I asked.

Seamus squeezed my hand. "He wouldn't dare. Not whilst I'm around."

CHAPTER 12

On the first full day of Felix and Chloe's visit, Seamus and I took them to the world-famous Loch Ness. Like everyone else, they wanted to spot the elusive Nessie in the cold waters of the loch. We enjoyed a boat tour of the loch, which included a trip to Urquhart Castle on the hillside above the water's edge. Though it was still summer, the wind whipped down the mountains and across the loch, assaulting our face with biting cold. Seamus and I enjoyed the day as much as our English guests because we hadn't visited Loch Ness in a while, and we had never toured the ruins of the castle on its banks.

Alas, we did not spot the monster of Loch Ness.

Chloe especially was eager to get off the main roads and explore the Highlands that most tourists didn't get to see. Seamus and I were only too happy to oblige. We took our friends on a long, lazy tour of the back roads and lanes leading away from Loch Ness and toward the interior of the Highlands.

We visited Cannich and then headed further west toward Muchrachd. Felix and Chloe were overwhelmed by the scenery and the raw, rugged beauty of the area. We got out of the car for a few short hikes, and the rest of the time we looked out the windows of the car, admiring the heart-achingly beautiful vistas.

We hated to go home that evening, but we were all hungry and we agreed that we would rather have Seamus's cooking than stop and take a chance on an unknown restaurant. So many little towns offered chippies, but not much more. And as much as I loved fish and chips, I wasn't sure our guests had that same fervor.

Mum was waiting for us when we got back to Gorse Brae. She wanted to hear all about our day and see the photos we'd taken, and she was excited to tell us of the sales she had made in our absence. For a second night, the five of us enjoyed a wonderful dinner. The talk around the table was boisterous and jovial.

The next two weeks continued in much the same way. We went farther afield on many days, with trips to the Isle of Skye, the Outer Hebrides, John o'Groats, Uig, Ullapool, and the Shetland Islands. Several times we camped overnight when we were too far from Cauld Loch to have a proper visit in just one day.

Felix and Chloe were overwhelmed by the beauty of Scotland. They told us countless times they wanted to plan a longer holiday sometime in the future.

Seamus and I were still tentative around each other during Felix and Chloe's stay. Chloe mentioned it one evening when Felix and Seamus had joined Callum at the pub.

"You two don't seem as happy as you were in London," she said.

"I really don't believe we are."

"Is it because of the money?"

"It's not the money—it's that Seamus lied about it. He won't tell me what's going on. I live with anxiety that there's another woman, and yet I'm afraid to talk to him about it. He gets angry and withdrawn. To me, this lukewarm marriage is better than knowing the truth and dealing with his anger," I replied.

"But you can't do this forever. What kind of a marriage would that be?"

I sighed. "Not much of a marriage, I'm afraid."

"So are you going to talk to him?"

"I don't want to."

"Do you think he'll just open up and tell you everything on his own?"

"No."

"I hate to see you like this. You're unhappy, he seems unhappy. You're not the same couple you were. Do you want Felix to talk to him?"

"No. I can't ask someone else to do my dirty work. I'll deal with it myself. I've just been putting it off because I'm afraid of what he's going to say."

"Whatever he says, you have a lot of friends and family who are behind you. We'll all help you if you need it."

I smiled sadly. "Thanks."

She was right, as Greer had been right, as James had been right. Seamus and I couldn't go on pretending we were happily married when he had a secret that was threatening to pull us apart. I had to talk to him.

A few nights before Felix and Chloe were to return to London, they went into Edinburgh for dinner by themselves. It was my chance to confront Seamus with an ultimatum: Either tell me the truth about the money and what happened to it, or risk losing everything we had together.

I asked Eilidh to invite Mum for dinner so she wouldn't have to witness the melee.

After I put dinner on the table, we sat down to eat. Seamus picked up his fork, but before he could eat his first bite, I stopped him.

"Seamus, we can't go on like this."

"Like what?"

"Like *this*. Pretending we're happy. Pretending you don't have a secret you're refusing to share with me. I have to know what it is you're hiding."

He put his fork down with an exaggerated sigh. "It's probably time you found out."

CHAPTER 13

"Found out what?" I asked. My throat was beginning to constrict. I put my fork down so he couldn't see my hand trembling.

"You know I was in prison," he began.

"Yes. That's not a secret."

"That's true. But what you don't know is what happened in the years before I went to prison." He paused.

"Yes?" I prompted.

He didn't say anything. He seemed to be searching for the right words. His mouth opened and shut twice as if he was going to speak, but no words came out.

"Seamus, tell me. What could be worse than you going to prison?"

"The fact that I was married before that."

I felt like a bomb had dropped on our kitchen. Silence rang through the house. Surely I had heard him wrong.

"I don't understand," I said. I truly didn't.

"I was married for a short time to a woman from Glasgow. Her name is Rose."

"I can't believe this! You were *married*? How come you didn't tell me? How could you think I didn't deserve to know about this? What other secrets are you hiding?" I was screeching.

"I'm sorry, love," he said.

"Don't you dare call me 'love,'" I seethed.

"But I love you —"

"How can you possibly love me?" I yelled. And suddenly I reached the obvious conclusion about the missing money.

"Did you give Rose the money you made at the Lundenburg?" I asked, gesticulating toward the studio.

He hung his head. He didn't have to answer—I knew where the money had gone.

"This cannae be happening," I said, half to myself.

"Please, Sylvie, let me explain."

"What's there to explain? You gave forty-five thousand pounds to a woman you were once married to and left us with fifteen thousand. It's perfectly simple," I sneered.

"But you don't know why I did it," he said, opening his palms toward me in supplication.

"I don't care why you did it. What's important is that you did it, and that you didn't tell me about Rose in the first place. How could you do this?!" My voice had risen an octave, and I was sure the neighbors could hear. I didn't care.

"Rose is sick. Very sick."

"So what?"

"Have some compassion, Sylvie."

"What?!" I shrieked. "*You're* asking *me* to have compassion? How dare you!"

"She's dying. She's in a care home and she has no money. She was destitute when she left me. We didn't have any money when we were married, neither of us had a good job. She began to run up bills—lots of them. When she was diagnosed, shopping became her therapy. She would open one credit card after another, run them up, and then couldn't pay. She asked me for a loan to invest in some scheme. Like an idiot I loaned her the money, then she lost it all."

"That's her problem, Seamus."

"I know, but I feel a responsibility for her. After she left me I met you and went on to be happy and successful, and I feel guilty about leaving her in the darkness behind me."

"How often do you hear from her? Where does she live?"

He looked down at his food, as if searching for an answer. "In Edinburgh."

"You've got to be kidding me, Seamus."

"I'm not. I sometimes visit her when we go in for the day."

I pushed myself away from the table. I couldn't bear to eat a bite. "You make me sick," I told him. "I want you to get out."

"Sylvie, don't say that. I'm sorry for everything."

"Get out. And please tell me what on earth she needed forty-five thousand pounds for."

"I paid off the mortgage on her house," he said in a whisper.

I could only shake my head.

"I'm sorry," he repeated.

"I couldnae care less how sorry you are. Now please, get away from me."

When Mum returned that evening after a lovely meal with Eilidh and Callum, Seamus was packing a bag in the bedroom. I told her what had transpired in her absence.

"Och, Sylvie, I'm so verra sorry. Where's he going to go?"

"I dinnae know and I dinnae care."

"It'll be good for you two to have some time apart."

"If I ever see him again it'll be too soon," I said, gritting my teeth.

He came out of the bedroom with a stuffed duffel bag. He looked at Mum, the woman who was like a mother to him. "I'm sorry about everything. I didn't mean to hurt you or Sylvie. I'm sorry."

Mum just gave him a sad smile.

I opened the kitchen door and waited for him to leave. His eyes caught mine before he walked out the door, but I looked away. He had no idea the pain he had caused me. I shut the door behind him and watched him walk down the drive. When he didn't get in the car, I knew he would be spending the night with Eilidh and Callum.

When Felix and Chloe returned from their romantic dinner in Edinburgh, they were shocked that Seamus had left—and even more shocked when I told them the reason.

Chloe put her arms around me. "This is my fault," she said, tears in her eyes. "I shouldn't have encouraged you to talk to him."

"It's most certainly *not* your fault," I replied. "The fault lies entirely with Seamus. You just gave me the nerve I needed to confront him. He's been lying for too long. Honestly, I don't know how he's been living with himself, the deceitful clod."

"Maybe I can talk to him," Felix suggested.

"And say what?" I asked. "Tell him he shouldn't have done something so stupid? Advise him to apologize? He already knows, and he's already apologized. Many times. Nothing is going to solve this problem." I said flatly.

I cried myself to sleep that night, embarrassed, ashamed, and sorry for myself and for a marriage that had failed.

CHAPTER 14

I woke up the next morning to a sunny day. I grimaced as I pulled up the covers and turned away from the window. But as the pain in my head slowly increased from dull to sharp to throbbing and insistent, I grudgingly got out of bed and shuffled into the kitchen for tea. Mum was already up and sitting at the table with Chloe. They stopped talking when they saw me.

"I made tea," Mum said. She knew better than to ask how I had slept or how I was doing.

"Thanks," I mumbled.

"Are you coming into the shop today?" she asked.

"I dinnae know. It depends on what Felix and Chloe want to do," I answered.

"I think we'll head back to London," Chloe said. "I don't think this is a good time for us to be here."

"Oh, no. Please don't leave now. Stay a couple more days. I'll feel terrible if you leave because of me and Seamus."

Mum looked at Chloe. "I think you and Felix could help Sylvie pass the time if you stayed for a bit longer. You can all go hiking or for a drive. Help take her mind off things."

Chloe looked up at me. "What do you think?"

"I'm not sure you could take my mind off Seamus, but it would be nice to have someone to spend the hours with. Mum, can you stay here and mind the shop? Chloe and Felix and I could go up to Speyside. Maybe they'd like to see the whisky trail."

"That sounds fun. I could use some whisky," Chloe said with a smile.

"You go and try to have a good time," Mum said, standing up and giving me a hug. I barely had the energy to return her embrace. "Now eat a good, big breakfast and get out there. Your headache will get better and so will your mood, once you have some food and do a whisky tasting."

How did she know I had a headache? Mum knew everything.

Mum went to her room and came back carrying her handbag. She handed a wad of bills to Chloe. "Take this and the three of you go out for breakfast. My treat."

"Mum, I can afford breakfast," I told her.

"No," she insisted. "My treat. Now shoo."

I smiled my thanks. I swallowed two headache tablets at the sink and turned to Chloe. "You heard Mum, tell Felix to get out here and let's go," I said, forcing a cheerful note in my voice.

Chloe looked at me with sad eyes and smiled. "All right. I'll get him. Do you mind driving, at least as far as a restaurant? Then you give directions and Felix will drive the rest of the day. You and I can have a good long day on the whisky trail."

It sounded good to me.

Though I'm sure all three of us feared that I would have a breakdown at any moment, it didn't happen. Felix and Chloe kept me talking all through breakfast, then they chatted during the entire drive to our first distillery. At the distillery our tour guide took over; Felix and Chloe were probably thankful to let him do all the talking for an hour. Then we enjoyed a tasting, bought a bottle of the smooth golden liquid, and went on to our next stop.

We visited quite a few distilleries that day—I lost count after six. Felix only had one or two small tastes and seemed content to be the designated driver. Both Chloe and I were a wee bit sozzled by the end of the day. But I was smiling, and that was exactly what I needed.

Chloe and I burst through the kitchen door when we got home. Mum was stirring something on the stove and turned around, startled, then laughed. Felix came in behind us, shaking his head and smiling.

"Had fun, did ye?" asked Mum.

I collapsed on a chair and started laughing. "Mum, a day of distillery tours was just what the doctor ordered."

Chloe sat down next to me. "It sure was. We had a wonderful time."

"What did you do today?" I asked Mum.

"I just worked in the shop. Not too many customers today."

The question I wanted to ask hung in the air between us. Chloe looked from me to Mum and back to me.

"Did he come by?" I asked.

Mum shook her head. "I think he's wise to give you some time."

"I wonder if he's painting over at Eilidh's."

My mention of Seamus had cast a pall over the gaiety in the room. It was a sudden letdown after a day spent keeping my mind off him, but I suppose it had to happen. I couldn't go forever without thinking or talking about him.

As the effects of the whisky wore off, I realized how tired I was. I bid everyone an early good night and was drifting off when my mobile phone buzzed. It was Seamus.

Missed you today. R U Ok?

I didn't want to answer. I wanted to forget all about him. But if I didn't answer his text I wouldn't be able to sleep.

I'm fine.

What did you do today?

Went to Speyside with Felix & Chloe. Distillery tours.

Sounds fun. Wish I could have gone.

I was glad he hadn't gone, so I didn't respond further. He didn't, either. I had a perverse desire to know how he had spent his day. I could call Eilidh, but I was afraid he'd hear her talking to me or worse, that she would share our conversation with him. I was never sure about Eilidh's common sense—she might not realize when a conversation was meant to be kept private.

I fell into an uneasy sleep. Whisky often had that effect on me. I'd paid for my day of no responsibility with a night of insecurity, indecision, sorrow, and little sound sleep.

I was grumpy when I woke up. Chloe was in the kitchen, nursing a hangover, she said. I almost wished I had a hangover—at least then I would have a better excuse for being a grouch.

Felix and Chloe would be returning to London the following day. My stomach twisted just thinking about their departure. They and Mum were keeping me from going mad with anger, sadness, and anxiety, though Mum couldn't stay forever, either. At some point I was going to have to grow up and face my problems on my own, without the crutch of houseguests to keep my mind and body occupied.

Chloe wanted to spend the day shopping in Cauld Loch and the nearby villages for souvenirs to take back to London. She wanted something to remind her of the most wonderful holiday she'd had in years, she said. Rather than showing her my favorite shops, I told her to take my car and explore to find her own favorites. I told Mum to take the day off, too. I wanted to spend the day working on my photos and getting back into the habit of taking care of things in our shop and gallery. Felix left in his hired car to do a last bit of exploring, so I was left at home by myself.

I wandered into the shop before opening the door to any customers. Running my fingertips along some of the pieces of artwork I'd grown used to seeing, I thought about Seamus and our marriage. I was afraid of what the future held. I went into the studio and glanced around at all my husband's paintings on the walls. There were several unfinished paintings on easels, stacked against each other on the floor and his table.

My eyes rested on his table. Looking over my shoulder though the doors were locked and no customers waited outside, I walked over to the table and pulled out the top drawer. I rifled through papers, newspaper clippings, and business detritus looking for...I didn't know what I was looking for.

There was nothing of interest in the top drawer, so I looked through the other three. I found art supplies, a get-well card he had received from Greer and James a year prior, two books on impressionist painting, and, on the bottom of the drawer, a letter. Ignoring the twinge of conscience I felt, I slid my finger under the flap and read the single sheet of paper that was inside:

Seamus,

I'm ashamed to write this, but I'm asking for a bit of help with my bills again. I invested in a company that turned out to be a scam, and I've lost everything. The people who convinced me to invest are gone. Can't find them anywhere. They took my money with them. I've gotten behind on my house payments and my credit cards. The bank is saying they're going to repossess the house. I don't know where I'll go if that happens. You don't owe me anything and I know you don't like to help me because you have a new life now, but if you don't I don't know what I'm going to do. Please, for the sake of our old friendship, please help me.

Rose

I read and reread the letter, trying to imagine what Rose looked like. Seamus had said she was sick—her handwriting was spidery, like that of someone who couldn't hold a pen firmly. My heart went out to her, despite my feelings of anger and pain. She was probably hurting far worse than I.

It wasn't her fault that Seamus had lied to me.

I put the letter back into the envelope and closed the flap. I placed it back where I had found it and put all the other items from the drawer back on top of it. Strangely, I felt calmer after reading the note from Rose. I suppose in the back of my mind I had worried that Seamus still had feelings for her, but somehow the note reassured me. At this point their relationship was nothing more than that of old friends. And one of the friends needed help.

But that didn't excuse Seamus deceiving me for years, letting me think that I was his first wife. I grimaced.

My mobile phone rang. I glanced at the caller ID. Seamus. I turned off the ringer and set the phone on my own work table, then went through the shop and unlocked the door. I didn't see anyone outside, but as soon as I turned around the bell above the door tinkled. I turned back and was shocked to see Alice standing in the doorway.

"Alice!" I cried. "How are you?"

But before I even got the words out I knew something was wrong. I knew Alice had been hiding somewhere near the front of the shop, waiting to come inside.

She stepped in and closed the door behind her, then reached for the lock and clicked it. She was standing between me and the door. Something told me that if I tried to get around her to unlock the door, I would be sorry.

"What can I do for you, Alice?" I could hear the quaver in my voice. How I wished I had answered Seamus's call.

"You can start by telling me where the painting is," she said in a low voice.

I was trying to stall for time, to figure out how to get away from her. To get help. "What painting?" I asked.

"You know what painting, Sylvie. Please don't act stupid," she answered with a sneer.

"The Leitch? We don't know where it is. We've been hoping the police will find it when they figure out who killed Florian."

"You're not telling the truth, Sylvie. What happened to the naïve little girl I had lunch with in London? She always told the truth."

"I thought we were friends, Alice. Why are you doing this?"

"You *assumed* we were friends. We were never friends."

"Why did you follow me to Westminster Abbey?"

She laughed, a hollow, mirthless sound. "You knew I was there?"

"Not until I got home. I noticed you in a picture I took."

"That was careless of me."

"Why were you there?" I asked again.

"I was following you, clearly."

"But why?"

"To find the painting. I figured you knew where it was, or that you would lead me to it. I figured you had it with you in London, to sell it there, or that perhaps you had sold it to that posh gallery where you spent so much of your time."

"It wasn't there."

"I know that now. So where is it?"

"I told you. I don't know. What do you want with it?"

"It belongs to me. I am Florian's heir, and he bought it before he died. That makes it part of his estate and, therefore, mine."

"Why don't you wait until the police find it, then claim it? They have to give it to you—it's yours."

She shook her head as if she felt sorry for me. "You don't understand, do you? That painting is worth *millions*. Do really think I'm going to get it back the conventional way? No. If I don't find that painting myself, I'm never going to see it."

"We don't have it, and we don't know where it is."

"You see, Sylvie, I don't believe you. That husband of yours is no stranger to bad behavior. Do you think I don't know he's spent time in prison? Do you think I believe he could keep his felonious hands off a priceless work of art?"

Instinctively, my anger flared up. How *dare* she talk about Seamus like that.

"Seamus would never do such a thing," I told her hotly. "He's a good and honest man." *At least when it came to art.*

She laughed, the sound erupting from her throat like a bark. "Ha! No one, let alone an artist living in the wilds of Scotland, can resist the historical importance of that painting and the money it would bring. Not Seamus, not anyone."

"You're wrong," I said, my fists clenched at my sides.

"It would have been so easy for him to take the painting after Florian left. He could have tampered with Florian's car whilst Florian was in the shop—it would have taken only a minute—then followed him, waiting for the inevitable. When Florian went off the road, Seamus could have taken the painting and disappeared before anyone knew Florian lay dying on some back road in the middle of nowhere."

"That's not what happened."

"How do you know?"

"Because I was here with him all evening, and he stayed here after Florian left, that's how."

"But how do *I* know you're telling the truth?"

I paused. I didn't really have an answer for that. "I don't care if you believe me or not. It's the truth. You're stuck with it." I couldn't believe the strength of my desire to defend Seamus from Alice's attack.

She advanced toward me and I stepped backward. "You need to leave, Alice, or I'll call the police."

"And what will you tell them? That you have a customer in your store who's asking questions?"

"I'll tell them there's a deranged woman in my store who's threatening me and won't let me leave."

"I haven't threatened you at all, Sylvie. You wouldn't lie to the police, would you?"

"Your very presence is threatening. Now go. Get out of here."

"I will, as soon as you tell me where the painting is."

"I don't know!" I yelled, exasperated. "What's it going to take to get you to believe me? And how do I know this isn't all a ruse to throw suspicion from yourself? How do I know *you* don't have the painting?"

That gave her pause, but only for a moment. She cocked her head and gave me a hard look. "Do you really think I'd come all the way up to this godforsaken place just to make you think I didn't have the painting?"

"I don't know," I said again. "Would you?"

She pushed past me and craned her neck to look around the shop. "If we had the painting, Alice, we certainly wouldn't hang it up in here."

That was the wrong thing to say. She barged into the studio and started rummaging through Seamus's unfinished paintings. "Maybe it's in here, then."

"Alice, I won't tell you again to get out." I started making my way toward my phone. But Alice was quicker than I. In two steps, she had reached my photography table and snatched my phone in her hand.

"You can't tell me what to do. Not when you have stolen property. Now where is your big lout of a husband?"

"He's not here."

"I figured," she said with a smirk. "He would have come to rescue his damsel in distress by now if he were. I asked where he was."

"I don't know."

She studied me for a moment. "Why do I get the feeling you're finally telling the truth?"

I was silent.

Her short laugh was loud in the silence of the studio. "Did he leave you? That's a hoot! What did you do?"

It only took me a moment to turn around and run for the door. Alice must have been startled by my sudden movement, because she didn't follow me right away. I was outside before she reached the door. It probably wasn't the smartest choice, because she locked the door behind me and had the shop, the studio, and our cottage to herself while I fumed outside, having left my keys indoors.

I banged on the windows of the shop. "Alice! Open the door!" But when I peered through the glass she had disappeared, no doubt to rifle through the entire house looking for something that wasn't there.

I looked up and down the lane in front of Gorse Brae and saw no one. Almost without thinking, I ran to the potter's shop and burst through the front door.

The potter, an older gentleman with thin white hair and thick glasses, blinked at me in surprise. "What can I do for ye, Mrs. Carmichael?" he asked.

"Is Eilidh here?"

"Nay. She'll be coming in a wee bit later."

"Thanks." I turned and fled out the door, no doubt leaving the potter to wonder what on earth was going on. I ran all the way to Eilidh's house and banged on the front door. Eilidh opened the door, a look of shock on her face.

"Sylvie! What's wrong? Come in, come in." She took my arm and led me inside, where Seamus was sitting at the kitchen table. He stood up quickly when he saw me.

"What's the matter?" he asked, his eyes wide.

"Alice. She's in the shop. She's locked me out and I'm sure she's ransacking the place. She's looking for the Leitch painting," I explained breathlessly.

"But the painting isn't there! We have no idea where it is!" Seamus exclaimed unnecessarily.

"I know that, but she doesn't believe it. She's convinced you orchestrated the whole accident to kill Florian and take the painting."

"Why would I do that?" he asked.

"Honestly, Seamus! We're wasting time! Please just do something to get her out of there. She's daft."

He bolted through the door and up the lane toward Gorse Brae. Eilidh and I followed behind. He could certainly move quickly for his size.

When Eilidh and I reached Gorse Brae Seamus was out front, banging on the shop window as unsuccessfully as I had.

"Can you see her in there?" I called to him.

"Nay."

Eilidh pulled her mobile phone out of her back pocket dialed quickly. She hung up just a moment later and said, "The constable's on his way."

"Thank you," I said.

"You two stay out front and watch for her to leave. I'm going around back," Seamus said.

He jogged away but returned after just a few moments. "She's gone. She must have left through the back door, because it's wide open." He shook his head ruefully. "She can't have gotten too far," he said, then looked at me. "What kind of car was she driving?"

"There was no car out front this morning when I opened up. I remember checking specifically. She walked in right behind me as soon as I unlocked the door, so she must have been hiding in the shrubs."

"So the car must have been hidden on a nearby lane," he said, rubbing his chin. Just then, the constable drove up and joined the three of us in front of Gorse Brae.

"What happened?" he asked.

I told him about Alice's appearance a short while before. "And now she's gone," I concluded. "I didn't see what she was driving."

"What was she wearing?" the constable asked.

"Typical Alice. She looked a wee bit out of place. Peasant blouse, long trousers, brogues, a fedora."

"I'll radio the information, but it'll be pretty hard to find her if we don't know what she's driving."

Alice was gone and they weren't going to find her—she had gotten too much of a head start. I suddenly realized she had been holding my phone when I left. "Seamus, did you go inside around back?"

"Nay. Why?"

"I'm hoping she left my phone behind. She was holding it when I ran out."

"Can we go in?" Seamus asked the constable.

"Aye, but let me go first." Seamus, Eilidh, and I followed him around the back of the house. The door stood wide open; he pushed it with his foot and peered around the edge of the door. Apparently there was no one inside, so he went in and we followed closely behind.

He methodically checked each room in the small cottage. Alice had done little damage in her search for the painting, if in fact she had searched at all. No drawers were open, no closet contents spilled on the floor. When we went in to inspect the shop and the gallery and the studio, we found them in much the same condition. She had pulled a few drawers open on Seamus's table, but the items inside were still stacked neatly, just the way I had left them when *I* had searched the table earlier in the day. I breathed a sigh of relief that I had put everything back as I had found it before Alice came in. Otherwise, Seamus would suspect that Alice went through his belongings and I would feel compelled to admit I had been the culprit. But I felt no such compulsion as long as no one knew the contents of the table had been touched.

My phone was on the floor near my work station. The screen was cracked; she had probably dropped it in her haste to get out of the cottage once I left. Seamus picked it up and handed it to me. "We'll get you a new phone, don't worry," he said, looking me in the eyes.

"That's okay. Maybe this one still works." I didn't meet his gaze. I didn't want him to be nice to me. I wanted to stay furious with him.

The constable asked me to sit down with him in the kitchen and give a more complete statement about what had happened, and I was happy to oblige. Now that the ordeal was over, I was starting to feel shaky. I had no idea what the woman was capable of—for all I knew I was lucky to be alive. He asked several detailed questions about Alice's appearance and her personality. I told him she was a bit odd. I explained that I had met up with her a couple times in London and that she had followed me on at least one occasion.

After promising to have local police remain on the lookout, the constable left to write up a report. Eilidh and Seamus remained at the cottage and I fixed tea for all of us.

"Do you think she really doesn't know where the painting is?" Eilidh asked.

"She certainly seemed serious about finding it," I declared. "She's so strange. Each time I met her in London she did something bizarre or out of character. I came away from each meeting realizing I really didn't know her at all."

Seamus was giving me an arch look. "Just how many times did you meet with Alice in London?" he asked, trying to keep his voice light.

It was then I realized I hadn't told Seamus about the second time I had seen Alice, and he still didn't know she had followed me to Westminster Abbey.

"Um, I guess…just twice," I stammered.

"But you only told me about one time."

"Yes."

"So you lied."

"No I didn't."

He let out an exasperated sigh. "All right then, but you deceived me." He gave me a pointed look.

I remained silent. The meaning of what he was saying wasn't lost on me.

Eilidh broke the uncomfortable silence. "Are you going to stay here, Seamus?"

"I dinnae know." He glanced at me. "I think I should."

"Why?" I asked.

"What if she comes back? You don't ever want to be alone with her again, do you?"

"No, but I doubt very much she'll be back. Besides, Mum will be back soon. And so will Felix and Chloe. We'll all be here. You should go back to Eilidh and Callum's for now," I finished in a low voice.

Eilidh looked at me sadly. "Sylvie," she began.

"What?" There was a challenge in my look.

"Nothing. Seamus is welcome to stay at our house, of course."

When the silence became too long, Eilidh and Seamus left. I watched them walk slowly down the front path. Seamus's shoulders drooped.

A tiny part of me wanted to call him back, to turn back the clock to the way things were before I knew about the money and Rose. Was it better to know the truth, or had I been better off in ignorance of Seamus's first wife?

CHAPTER 15

When Mum returned I didn't mention Alice's visit. She asked why I was so quiet and said I appeared nervous, but I blamed it on the situation with Seamus. She seemed to accept that explanation, though I wondered if she really believed me.

When Chloe returned she wasn't as accepting. "What's the matter?" she asked in a quiet voice, drawing me into the studio so Mum couldn't hear us.

I didn't want to alarm her with my tale about Alice, so I lied to her, too. "It's Seamus. I'm just upset about the whole thing."

She looked at me askance. "I'm sure that's true, but I have a feeling it's more than that. When I left here this morning you were angry. Now you seem scared. I know you're not scared of Seamus, so what's up?"

I couldn't keep lying to my friend. "It's Alice," I whispered. "I don't want Mum to know, so please don't say anything." I went on to tell her about Alice's visit. She was shocked.

"And the police are out looking for her, right?" she asked with alarm. "She can't be allowed to bully and scare you like that."

"The constable said he would put out a bulletin, but no one saw the type of car she was driving. She didn't park anywhere near Gorse Brae, so when she left through the back door she could have gone in any direction, maybe to a waiting car."

"Could someone have been waiting for her?"

"Definitely. But I wouldn't know who to tell the police to look for."

"I don't think Felix and I should leave yet," she said, her face wrinkled with worry. "I want to make sure you're all right."

"I'll be fine," I waved my hand dismissively, trying to reassure her. "Mum's here, and Seamus isn't far away if I need him."

"He wasn't here when Alice showed up," she said pointedly.

"But I went to get him, and it only took a minute," I replied, hoping she would drop the subject. The truth was that I wanted Chloe and Felix to stay, but I knew they had to get back to London. They couldn't rearrange their lives for me. I needed to summon the courage I would need to live at Gorse Brae without Seamus, without my mother, without my friends.

"Let me talk to Felix when he gets back," she said.

My head was aching. Rather than work through the pain I took some medicine and let Mum watch the shop and the gallery while I rested on the air mattress. The only positive result of my friends' departure would be to have my own comfortable bed back. I could at least look forward to that.

When I woke up an hour later, Seamus had been and gone. Mum told me he had come to retrieve some of his painting supplies—and he had told her about Alice's visit. I silently cursed him for making her worry.

"You should have told me," Mum scolded. "I wouldn't know anything if it weren't for Seamus. He's worried about all of us in the cottage with Alice on the loose."

"If you're suggesting that I ask him to come back, I can't do that," I replied.

"I'm not suggesting anything," Mum said. "I'm just telling you what he said. He said he's worried."

"So am I," I admitted. "But if Seamus and I split up, I'm going to have to get used to being on my own. I can't go running to him every time I'm scared of something."

"Don't you think it's a wee bit too soon to be talking about splitting up?" she asked gently.

My head and shoulders drooped. "I don't know what to think," I told her in a plaintive voice. I hated to hear that tone coming from my own mouth. "I just can't imagine having him back here right now. He lied to me, Mum. It was a pretty big lie."

"You're right," she conceded. "But maybe he's paying for it now. It's not as if he had an affair."

"I know that, but he *has* been involved with another woman since we've been married, even if it wasn't a romantic relationship. And he deceived me about it."

"What would you have said if he had told you?"

"I honestly don't know. Does it matter?"

"I think it matters. If you would have reacted with screaming and threats to kick him out, then it's no wonder he didn't tell you. He would have been afraid of your reaction."

"Seamus? Afraid?" I let out an ugly laugh. "He's never been afraid of anything in his whole life!"

Mum continued as if she hadn't heard me. "On the other hand, if he thought you'd react with understanding, he might have been willing to discuss it with you."

As much as I hated to admit it, Mum had a point. Was it possible Seamus had wanted to talk to me about Rose for a long time, but apprehension over my reaction stopped him? Was I really that much of a shrew?

But that didn't excuse his behavior. I still had a right to know how much he made and where the money was going. Married people talked to each other. Married people shared things with each other. And if Seamus thought I was being a shrew, he should have talked to me about it.

"I'll think about it, I promise," I told her. "I want everything to work out, but I need to be able to trust him. Now I understand how Greer's been feeling about marrying James. I didn't realize I had a reason to distrust Seamus, but now that I know he's been hiding something, it's hard to move forward."

"Just don't make any decisions until you've talked to him," Mum said, her eyes filled with sadness. She and Dad had enjoyed a long and happy marriage before his death years before, and it would be very painful to watch *both* her daughters' marriages fail—even if it was a good thing Greer's marriage to Neill had ended.

When Felix came home later that afternoon, he and Chloe disappeared into the bedroom, no doubt so Chloe could tell him what had happened and to ask if they could extend their holiday.

When they emerged Felix found me in the studio, poring over photographs. "Chloe told me what happened this morning," he said. "I'm so sorry we weren't here to help you. I think we should stay longer, at least until Seamus comes home or Alice has been caught."

I shook my head. "No, Felix. I appreciate your concern, but this is something I need to handle myself. I have to prove to myself that I can. If Seamus leaves for good, I need to know that I'm capable of living on my own, without falling apart or being paralyzed by fear." I smiled at him. "You and Chloe need to get back to London and stop worrying about me. I've promised Mum that I won't make any rash decisions about my marriage without talking to Seamus, and without serious thought."

"If you're sure…" he said. He sounded doubtful.

I gave him a quick hug. "I'm sure. It's been wonderful having you here, but you have a life to get back to, and if you stayed I would feel so guilty that I couldn't live with myself."

"Then we'll stick with our plan to head back to London in the morning."
"I'll miss you both, but that's the right decision."

When they left early the next day, I was sad to see them go. Seamus came to say goodbye. He gave Chloe a peck on the cheek and shook hands with Felix.

"Och, I'm so sorry for the way things turned out. I hope I didn't ruin your holiday," Seamus told Felix as he glanced at me. I pretended not to notice. "Will you come up again?"

"Of course we will," Felix assured him. "I hope you two are back under the same roof when we return."

I didn't know what to say, so I didn't say anything. Seamus gave me a hopeful look, but I turned away to give Chloe a hug.

"Come down to London anytime you want," she said. "You're always welcome in our home."

I wiped away a tiny tear that had made its way into the corner of my eye. Felix and Chloe slid into the hired car, dressed once again in the London idea of country clothes, and left for the train station. Seamus, Mum, and I waved until they were out of sight, then Mum abruptly went into the shop. Seamus lingered after she left.

"It was nice to see them, aye?"

"It was," I agreed.

"We should go down to London to see them again before too long," Seamus said.

"Maybe." I was noncommittal. I didn't want him think I was making plans with him.

"Well, I guess I'll see you later." He gave me a hopeful look, and when I didn't respond he walked down the drive and toward Eilidh's house.

Gorse Brae seemed so empty that day. I moped around until closing time, then Mum said she was taking me out for dinner at the pub.

"I don't really want to go out," I protested.

"I don't really care," she responded. "I'm not going to watch you slink around here all night the way I watched you all day. You need to get out. Come on." She held the door open as I walked outside, then locked it behind her and checked it by rattling the doorknob.

When Mum and I got to the pub we sat in a booth in the back at my request. A game of darts was in full swing, and when the fellows playing saw me come in, they hailed me over.

"Sylvie! Come take a turn!"

"Nay, I can't. I'm here to have dinner with my mum," I replied.

"Of course ye can play," she exclaimed. "I'd love to watch!"

"Och. All right," I said with a sigh.

I accepted a dart from one of the men, aimed carefully, and let the dart fly. Bull's-eye! The men cheered and their wives, sitting nearby, clapped and laughed. I walked over to introduce Mum and to chat for a few minutes. They were full of questions about me and Seamus. I guess word had gotten around that I had kicked him out and that he was staying with Eilidh and Callum.

I was grateful when my turn came around again so I could step away from the women and their nosy questions. I left Mum talking to them while I finished the game, then Mum and I went back to our booth and chatted quietly until our food came.

We hadn't been eating long when Seamus, Eilidh, and Callum walked into the pub. I saw them immediately and groaned inwardly. This was sure to be awkward. The people who had seen then looked at me, as if expecting some vehement reaction, but I disappointed them and remained silent and still, trying to ignore what was going on.

"Don't turn around now, but Seamus, Eilidh, and Callum just walked in," I told Mum in a low voice.

She turned around. "Mum! I told you not to turn around," I whined.

"Oh. Sorry about that," she said. Eilidh had seen Mum and she made a beeline for our table. "Sylvie! Aunt Margot! What a surprise to see you here!" Her eyes widened and her smile was broad and toothy.

Eilidh was a wee bit *too* surprised, though, and suddenly I knew she and Mum had planned this. I glowered at them. "I know what you're doing," I almost growled. "And I don't appreciate it."

"What?" Mum asked, a picture of innocence.

"I know you two planned this, to get Seamus and me together to talk."

"Well, now that he's here you might as well," Mum said. Eilidh nodded her agreement.

"What if I'm not ready?" I asked.

"You don't have to talk to him if you don't want to," Mum said. "But if you want to..." She nodded and raised her eyebrows in his direction. He hadn't even noticed me yet—he and Callum were busy talking to the men playing darts.

Seamus stopped short when he saw me. It was clear he hadn't been part of Mum and Eilidh's ambush plan. He stepped forward tentatively.

"I dinnae know you two were here," he said to Mum, then he turned to me. "Do you want us to leave?"

I hesitated, then replied. "No. Eilidh and Mum arranged this whole thing so you and I would have to talk to each other."

"You don't *have* to," Mum began, but I stopped her by putting my hand up.

"Maybe it's a good idea. If we're in a public place, it might keep us from screaming and getting too out of hand," I said to Seamus.

Seamus slid into the seat opposite me while Mum joined Eilidh and Callum at a table nearby.

"This is awkward," Seamus said. "I dinnae have anything to do with their plan."

"I know. I could tell from your reaction when you saw me sitting here."

"I've missed you," he said.

"The truth is, I've missed you too. But I still don't know how to handle what's happened between us."

"I'm sorry for everything. It's all my fault," he said, placing his hands palms-up on the table.

"Actually, I don't think that's true. I've been thinking about it," I answered. "There had to be something in my nature that made you want to keep Rose a secret. Maybe I'm too judgmental, too angry, too nagging—I don't know. But what I *do* know is this: We both have things to work out before we can move forward."

He pondered that for a few moments. "Does that mean you don't want me moving back yet?"

"I'm afraid it does."

"Because we both have things to work on?"

I nodded. I hated to make him stay away, but I had to do it to save our marriage. We had problems that we hadn't even known we had, and we both needed time to examine ourselves.

We ate our meals in silence. I glanced out the corner of my eye to see Mum, Eilidh, and Callum watching us. They would be disappointed, but their plan hadn't been a total failure. Seamus and I had spoken civilly to each other, without vitriol, and with a view toward making our marriage work. We had both acknowledged fault, and that was a big step. Seamus put his hand over mine before we stood up to join the others. My instinct was to pull my hand away, but I left it where it was.

Mum and I left Eilidh, Callum, and their reluctant houseguest at the front of the pub and took the long way back to Gorse Brae. I thanked her for trying to get Seamus and me to speak to each other and explained why he wasn't coming home with us. She seemed to understand and was happy that Seamus and I had taken one tentative step toward acting like husband and wife again.

CHAPTER 16

The police were no closer to figuring out who had killed Florian McDermott. They questioned me again, and I heard from Eilidh and Callum that they had questioned Seamus, too. Scotland Yard was apparently still working on the case, we were told, but had requested that the local police reinterview people in Cauld Loch.

Autumn was fast approaching and Eilidh's job at the potter's came to an end. The potter hated to let her go, he said, but with a dwindling number of tourists to visit the shop and buy souvenirs, his income was also dwindling. Eilidh had known from the beginning that her job would only be temporary, so she was accepting. She missed it, though, and often visited me in the shop and studio while I worked.

One morning she came in wondering whether Seamus might come to the studio to work.

"Of course he can," I told her. "This is still his house, and he's welcome to come over. I just don't want him here when he's not working."

She rang him up and told him. I had been giving more thought to hiring Eilidh as an assistant—her help would be even more appreciated now that Seamus was spending most of his time at her house and I had my own work to do in the studio. The main reason we hadn't offered her the job after our trip to London had been financial. But now that I knew Seamus had made a great deal more at the Lundenburg, it was time to tell Eilidh the job was hers if she still wanted it. I would tell Seamus later.

"Remember we talked about possibly hiring you when your job at the potter's ended?" I asked her.

"Yes."

"Well, if you're still interested, I'd love to have you come to work here."

"I'd love to!" she exclaimed. "Is it okay with Seamus?" She looked toward the door as if she expected him to be standing there.

"I haven't discussed it with Seamus, but believe me, we don't have to worry about not having the money to hire you. Seamus knows how wonderful it is to have an assistant around here, especially when I'm busy shooting photos or getting them ready to sell. He won't have any problem with it—trust me." Seamus knew better than to thwart me on this. The last thing either of us wanted right now was another fight.

"And I have a gift for you," I said over my shoulder as I walked into the kitchen. Eilidh followed me. "I bought it over a week ago when I was out shopping with Chloe." I handed her a gift bag with tissue crowding its opening.

"Ooh, this is exciting!" Eilidh said, smiling into the bag. She pulled out a leather pouch and untied the thin strings keeping it closed. "Darts!" she exclaimed. "My own set of darts! Thank you verra much."

I watched her proudly, pleased that I had made her so happy. "I promised I'd teach you, remember?" I asked.

"I remember. When can we start?"

"Tonight. You and I will go over to the pub and have a throw."

She hugged me again. "Now Callum won't be able to laugh at me for being such a terrible dart player."

I wagged my finger at her. "It will take you some time to learn, so Callum may still laugh. But not for long," I added with a smile. "Pretty soon you'll be playing with the best of them."

She grinned as she examined her new darts more closely. "They're really quite beautiful," she said.

"They are," I agreed. "My set is similar. You can feel the quality—they feel good in your hand."

She put them aside and turned to me. "Where should I start? You want me to start today, right?"

"Uh, sure. I hadn't really thought about it. But there's a lot you can do to help around here. Mum will help, too." I gave her a list of jobs that would keep the two of them busy for the next three days, then went out to shoot some photos on Cauld Loch. I didn't want to be around when Seamus came over.

The loch was at its most glorious in the late summer and early fall. The trees lining its banks were beginning to lose their green and gain a tinge of yellow and orange. When the sun was shining and the wind wasn't blowing, I could see a perfect reflection of the trees in the chilly water that gave the loch its name. An otter family splashed in the water, playing games with each other. I sat quiet and still, watching them until they tired of their activities and swam off. I took as many photos of them as I could, but I didn't want them to hear the shutter clicking so I used the camera on my mobile phone. I hoped the photos would turn out well. I sat for a bit longer, waiting to see what other animals might appear. I was rewarded with two kestrels and a hawk soaring high above the loch, no doubt searching its cold waters for a meal.

It can be frustrating to be a photographer, as I discovered soon after Seamus gave me that first camera. It can take all day to get a perfect shot—an unlucky photographer could wait many hours for a shot that never comes.

But this day was an anomaly. Shots appeared in front of me—the otters, the kestrels, the hawk. The sun playing on the water was an exquisite backdrop for the birds and the animals. I couldn't have planned a better time to take the photos. To think I had gone to the loch simply to get away from Seamus.

It was quiet at the loch. The tourists had disappeared, along with the traffic, the noise, and the litter they left behind. I took hundreds of shots. Normally I would be anxious to get back to the studio to see the photos on the computer, but on this day I was content to sit and wait for the photos to reveal themselves to me. My time at the loch gave me a chance to think uninterrupted about Seamus, our marriage, his lies, and my tendency to judge others.

As the sun moved across the sky and the shadows on the water shifted, I decided to move to another spot for a different angle. I packed up my lenses, my tripod, my camera, and my rucksack. Before leaving my spot under an ash tree, I stood up and listened to the sounds around me—the lapping water of the loch, the unseen birds chirping, the leaves rustling in the trees over my head.

But then I heard another sound, like a twig snapping. I stood as still as a statue, straining my ears to hear the sound again. But it didn't repeat itself. It could have been anything—a fox, a badger, a weasel. Or a person.

When I moved, I did so tentatively. I took a step, then paused, then took another step. No sound. I shifted the rucksack on my back to make it more comfortable, and as I did so I thought I heard the sound again. I looked around but saw nothing. The trees were thick where I stood, so I might not see a person who wanted to remain unseen. I was beginning to feel nervous—if the same thing had happened six months earlier, I wouldn't have given the noise a second thought. But after the break-in and the visit from Alice, I was easily unnerved. I didn't want to flee to the safety of

Gorse Brae, though, because I wanted to show myself, and any person who might be nearby, that I wasn't afraid.

So I kept walking. I moved out of the woods and toward the edge of the water—it felt safer to be exposed and visible rather than hidden among the growth of trees. I glanced over my shoulder occasionally as I walked, but I didn't see anything.

It wasn't until I found a new place to set up my camera equipment that I heard the sound again. Something—or someone—was following me. I was sure of it. I reached into my back pocket for my mobile phone to call Mum or Eilidh, then realized with a jolt of anxiety that I had no service. I was out here alone, with no way of communicating, and possibly in the sights of someone who meant me harm.

I decided to forget about proving how brave I was. I needed to get home and back among other people. I packed up the camera equipment again, without taking a single photo in the new spot, and started back in the direction from which I'd come.

I hadn't gone more than twenty steps when I saw a gorgeous red fox standing in front of me. He stared at me in curious wonder, but didn't run away as I expected him to do. Moving in slow motion, I reached back and gently slid the rucksack off my shoulder. I bent down to unzip the bag and get my camera out. I glanced up to make sure the fox was still there; he was, watching and waiting to see what I would do.

I lifted the camera to my face, squeezed one eye shut, and focused on the fox. Miraculously, he was standing regally still, almost as if he knew I wanted to take his picture. When I had snapped the shutter several times, he took off running through the woods. I smiled in satisfaction, knowing I had gotten some excellent photos. I bent down to put the camera away. Zipping up the bag, I glanced out of the corner of my eye and noticed a pair of boots standing behind me. With a gasp I stood up and wheeled around to face the person.

It was Hagen. He looked different from the last time I had seen him. Now he sported a long, ragged-looking beard, rumpled clothing in camouflage colors of green and brown, and a hat pulled low over his eyes.

"Hagen!" I exclaimed, looking around warily for the quickest escape. "What are you doing here?"

"Hiking," came the reply.

"But why here?" I could hear the suspicion in my voice. "Why in Cauld Loch?"

"Because I saw what a beautiful place it was when I came up to have a look at that painting, and I wanted to come back and explore. I took a sabbatical from my position at the university to spend some time getting back to nature."

"Chloe mentioned that you had taken a leave from your job. No one knows where you are, and I think some of your colleagues are a wee bit worried." I had the feeling he wasn't telling the truth. "Have you been following me?" I asked him, feeling a little more courageous now that I knew the source of the noises I had heard in the woods.

"I have," he answered. "I'm sorry if I scared you. I know you're a photographer, and I saw you come into the woods and head down toward the shore. I figured you'd know the most beautiful places, so I followed you."

"You should have announced yourself," I said. "I could have talked to you about the loch, given you some tips on where to go next."

"It seemed like you were trying to be quiet, to take pictures, so I didn't want to disturb you."

Something about this conversation was unreal. I was sure he was lying, and he probably suspected my thoughts, but I continued speaking to him as if I believed him and he believed me.

"Well, it was nice running into you, Hagen. I have to be getting home. Take care of yourself."

"Wait a minute," he said, reaching for my arm. I pulled it out of his grasp.

"What do you want?" I asked.

"Tell me what you know about the painting."

I didn't bother pretending not to know which painting he was referring to. "I don't know anything about it, and I don't know where it is."

"Are you trying to tell me you don't know what happened to the painting after Florian was killed?"

"That's exactly what I'm telling you. Now I have to leave." I marched away quickly, only looking back once or twice to see if he was watching me. He was. I shivered. I wouldn't be venturing into the woods again soon, no matter how lovely the view.

When I returned to Gorse Brae Eilidh was waiting for me. "Chloe phoned," she said. "She tried to reach you on your mobile, but it went right to voicemail."

"Did she leave a message?"

"She just said she was trying to find you."

I tried calling her back, but there was no answer. Her phone went straight to voicemail, too. I left her a message asking her to ring me up when she got a chance.

I spent the rest of the day going through the photos I had taken at the loch. Some were very good, some were just average. My favorites were always the ones with heavy dark and light contrasts, but those photos weren't always my customers' favorites. I'd put all kinds of pictures online and had discovered an audience for each type.

Chloe rang me up that night as I was getting ready for bed. Mum had announced that she would be going back to Dumfries in a couple days, so she and I had stayed up late talking. I hated the thought of her leaving—I had gotten used to having her around and suddenly I didn't want her to go.

"Sylvie, you'll never guess what happened. Remember Thea? Hagen's ex-wife? She was found murdered in her house." Chloe said breathlessly.

I was stunned. "Do they know who did it?"

"The police don't know. Her body was found yesterday. She had been dead for several days."

"I can't believe it. Because you'll never guess what happened to me today. I was in the woods down by the loch taking pictures, and who should be following me but Hagen!"

"You saw Hagen?" She sounded incredulous.

I nodded as I spoke. "Yes. He looked terrible. He hadn't shaved in ages and he was dressed in clothes that looked as if he'd slept in them for days."

"The police have been looking for him everywhere down here," Chloe said.

"Will you tell them to come up here?"

"I have to. They say he's not a suspect, that they're looking for him because they want to talk to him."

"You know what it means when the police say they just want to talk to someone. I'm sure he's a suspect. How could he not be?"

"He'll be crushed when he hears the news," Chloe said.

"If he doesn't know already," I said pointedly. "If he knows, he must also know the police are looking for him. And yet he chose to disappear and come up to the Highlands, allegedly to get back to nature."

"Where did you say he was?" Chloe asked.

I told her I had been walking near the shore of Cauld Loch when I saw him. It wouldn't be long, I knew, before the peace of our tiny village was disrupted again, this time with police looking for a possible murder suspect. The world was indeed becoming a scarier place.

I was right—it was only an hour or so, during which I tried unsuccessfully to sleep, before I heard sirens breaking the silence of the darkness, no doubt speeding toward the woods by the loch and their grimy inhabitant. I texted Chloe to let her know the police had wasted no time in their search for Hagen.

Let me know if they find him, will you? she replied.

I don't know if I'll even find out, but I'll text you if I learn anything. I answered.

The next day I drove by the loch, hoping to see some evidence of activity that I could report to Chloe. There were several police cars parked along the side of the road near the spot where I had exited the woods, but no sign of any people. I wondered if they had found the elusive professor yet.

Later that afternoon I checked the local news online. Indeed, a man wanted for questioning in connection with a crime in London, a Dr. Hagen Ridley, had been apprehended in the woods near Cauld Loch. I texted Chloe with the news. She was grateful, and said she would pass the information along to the people in Hagen's department who were worried about him.

Seamus had seen the news, too, and he came straight to Gorse Brae to talk about it.

"You've heard about Hagen, I assume?" he asked as he came in through the door of the shop.

"Yes. Chloe called last night and told me the whole story."

"Do you think he did it? Murdered his ex-wife?"

"How would I know that?"

"You met him."

"So did you."

"Aye, but don't women have a sense about those things?"

"I wouldn't think so. Otherwise all crimes would be solved by women and their 'sense,'" I answered, wiggling my fingers like a magician.

"Och, you know what I mean. You read people better than men."

"Sometimes," I conceded. I didn't add, *If I read people so well, how come I didn't know about Rose?*

As if he was reading my mind, Seamus blushed and looked away.

"How did you hear about Hagen?" I asked, trying to find a way to peek through the curtain that had suddenly fallen between us.

"Saw it online. I wonder how the police knew to look up here."

"I saw him yesterday in the woods, that's how."

Seamus looked at me in shock, his mouth agape. "You saw him yesterday?" he repeated.

I nodded. "I was down by the loch trying to get some good shots and he appeared behind me."

"He just happened to bump into you?" Seamus asked, a skeptical look on his face.

"He had been following me."

"Why?"

"Why do you think? Why has anything happened lately? Because of that Leitch painting, that's why."

"What did he say?"

"At first he tried telling me that he wanted to get back to nature, and that he followed me because he knew I was trying to take photos. But I didn't buy it, and I think he realized it. Eventually he fessed up and asked what I knew about the painting. I told him I didn't know anything."

"And he just accepted that and walked away?"

"No. I walked away. He watched me leave."

"Och, you shouldn't have been in the woods by yourself, Sylvie."

"I know that, but I've never had an issue in the past. It's always been peaceful and quiet down by the loch."

"Please take someone with you next time."

"I will." I expected him to suggest taking him, but he didn't.

Seamus didn't say anything for a few moments, and the silence started to feel awkward. "Are you staying here to work this afternoon?" I finally asked.

"If it's all right with you. I'm working on a big piece, one that's too big to paint at Callum and Eilidh's house."

"That's fine. I'll do something in the shop."

"You can stay in the studio. It would be nice to have you in there with me." His tone was light, hopeful.

"I don't think so, Seamus. Not yet." It was getting easier to say that to him, even with the look of sadness that crossed his face when he turned to go into the studio.

"Where's your mum?" he asked, turning around at the doorway of the studio.

"She left this morning."

"Oh. I didn't know she was leaving."

"I'm sure she wanted to say goodbye, but with things the way they are right now, it was probably best for her not to."

"Oh."

I left him alone while he worked and eventually went into the kitchen to make dinner for myself. I was stirring the contents of a pot when Seamus poked his head in.

"I'm headed back. Anything you need done here?"

"No, I'm fine."

"What are you making?"

"Tomato soup."

"From a *can*?" he sounded incredulous.

"Yes, from a can," I replied testily.

"At least let me show you an easy way to have homemade soup. Throw that rubbish away," he said, pointing to the pan.

I looked dubiously at him. "I don't mind tomato soup from a can," I said. "It's horrible. Get rid of it. I promise you'll like mine better."

I shrugged. I was secretly happy he had caught me making my dinner. I wasn't looking forward to soup from a can, but now that Mum wasn't doing the cooking I didn't know how I was going to survive. I didn't know how to cook a thing. Mum had tried to teach me a thousand times, but I was lucky enough to have married a man who knew his way around a kitchen.

And I had kicked him out.

This didn't mean I was letting him come back to Gorse Brae—it simply meant I was accepting his help in becoming more self-sufficient, more independent.

He sautéed onion and garlic, then added a large can of tomatoes, some broth, a wee splash of cream, and salt and pepper. He handed me the immersion blender and showed me how to use it. It was easy—and fun. We didn't talk much while we worked side by side, but the silence wasn't unbearable. It wasn't a comfortable situation, but it wasn't terribly awkward, either.

While the soup was simmering I cut thick slices of bread and offered to let Seamus stay for dinner. To my surprise, he said he would go back to Callum and Eilidh's house and eat there. I thanked him for helping me and he left.

While I ate I contemplated everything going on with Seamus. Was it possible he was getting along fine without me? Did he miss me?

I thought about ringing up Eilidh and asking her, but it seemed such a teenaged thing to do that just thinking about it embarrassed me.

I had no choice but to accept that I was by myself for the present, and I would have to get used to it. *Maybe it'll get easier*, I thought.

But when it came time to get ready for bed, I was afraid. Memories of Florian's murder, the attack in the cottage, of Alice's visit, and of Hagen's mysterious appearance in the Highlands crowded their way into my mind and prevented me from falling asleep. I couldn't stop thinking about what happened the last time I was alone for a night—the night Seamus went camping in the Cairngorms. The attack had been horrifying, and as I lay in my bed, listening for every sound, I tried to think of happier times. I thought about the day Seamus and I were married, the day Greer was reunited with Ellie after Neill had kidnapped her, and the fun I had had with Felix and Chloe when they visited. I thought about getting together with Greer on trips to Edinburgh and came up with a bucket list of places I wanted to photograph.

Eventually sleep came, but it didn't last long.

The phone rang in the middle of the night. It was Eilidh. She was crying.

"Sylvie, I'm so sorry to bother you at this hour," she sobbed.

"Eilidh, what's wrong?" I threw off the covers and propped myself up on one arm, reaching for the lamp on the nightstand. When light flooded the room I blinked, still confused.

"Callum and I had a fight."

"About what?"

"My job at your shop. He thinks I should be looking for something in accounting, like I had before."

"Why? Doesn't he approve of you working in our shop?"

"He just thinks I could make more money if I had a full-time job that didn't fluctuate with the seasons."

"But your job with us is a stable position—we talked about that, remember? Seamus has made enough money that we don't have to worry about being able to pay an employee…an assistant," I corrected myself. I didn't want Eilidh to think we considered her to be nothing more than an employee.

"I think he wants me to have a job that sounds more posh, not just working in a shop somewhere."

"Do you want to come over?" I asked. I rubbed my eyes with my free hand.

"I'd better not leave. He'd be mad."

"What can I do to help you?"

"Nothing, I guess. I was just so upset. I needed to talk to someone and Seamus isn't really an option. I don't want to ask him to take sides when he's staying right here in our house."

"Come over in the morning. I'll make tea. We can talk then."

"Okay," she sniffled. "I'll be there early."

I never did get back to sleep after she called. I was worried about her—she was such a sweet soul, and she didn't take criticism well. Callum, for as much as he loved her, sometimes didn't think before he spoke. I wondered if she would start looking for another job. I had gotten used to having someone around the shop to do the little, time-consuming chores I didn't have time for when I was working on my photography. And it was nice to have some company, as much as I was trying to get accustomed to being alone.

I was on my third cup of tea by the time Eilidh showed up in the morning. I had spent the rest of my night watching television, and a very dull show at that. If that show couldn't put me to sleep, nothing would.

Eilidh's eyes were red and puffy when she walked in. She turned to face me and sniffled, placing a tissue against the end of her nose.

"I've cried so much my nose hurts," she said with a little smile.

I put my arms around her. "I'm sure Callum was just in a foul mood and he took it out on you. I bet you'll find that he's in a much happier frame of mind today. Have you seen him?"

"No. He left for work whilst I was in the shower."

"You'll see him later. Maybe the two of you can talk things over."

"Here's my problem, Sylvie: If you and Seamus aren't living together right now, why should it be any easier for me and Callum? You and Seamus are the last people anyone thought would have problems."

I didn't know what to say to her. I thought for a few moments before answering. "Seamus and I are going through a rough patch, that's for sure. But it's because of a lie. Or a deception, or whatever you want to call it. That's the difference. There's been no lying between you and Callum—just a disagreement over money, and lots of couples deal with that. And they get through the problems just fine. And so will you and Callum." I gave her another squeeze.

Eilidh was subdued the rest of the day. She didn't engage with the customers in her usual jovial way, and she moped around like her world was coming to an end. Finally I pulled her aside and told her to go into the kitchen, ring up Callum at work, and talk to him.

"Your glum face is driving away business," I told her with a smile. She managed to smile in return and left.

She didn't come back for over thirty minutes, during which time I happily waited on customers and talked to them about art and photography. I gave them the experience they expected to have in a Highlands art shop.

"Well, how did it go?" I asked when the only remaining customer had left. "You certainly look happier—you're smiling, and you look more relaxed."

She beamed. "Callum apologized for everything and wants to take me out to dinner. He's so sweet. He said it was all his fault—which it was—and that he's lucky to be married to me."

It didn't take much to appease Eilidh, I decided. I was a little disappointed that she should accept his apology so readily, but I had to remind myself that Eilidh and I were different, and just because I expected more from Seamus didn't mean she needed to expect more from Callum.

That night I finished the soup Seamus had made, wondering if I should make it last another day so I wouldn't have to worry about dinner the next night. But it was too good—I decided I would handle tomorrow's dinner somehow. I spent a quiet evening in the cottage after making sure the doors were locked and the closets were empty of people. I don't know what I would have done if I had actually found someone in one of the closets, but I felt better after I had checked.

I had just curled up to watch television when my mobile phone rang. It was Chloe. She had talked to Hagen.

"First of all, is he still near here, or is he back in London?" I asked.

"He's in London."

I breathed a small sigh of relief. "So has he been arrested?" I asked.

"No. He talked to Scotland Yard and they let him go. I don't know what to think about the whole situation."

"Tell me what he told you."

"I was actually a little surprised to hear from him. I thought he'd call family, but I think he feels comfortable talking to me.

"He and Thea divorced about five years ago. He dated a few women over those years, but nothing serious. He and Thea remained friends throughout that time.

"Recently—within the past few months—Hagen mentioned that he and Thea were having dinner together. After that night, her name began coming up more often, and before long he told me that things were heating up and that he had been spending lots of time with her."

"She lives in London? I mean, she lived in London?"

"Yes."

"Go on."

"Before he went on sabbatical, he told me he had given some thought to moving in with her. I was pretty sure they were going to reconcile."You want to know my opinion? They were made for each other. When they divorced, neither one could find someone who lived up to the other's memory, so neither one found love again."

"That's sad."

"It is. Hagen, I think, was willing to scale back at work just as Thea was reaching the end of her childbearing years. They reached the decision that although they simply weren't meant to have children, they could spend the rest of their years together happily."

"So what happened?"

"Hagen hasn't said why he took a sabbatical, but it's my opinion that he wanted one last chance to think everything through before marrying Thea again. He has a sister who didn't approve—she said Thea had hurt Hagen too deeply when she left him—and I think he wanted to affirm his own feelings for Thea.

"So he left town. No one knew where he had gone, including Thea. At least that's what she told people. She may have known exactly where he was, but she wasn't telling anyone.

"And then she was killed whilst he was away. The police haven't released any information about the crime, but Hagen said she was stabbed. That's a very personal crime."

"Did Hagen say why he was in the woods, so close to the place where Florian died, or why he asked me about the painting? It seems that he wouldn't be focused on those things if his goal really was to get back to nature and do some serious thinking about his relationship with Thea."

I could almost hear her shrugging. "I can't explain that. Maybe he got tired of thinking about marrying Thea and wanted to focus on something else."

"How was he doing when you talked to him?"

"He was in pretty bad shape. Crying, snuffling, you know."

"I would cry and snuffle, too, if my maybe-almost-fiancée was murdered." I paused, then asked, "So who do the police think killed Thea?"

"They're not saying. They told Hagen they're working on a couple leads, but no one is in custody and no one besides Hagen has been questioned as a possible suspect."

"Is Hagen definitely off the hook?"

"No. They told him to stay in London. He doesn't have an alibi because he was off by himself in the woods, so I'm sure they're still looking at him."

"What do you think happened? I mean, you've talked to him. Do you have a feel for what went on?"

"I really don't. He and Thea were getting along so well, at least according to him. It doesn't seem like he would do anything to hurt her."

"Well, someone did."

"Do you think it was Hagen?" Chloe asked, her voice hushed.

"I don't know. Like you said, stabbing is a personal crime. They say that stabbings happen between people who know each other very well. But aside from that, Hagen is the one person with ties to both Florian's death and Thea's death. Of course, it's also possible that he's the unluckiest man in the world and the two events have nothing to do with each other."

"I'll let you know if I hear anything else," Chloe said.

We rang off and I sat lost in thought. Was there a connection between Florian's death and Thea's? Hagen was the only person who could connect the two crimes. But what did Thea have to do with the Leitch painting?

Or maybe Hagen was just unstable. I hadn't considered that possibility. He definitely hadn't seemed stable when I saw him in the woods by Cauld Loch. But he was a professor and an important person in London's art scene. How could someone who was so smart and so successful come undone so spectacularly?

But why would someone who was so smart and so successful leave London's art scene for the forests and lochs of the Highlands if he didn't have something to hide?

CHAPTER 17

The days lapsed into a routine that was both comfortable and uneasy at the same time. Seamus would come to the studio early in the morning and work all day. Eilidh continued to work at the shop, with Callum's blessing. I worked on my photography and ventured out to take more photographs of the ever-changing Highland vistas during the brilliantly colored autumn. Seamus demanded that someone accompany me on my photo excursions, so I took Eilidh and left him in charge of the shop. Eilidh liked to suggest places we could visit to take photos.

But there was no change between Seamus and me. I let him in every morning and locked the door behind him every night, but I wouldn't let him stay at Gorse Brae. I think he worried that I was in the house by myself at night, but I was careful about checking the locks and closing the blinds after he left. I always left a lamp on in the living room while I slept. It made me feel safer, even if it was just my imagination. I was becoming more accustomed to being by myself, and it was an empowering feeling, especially given the events that had occurred at Gorse Brae since the spring.

But one night all that changed. There was a call on my mobile phone. I answered it without looking at the caller ID, then immediately regretted it when I heard a crackling voice on the other end.

"Sylvie, I'm coming for you," the voice said. I couldn't tell if I was listening to a man or a woman. Whoever it was had disguised his or her voice.

"Why?" I asked, my own voice an octave higher than normal. I should have turned the phone off immediately, but I didn't. I engaged the person, which was the worst thing I could have done.

"You know why," the voice said.

"No I don't," I answered.

"The painting. You have it. I want it."

"I don't have the painting! I promise!" I screeched into the phone.

The person hung up. I was trembling and sweating. My heart beat so fast I thought I might die of fright before I could get help. My first reaction was to call Seamus.

"Hullo?" he answered.

"Seamus, it's me. Someone just called and said they were coming for me and I don't know what to do. I need help. Can you come over?"

"Hold on," he said. "I can't understand you. Tell me again, but slower this time. What happened?"

I took a deep breath. "Someone just called. I couldn't tell if it was a man or a woman. The person said they're coming for me because they think I have that stupid painting."

"Have you called the police?"

"No. I called you first."

"You call the police. I'll be over as soon as I can. And try to find out the number the person called from."

I hung up and phoned the police. When I explained what had happened, they promised to send someone over as quickly as possible. I tried to figure out who called by punching numbers into the phone, but the caller had blocked all identification. I turned on every light in the house and sat on the sofa to wait for Seamus.

I only had to wait a couple minutes. He banged on the door, making me jump, and I ran to open it. When he swept into the room he locked the door behind him and wrapped me in a big hug. I wept into his chest as he smoothed my hair, not saying a word.

"I'm so scared, Seamus. I wish we had never seen that painting. It's brought us nothing but danger and stress," I cried.

"We'll get to the bottom of it, I promise," he said.

"It's got to be Alice. Or Hagen. They've both expressed an obsessive interest in that painting."

"You're probably right. We'll send the police looking for both of them when they get here."

As if on cue, a knock sounded on the front door.

"Stay here," Seamus instructed me.

He walked to the front door and peered out the window before unlocking it and admitting two police officers into the house. They introduced themselves and listened, taking notes all the while, as I told the story of the phone call.

Then they asked questions of me and Seamus. We had to tell them we had been living apart, which increased my worry that they would think Seamus was behind the incident. Would they think he had done this to force me to ask him to come back and live at Gorse Brae? Would they wonder about his time in prison and assume he hadn't changed his stripes, that he was capable of doing me harm? Because I knew none of that was true, and I was prepared to argue the point with them all night if necessary.

But their questions didn't focus on Seamus. When we told them about Hagen and Alice, they promised to investigate both of them. They found it especially interesting that Hagen was currently under police orders not to leave London due to his possible role in a murder investigation. They noted that the caller had blocked his or her number from identification and said they would try to get around the blockage and figure out the source of the call. "We'll have our counterparts in London look up both Alice and Hagen, and we'll get back to you with any information they're able to gather. In the meantime, I suggest you install an alarm system," one of the officers cautioned.

I looked at Seamus. No one in Cauld Loch had an alarm system. Nothing ever happened in the village. That is, until it was discovered that Seamus had the Leitch painting in his shop. But as much as I hated the idea of getting an alarm system, I knew it was necessary. We didn't have to use it once Florian's killer, and possibly Thea's, had been caught.

After the police left, with assurances that they would be in touch soon, Seamus and I sat down at the kitchen table. I made tea and we talked about the phone call.

"I don't think you should be here alone," Seamus said. "I know you don't want me here right now, but I don't really believe you have an option."

"What about the alarm system? If someone can install one in the next day or two, then I should be fine, right?" I asked.

"We can check on that first thing in the morning. For tonight, though, will you please let me stay here? I won't sleep if I'm at Eilidh's wondering if you're all right. I'll sleep in the guest room or on the sofa."

I was torn. I wasn't ready for him to come home, but I was scared to be alone. In the end, my fear won and I found myself agreeing to let him stay in the guest room. He still had plenty of clothes at the cottage, so he didn't have to fetch anything from Eilidh's. I called her to let her know that Seamus was spending the night.

"Really?" she squealed. "That's great news!"

"Easy, Eilidh. It's not what you think. He's staying here so the lunatic who rang me up and threatened me doesn't break in whilst I'm sleeping."

"You're kidding."

"No," I said with a sigh. "I'll tell you all about it tomorrow morning." I hung up with a yawn. My exhaustion proved to be a blessing in disguise—normally I wouldn't have been able to sleep after such a terrifying experience, but I was so tired that I thought I might just be able to get some rest.

Having Seamus sleeping in the next room did indeed prove to be a balm for my nerves—I slept soundly. When the alarm went off in the morning, he was already in the kitchen making breakfast. The tea was ready.

"Wow. Thanks for doing this. Did you get any sleep?" I greeted him.

"A little," he answered, stirring a pot on the stove. "Want porridge?"

"Mmm," I nodded. I accepted a bowl of the steaming cereal and got cream and berries from the refrigerator. We ate without many words. I was suddenly shy and didn't know what to say. I didn't want to talk about him moving back yet, and I was afraid that was what he was waiting for.

Finally he spoke. "Are you going to call an alarm company this morning, or do you want me to do it?"

"I'll do it," I said.

After breakfast I did the dishes and Seamus went to Eilidh's to shower and change his clothes. He and Eilidh arrived at the shop together not long after that.

"Seamus told me everything," Eilidh greeted me, giving me a hug. "I can't wait until this whole thing is over. They just have to catch the person who's doing these things to you. I mean, we know Alice was here and we know Hagen was here, but we don't know who rang you up last night or who attacked you. I'm scared for you, Sylvie. Maybe you should come stay at my house, too."

"I don't think I need to do anything as drastic as move out to hide from someone. I'm going to ring up an alarm company in just a minute and get someone over here right away."

Eilidh gave me a worried look and turned to Seamus. "Seamus, do you agree with me?"

"Och, I'm staying out of that conversation. I've learned a thing or two about women lately." He smiled and shook his head. For the first time in a long while, I smiled back at him.

Eilidh went to work in the shop and I found an alarm company with good reviews online. When I talked to the manager, he promised to send a team over in a few hours to have a look at the cottage.

When the men arrived, they quickly surveyed the cottage, the wiring, and the windows and doors, then pronounced Gorse Brae an easy job.

And better still, they were able to start that afternoon. I was relieved and asked them to get to work right away.

When they left for the day, they promised to be back in the morning to finish up the job. I felt suddenly nervous about spending the night alone before the alarm was completely installed. Seamus must have sensed that I was anxious, because he came up behind me in the studio and tapped me on the shoulder at the end of the day.

"Sylvie? You okay?"

I jumped at his touch, then smiled ruefully. "I'm sorry. You startled me. I guess I'm okay."

"No, you're not. I can hear it in your voice. Do you want me to stay one more night, until the alarm is fully installed?"

I took a deep breath. "Do you mind? I'm sorry, I just don't feel comfortable staying here by myself without an alarm."

"Sure, I'll stay. I'll grab dinner at Eilidh's and then I'll be back."

Part of me—my heart, I think—wanted to stop him, to ask him to have dinner with me. But my brain let him go. We weren't ready to take the next step, and I didn't want to encourage him. I made myself a grilled cheese sandwich for dinner and waited impatiently for him to get back. When he arrived we watched television for a while before I went into the bedroom to read before going to sleep. When I told him goodnight he gave me a hug and kissed my forehead, telling me not to worry, that I was safe for the night. There was a question in his eyes, but I just couldn't let him sleep with me in the bedroom.

"Seamus, we can't. Not yet. I'm sorry."

He dropped his arms to his sides and sighed. "Och, it was worth a try. I'll wait." He chucked me on the chin and unbidden tears sprang to my eyes at his familiar gesture. I blinked them away rapidly.

"Thank you," I said.

"For what?"

"For understanding that we still need some time before we're ready to act like married people again."

He smiled and I went into the bedroom.

The men from the alarm company were back first thing the next morning. They finished the installation before lunchtime. What a relief it was to see the little electronic box attached to the wall, ready to alert me if anyone who didn't belong tried to enter Gorse Brae. I almost looked forward to bedtime so I could try it out.

And indeed, I slept well that night. Seamus had returned to Eilidh's and I was alone. I armed the windows and doors and sat on the sofa reading a book, not worrying about anything outside the walls of my house.

But reality encroached the next morning when Chloe rang me up. "They've arrested Hagen for Thea's murder," she said.

I gasped. "You're kidding. Even though it seems logical, I still can't believe it."

"They went to his house last night to arrest him. Came flying down his street with lights flashing and everything. It was late, but they created enough of a ruckus to alert the neighbors and everyone watched the whole thing from their front doors. I feel sorry for Hagen. I still can't picture him doing something like that."

I didn't say anything, but I could picture it, given how he looked and his state of mind when I saw him in the woods by Cauld Loch.

"Have you been to see him?" I asked.

"Not yet, but I think I'll be allowed to go in later today."

"Let me know when you've talked to him. I'd like to hear what he has to say." I wanted to ask her to question him about his trip to Cauld Loch and his insistence on knowing more about the Leitch painting, but I felt that would be asking too much. Better to wait and see what he wanted to talk about, then ask her to follow up if necessary.

When she called me later, I could tell from the tone of her voice that she had been disheartened by her visit with Hagen.

"So what happened?" I asked.

"He's in a cell with the most disreputable looking people" she began, probably forgetting that Seamus had been in jail at one time. "He's sad and angry. He swears he didn't kill Thea."

I was caught between wanting to soothe Chloe's nerves and wanting to point out to her that the police wouldn't have arrested Hagen without a strong suspicion that he killed Thea.

"Did the police have anything to say?"

"No, they wouldn't talk to me. But Hagen said they told him Thea's house showed no sign of a break-in and she clearly knew her killer. I guess we already figured that, since we knew Thea died from a stabbing."

"Unfortunately, Hagen fits those criteria," I said. "He probably had easy access to Thea's house, and he obviously knew her very well."

"That's true. But he's an art professor, for God's sake. How could he do something like this? He's so mild-mannered."

My mind reached back to the night Florian was killed. Indeed, Hagen had seemed unperturbed at the prospect of having lost the painting to another bidder. But was his calm a mask for anger and the desire for revenge? Or the desire to obtain the painting at all costs? It was possible that Hagen himself had the painting and that he came to Cauld Loch under the guise of looking for it, with the intention of throwing suspicion away from himself.

There was no telling how much that painting, with its storied history and hidden map, might be worth. And there was no telling how much the jewels themselves might be worth if someone got their hands on the map, followed it, and found the ancient gems. What might a person do to get that kind of fame and wealth? Even an art professor could be tempted to sacrifice their principles for such a prize, but I didn't voice my thoughts to Chloe.

"How long did you get to visit with him?" I asked.

"Not long. The inmates are only allowed a short amount of time to see visitors, and his sister was already there when I got there. I had to wait for them to finish their visit."

"Did he have anything else to say?"

"He asked me to bring some books from his office. I think he's already bored to death. Sorry—wrong choice of words."

"So you'll visit him again soon?"

"Not for a few days. He's only allowed visitors every so often, and I think he's used up his allotment for this week."

"Ring me up when you see him again. I'd like to stay in the loop."

"Absolutely. Talk to you soon."

Eilidh and I went to the pub that evening for dinner. I told her to bring her new darts along so I could start teaching her how to play. I was already at the pub when she arrived. She walked in with the pouch of darts clutched in one hand and smiled broadly when I waved her over to the table.

"When can we start?" she asked as soon as she sat down.

I laughed. "Let's eat first, then we'll play. There's a game going on now, anyway."

She clearly didn't want to wait. "All right," she said with a loud sigh. We arranged our chairs so we could watch the game going on. I instructed Eilidh to watch the hand movements of each player as I explained what they were doing right or wrong.

"It sounds cliché," I told her, "but it's all in the wrist. You have to flick it just right to get the dart to go where you want it to go. Ideally, that's the bull's-eye." She nodded.

Our server brought our orders and I continued to critique the players while we ate. Eilidh gobbled her meal quickly, probably hoping the quicker she ate the quicker I would show her how to play.

Finally the men playing the game sat down. Eilidh and I walked over to the dartboard and I showed her the basics. The concentric rings, each worth differing point values, the size of the bull's-eye up close, and where darts had gone astray and poked holes in the wooden frame around the board.

"Okay, okay," Eilidh said impatiently. "Let's get started."

For the next thirty minutes I stood behind my cousin, positioning her hand just right and demonstrating how to flick her wrist so that she could aim the dart directly at the middle of the board. Eventually she was ready to take a break. "My wrist hurts," she complained.

"That's enough for one night anyhow," I said. "Ice your wrist when you get home, and if it feels better tomorrow we can come over tomorrow night and try it again."

She agreed, and we parted ways at her house. I walked the short distance to Gorse Brae by myself, looking over my shoulder constantly for anyone who might be lurking nearby. I would have loved someone to walk home with me, but I didn't want to ask Eilidh. If she walked me home, then she would have to return to her own house by herself and she might not be safe.

I slept well that night. I had enjoyed my evening out with Eilidh; Callum and Seamus had probably enjoyed a men's night at Eilidh's house. I was learning how easy it was to have fun without a man around.

The next day Eilidh said the ice on her wrist had worked and she was ready to try again. I didn't want to eat dinner at the pub again, so I suggested she eat at home and meet me at the pub afterwards.

I ate dinner by myself—a can of chicken noodle soup. After I had cleaned up the few dishes I had dirtied, I fetched my own darts from the closet next to the front door and set the alarm. The system was set up to give me thirty seconds to leave the house before disturbing the entire village with its keening wail, so I hurried to lock the door behind me. I didn't see anyone standing next to the rowan tree beside the door.

Just as I turned the key in the deadbolt, a hand reached from behind me and gripped my wrist with an iron-like strength. I gasped and turned around.

CHAPTER 18

Alice was glaring at me, pure malice in her eyes.

"Get back inside," she ordered.

"What do you want?" I asked, trying to keep my voice even.

"I want you to get back inside," she growled, pushing me with a strength that surprised me.

Once inside, she closed the door behind us and demanded that I give her the alarm code. "And don't even think of giving me the wrong one or I'll kill you right here, right now." My mind warred with itself—did I dare give her the wrong code? I didn't know what would happen if I did. The alarm might keep beeping and alert Alice that I had lied. Then what would she do?

I gave her the correct code. She punched it in and then ordered me into the kitchen. She turned on the light and motioned me into one of the kitchen chairs, where I sat down slowly, my eyes never leaving her face.

"You know more than you've been telling me," she snarled, sitting down across from me and folding her hands before her on the table.

"I have no idea what you're talking about."

"The painting. It's always been about the painting. I know you know where it is, and you're not leaving here unless you tell me."

"I've never lied to you about the painting, Alice. I have no idea where it is."

"Stop it!" she shrieked, slamming her fist on the tabletop. She rooted through a bag she was carrying over her shoulder and held up a roll of duct tape, a triumphant look in her eyes. She stood up and moved to the side of the table where I sat. I didn't know if I dared to try to run.

I did. I leapt to my feet, the chair falling backward onto the floor with a loud crash. All I had to do was get to the back door so I could get outside, where I would be safe. There was no telling what Alice was capable of. She had surprised me every time I'd seen her since she first visited Gorse Brae after Florian's death.

But this time I surprised her. She blinked, momentarily thrown off guard. She must have expected me to sit still and obey her commands, but I had no intention of letting her decide how this would end.

She tripped over the fallen chair in her haste to reach me. That gave me an extra second to reach the door, but she recovered herself quickly behind me. My hand trembled as I tried to unlock the small lock, and I fumbled once.

That was all Alice needed to reach me. In a shocking display of strength, she yanked my arm behind my back just as I twisted the lock to the open position. I had almost made it to freedom. I had a feeling she was going to make me regret having tried to escape.

I was right. She slapped me hard across the face. I put my hand to my cheek where it was stinging. She still held my free arm behind my back and she wrenched it upward. The pain was blinding. Holding my arm, she propelled me toward the living room. She had surprising strength for such a slight woman. Once in the living room, she pushed my back with such force that I fell, knocking my shoulder against the edge of the coffee table. I could feel her let go of my arm as I pitched forward.

The pain in my shoulder was terrible. Tears sprang to my eyes, but I refused to let them fall. Alice wasn't going to see me cry. I was at her mercy on the floor, so I tried to struggle to my feet. But she was not going to give up her advantage. She leaned over me and punched me in the mouth. I saw blood spatter on the floor even before I was aware of the pain.

"Now tell me where you've hidden the painting!" she yelled.

My only choice at that point was to try to buy some time, so I tried to think of a place to send her to search to give me time to escape.

"It's in the studio," I said. "Seamus hid it in there, but I don't know where."

She produced the roll of duct tape again and I tried scrambling away, only to find that the arm she had wrenched behind me was useless. Alice saw immediately what I was trying to do and she kicked me into position against the leg of the coffee table. When I was seated to her satisfaction, she used her teeth to rip a long piece of tape from the roll, then she taped my arms behind me and then to the leg of the table.

I couldn't move. My mouth was still bleeding, my cheek hurt, and my arm was probably broken. It was useless to me, of that I was sure.

She turned off the lights and used a torch to make her way into the shop and toward the studio. I cursed myself for not locking the door between the kitchen and the shop, because I would have had an additional few precious seconds to try to extricate myself from the duct tape if she had needed to take the time to unlock the door. I wished I had the use of both arms. I struggled in vain against the tape, trying to rip it by twisting my arms against the edge of the table leg, but it didn't work. I tried pulling the table along the floor to the front door, but the pain in my arm was crippling and I was only able to move a few inches. I vowed to get rid of the coffee table if I made it out of this alive and in one piece.

I stopped struggling to listen for Alice; I could hear her footsteps approaching. She was moving slowly, probably because it was so dark in the house. After only a few seconds the beam from her torch cut through the darkness and shined directly into my eyes. I ducked my head to avoid being blinded.

Alice came over to the table and squatted down next to me. She squeezed my useless arm, causing me to cry out in pain. I hated to show any weakness in front of her.

"You lied to me, Sylvie. You knew all along that painting wasn't in the studio." Her voice was calm, deadly. I was terrified of what she might do.

"I thought that's where Seamus had it. He must have moved it," I lied, my throat constricting.

"I don't believe you. I'm going to leave you in here whilst I have a look around. I'm not worried that someone will interrupt me now that your dear husband isn't living here." She barked out an ugly laugh.

How did she know Seamus and I were living apart?

Leaving the lights off and taking her torch, Alice returned to the shop. I could hear her moving paintings around. My head slumped against my chest. Alice had defeated me. I couldn't reach my mobile phone to call anyone, and every part of me hurt.

It took Alice several minutes to go through the paintings in the shop since there were so many. I willed my brain to think of a way to keep her talking, to keep her from hurting me again—or worse.

After she finished searching the shop, she moved to the kitchen. I could hear her opening cupboards and knocking their contents onto the floor. She probably emptied every cupboard. Next I could hear her in the laundry room. She shuffled around the laundry closet, obviously not finding anything of interest. I could hear her muttering to herself. I was becoming more and more worried as each second ticked by, as Alice's mental state appeared to be deteriorating as she searched.

When she didn't find the painting in the laundry room, she went into the guest bedroom. The closet was directly behind the bedroom door, so Alice had to close the door in order to open the closet door.

She had just closed the bedroom door when I heard the front door handle rattle. Someone else was at Gorse Brae. I didn't know whether I should laugh or cry. Was it someone who meant me further harm, or was someone here to help?

The door opened slowly. I could see Eilidh's silhouette outlined against the moonlight.

"Eilidh," I called softly.

"Sylvie?" she asked.

"*Shh*," I whispered. "Alice is in the guest room. I'm tied up over here by the coffee table."

"Are you all right?" I could hear the alarm in her voice.

"I'm okay, just banged up a little."

"I'll get Seamus," she said, and started to turn away.

"No," I whispered urgently. "There's no time. Try to get me out of this."

Leaving the door open, she came and knelt next to me, setting a small package on the sofa. We could hear Alice tossing things aside as she searched through the closet in the guest bedroom.

"When you didn't show up for darts, I got worried," she whispered. "I'm so glad I came over to find you."

"Hurry," I urged.

Just then Alice slammed the closet door shut. Eilidh scrambled behind the sofa, leaving me slumped against the coffee table leg. Alice opened the bedroom door and came over to where I sat.

"I'm running out of places to look, and you're running out of time to tell me where the painting is," she said in a low voice. "I may have to take a look around the kitchen again. Maybe you've got a nice sharp knife I can use to convince you to talk a little faster."

"It's got to be around here somewhere," I said in a rasping voice, hoping she would leave the room quickly so Eilidh could help me.

"You'd better be right," Alice said. She gave me a swift kick in my shin. Wincing, I shot a glance in the direction where I knew Eilidh was hiding. It was reflexive; it was dark enough that I couldn't see anyone. So far Alice didn't seem to realize there was someone else in the house.

When Alice went into my bedroom, Eilidh clambered out from behind the sofa and felt her way to where I sat on the floor. I could hear her groping for furniture. When she reached me, she tried ripping the duct tape with her hands.

"My hands are verra sweaty," she whispered, her voice trembling. "I'm so sorry." She continued tugging fruitlessly.

"Can you get a knife?" I asked, wishing she would give up trying with her bare hands and move onto another solution.

"I'll look."

"Hurry," I urged her.

She stood up and I could hear her moving toward the kitchen. But before she got more than a meter away from me, Alice appeared in the bedroom doorway.

"What's going on?" she asked. "Who's here?"

Silence. I prayed Eilidh would stay still and that Alice would decide to keep the lights off.

"I asked, who's here?" Alice demanded in a rough voice. I could hear her walking toward the front door. I knew what she was doing.

The room lit up as Alice touched the switch on the wall. Before I even glanced in her direction, I raised my head to see Eilidh standing in the kitchen doorway, looking like a hunted animal. Her eyes darted this way and that, seeking an escape from what she knew was about to become an even more dangerous situation.

Eilidh locked eyes with Alice. "Who are you?" Alice asked.

"A friend of Sylvie's."

"You picked the wrong time to visit your friend," Alice sneered. Eilidh said nothing.

"Alice, let her leave. She has nothing to do with the painting," I pleaded.

"She can't leave. What do you think will happen? I'll tell you. She'll call the police before she can get down your front walk, that's what. Of course I'm not going to let that happen."

"No she won't," I insisted. "You won't, right, Eilidh?" I asked, looking at her. I meant it. If Eilidh could get out of Gorse Brae unharmed, I would trade that for police help.

"Of course I'd call the police!" Eilidh declared. I groaned inwardly. If there had been the slightest chance that Alice would let her go, it evaporated before my eyes. But I should have known Eilidh would remain loyal to me no matter what.

Alice started to move slowly around the perimeter of the room toward Eilidh, just as a hunter might stalk prey. Eilidh saw what Alice was doing and started moving, too, away from Alice. The two women stared at each other. The room was strangely silent as I watched this bizarre dance between my cousin and my captor. Suddenly Alice lunged at Eilidh.

Eilidh's courage since finding me on the floor, duct-taped to a table, had been surprising. I wouldn't have expected her to exhibit such strength in the face of danger. But she had another surprise in store for me.

Before Alice could reach her, Eilidh swooped toward the sofa, where she had left her pouch of darts. Alice and I figured out what was happening simultaneously. Though the darts wouldn't have been useful to cut through the thick tape that held me in place, they were just the right tool to put a stop to Alice's reign of terror.

Eilidh untied the pouch, her eyes never leaving Alice's face. The pouch fell to the floor and Eilidh held the darts in one hand. She held out the other hand as if she were trying to keep her balance, but I think she was feeling for furniture. Even though it was light in the room, she was so focused on Alice's movements that she probably didn't see the furniture in her peripheral vision and wanted to be sure she didn't stumble over anything and give Alice an advantage.

Everything seemed to be happening in slow motion. I desperately wished I could help Eilidh, but there was nothing I could do.

Or was there?

I may have lost the use of my arms, but I still had power of my voice. I used it.

"Alice, the painting is in the bedroom, under the mattress."

When Alice jerked her head to look at me, Eilidh took the opportunity I had given her and lunged toward Alice. Stepping onto the corner of the coffee table, Eilidh jumped off and landed on the floor next to Alice. Alice took her eyes from me again and, realizing she had been duped, swung her arm wildly toward Eilidh and connected with Eilidh's neck. Eilidh let out a grunt and stepped back; I feared she had lost her courage to face Alice. But she hadn't. She stood up again and swung her own arm in a long arc, grazing Alice's shoulder. Alice continued as though she hadn't even felt the punch. Glancing behind her, she reached for a heavy wooden candlestick on the mantel. I cried out, "Watch it, Eilidh!"

But she was already watching. When Alice thrust the candlestick toward Eilidh's face, Eilidh dodged out to the side, narrowly missing being hit on the side of her head. And that's when Alice made her mistake. She threw the candlestick at Eilidh, probably hoping to hit her hard enough to stun her and make her drop the darts. But Eilidh jumped out of the way and the candlestick dropped to the floor with a thud. Now Alice had no ready weapon and Eilidh knew it was time to press her advantage. She lurched to one side and Alice mirrored her movement, probably hoping to meet her in a hand-to-hand fight, but, quick as lightning, Eilidh lunged in the other direction, leaving Alice to stumble forward in surprise. And when Alice stumbled, Eilidh reached out and plunged a dart deep into her shoulder.

Alice howled in pain. A small circle of blood began to widen and spread across her shoulder. She became a wild woman, shrieking and flailing her good arm, thrashing out toward Eilidh as she stood over her, poised to strike again with the dart. When Alice kicked Eilidh's ankle she cried out, then fell onto one knee and plunged the dart into Alice's skin again and again. Circles of blood appeared on Alice's clothes, spreading with each thrust of Eilidh's arm. Before she drew her arm back, breathing heavily, Eilidh had stabbed Alice in the arm, the leg, the abdomen, and the throat.

As Alice lay on the floor, whimpering and cursing and unable to move, Eilidh ran to the kitchen for a pair of scissors and returned to the living room to cut me loose. As I stood gingerly and went to stand guard over Alice, Eilidh went to the kitchen and rang up the police, then Seamus and Callum. Then she returned and held me in a long embrace while I sobbed into her shoulder, thanking her over and over again for saving me.

Our husbands arrived before the police, but only by a few moments. When the police arrived they discovered pandemonium at Gorse Brae, between Seamus's shouts at Alice, Callum's shouts at Eilidh for getting herself into such a dangerous situation, and Eilidh and me trying to explain what happened. The police quieted us all down quickly. They called for two ambulances—one for me and one for Alice—then asked me questions while we waited for them to arrive. Alice was handcuffed on the floor, the looks on her face alternating between dejected and furious.

When the officers learned who Alice was, they quickly rang up Scotland Yard to tell them they had Florian McDermott's widow in custody. Someone promised to be in the village by morning to begin questioning Alice.

Seamus went with me in the ambulance, and at hospital I was checked over quickly and x-rayed. I had, indeed, suffered a broken arm, which was put into a cast. They bandaged the less serious injuries and I was released by morning. I returned to Gorse Brae to begin cleaning up the mess that had been left in Alice's wake.

Alice had been thorough in her search of the house. The only room she hadn't destroyed was my bedroom, which remained relatively intact. I decided it would be best to start in the studio and make my way toward the inside of the house.

With only one useful arm, cleaning was tedious and painful. But Eilidh came over to help, as did Seamus and Callum. I decided against telling Mum what had happened, because I had worried her enough lately. I rang her up to say hello, but never mentioned a word about Alice or the painting.

I instructed Seamus, Eilidh, and Callum to keep Alice's visit a secret from everyone, including Greer and James. I didn't want them worrying, either.

The next day I spoke to Chloe on the phone. When I told her everything that had happened, she was shocked. But she had news of her own, and after assuring herself that I was going to be fine and that Eilidh had suffered no ill effects from her encounter with Alice, she launched into her story.

"Hagen is going to be formally charged with Thea's murder."

"Have you been to see him?"

"Yes. I talked to him for a bit and he swears he didn't do it. He can't think of anyone who would hate Thea enough to kill her."

"Do you believe him? I mean, do you think he didn't do it and that he really has no idea who did?"

"I think I believe him, but he and I have been friends for a long time. I'm biased."

"I can't help thinking that it's a huge coincidence that Hagen shows up in the Highlands looking for a painting, then he's found up here again when his ex-wife is murdered. Do you think Thea's murder has something to do with the painting?"

"It's possible," Chloe said. The skepticism in her voice was obvious. "But Hagen says Thea didn't know anything about the painting."

"She didn't have to know anything about it to be involved. Maybe she knew he was looking for something valuable in connection with his work in the art world. Maybe she knew something and didn't even realize it."

"That's true." I could envision Chloe nodding slowly. "Well, I'm going to see Hagen again in a few days. If I learn anything else, I'll be sure to let you know."

I went back to my cleaning, which felt painstakingly slow. When there was a knock at the door, I jumped.

"Seamus," I scolded as I let him in. "You scared me."

"Sorry, Sylvie. I don't have my keys and I didn't think to ring you up before I came over." He looked me up and down. "How are you feeling?"

"I've been better, but I'm refusing to sit and sulk. Want to help me clean up this mess?" I asked, indicating the studio with a sweep of my good arm.

"That's what I came over for," he said with a smile. "Eilidh said she'll come over later, but the police are interviewing her again." Not surprising, since she had assaulted someone, but I hoped they would let her go quickly since it was obviously a case of self-defense.

"Thanks for coming," I said. "Where would you like to start?"

He joined me in the studio and we worked for a long time in silence, each of us concentrating on our own work spaces, tools, and materials.

Seamus had far more to do than I did, since much of my work was done on a computer and I didn't use too many implements to take photos. Seamus had an untold number of art supplies and accoutrements, so when I was done I began helping him.

After a while the silence got to be oppressive. Seamus was rearranging stacks of cold-pressed and rough papers containing hundreds of watercolors he had experimented with for larger works, so I sat down on the floor to help him. I knew how he liked his papers organized, so I was able to jump right in and help without needing any instruction.

I looked at him out of the corner of my eye and saw that he was watching me.

"What?" I asked.

"Nothing."

"What are you thinking about?" I asked.

"I was thinking that I don't have to explain what to do because you already know." His mouth curled in a tiny smile.

"Tell me about Rose," I said. I surprised even myself when I said it. Unbidden from the depths of my mind, my husband's first wife had emerged.

Clearly I surprised Seamus, too. "Well," he stammered, "what do you want to know?"

"Just tell me what she was like."

He pursed his lips.

"We met when we were just bairns. We were schoolmates in Glasgow, grew up in the same neighborhood. When we got out of school we lost touch, then met up years later. She was lonely, I was lonely, and we decided to tie the knot. We didn't give it much thought before we did it. It was more for the sake of convenience, for the sake of having someone to come home to every night. I was married to her when I started taking cooking classes.

"We fought a lot, mostly about money. I didn't have much money growing up, but she had even less. And when we both started earning paychecks, it seemed like a lot of money to two people who had never had much. I didn't realize at the time how little money we really had then. Not enough to live on comfortably.

"Anyway, she was furious when I started taking cooking classes. Thought it was a waste of money, though she didn't consider drinking with her friends to be a waste. She said she worked hard enough and her life had been hard enough that she deserved a break. But I continued to take cooking classes.

"Eventually she left me. She didn't want to be tied down to a man who would rather cook than go out with his mates."

"So she left you, not the other way around," I said. I had hoped Seamus had had the good sense to leave her.

"She did, but I was glad to see it happen. If she hadn't left me I would have left soon enough. We were never suited for marriage to each other. But we stayed friends, and I've watched for several years now as she's gone to a dark place in her drinking. And the spending never stopped, even though her income did."

"How was she able to spend money she didn't have?"

He looked down at his hands. "I've paid a lot of her bills, so the credit card companies haven't realized she's broke."

I gave him a long look. "It's funny it took me so long to realize what was going on. And even when it practically hit me in the face I didn't realize it. Or didn't want to believe it. Why didn't you tell me about her?"

He looked beyond me, as if he were looking back into the past. "It never came up. And I was embarrassed by the whole thing, and the longer we were together the harder it got to say something out of the blue. Rose is very sick. She's not going to live much longer. I figured that when she passed I would stop paying for stuff and I would never have to tell you about her."

I sighed. His story seemed so logical, and yet I knew in my heart it was a deep betrayal of my trust. I longed to understand his reasoning, if the story he told me was true, but I just couldn't. Not yet. Maybe not ever.

"Are you going to see her again?"

"I think it would be wrong not to," he said, making a resigned movement with his hands.

"It would be wrong not to see your first wife before she dies, but it wasn't wrong to neglect to tell your second wife about her?" I knew I shouldn't have said it, but I couldn't help it.

"I never said it wasn't wrong to keep Rose a secret. It was wrong, I admit that. I was stupid. And I'm verra, verra sorry." He looked at me with tired eyes and it occurred to me for the first time that this separation may have been harder on him than it had been on me, at least physically. He had been sleeping in a house that wasn't his own, in a bed that wasn't his own, living with people who weren't his own wife. He probably didn't have all the tools he needed to cook the way he wanted to at Eilidh and Callum's house, and I knew he missed his own kitchen.

But none of that was enough to make me take him back. I couldn't get past the hurt he had caused. I stood up and pushed my stool back. "I'd like to go with you when you see her again." My words surprised even me.

Seamus looked at me with shock. "Why?"

"I don't know. I just want to meet her, that's all."

"I'm not sure that's a good idea, Sylvie."

"Why not?" I asked, lifting my chin in defiance.

"Because she...because...I don't know. It just doesn't seem like a good idea."

"It's only fair. She knows about me, right?" Seamus nodded. "Then it won't be a shock to her to meet me. I wouldn't go if she didn't know I exist. But I guarantee you she wants to meet me, even if she's never mentioned it."

"What makes you think that?"

"I just know. Trust me."

He shrugged. "Maybe. No promises."

Just then Eilidh came in. She looked haggard. "What happened?" I asked.

"I've been talking to the constable. Alice wants them to charge *me* with a crime because I stabbed her with my dart! Can you believe it?"

"I've learned not to underestimate Alice," I said ruefully. "What does the constable say about it?"

"He said not to worry, that they need to gather more information before they can make a determination about charging me with anything." She shook her head. "I'm a nervous wreck. What else could possibly go wrong?"

CHAPTER 19

Mum rang me up that night, eager to know if Seamus and I had solved our troubles. I told her we hadn't, but then explained that I would be going to visit Rose at some point.

"Is that a good idea?" Mum asked.

"You sound like Seamus," I said, exasperated. "If you were Rose, wouldn't you want to meet your ex-husband's new wife?"

"I don't know that I could put myself in her shoes," Mum said, avoiding the question deftly.

"What else is going on?" I asked.

"Have you talked to Greer?"

"No. Why?"

"Just wondered."

"What's up?" I asked, starting to get worried.

"Nothing. You might want to give her a call."

I couldn't concentrate on anything else Mum had to say. I finally told her I had to ring off and call Greer. "I'm sure I'll talk to you soon, then," she said.

Now I was beside myself. I dialed Greer's mobile phone and waited, my fingers tapping the counter, until she answered. It was noisy in the background.

"Greer, it's me. What's wrong?"

"Nothing. Who told you anything was wrong?"

"Mum."

"What did she say?"

"She just asked if I had talked to you. Please tell me what happened. Is Ellie okay?"

Greer laughed. "Everything is fine. Better than fine, actually. I was going to wait to tell you in person, but I guess Mum is forcing my hand. James and I are getting married." I could practically see her wide smile.

"That's wonderful news!" I cried. "When? How did it happen?" I had a million other questions for her.

"Let me..." I heard shuffling. "Let me get out of here," she said. "We're celebrating with Ellie at a restaurant and it's a wee bit loud."

She told me everything when she was out on the street. "He must have known I was getting closer to saying 'yes.' He hadn't asked me about it in a long time," she said. "But then this afternoon the three of us were at a park and he enlisted Ellie's help. Her job was to pretend to need help tying her shoes, which I thought was strange, then whilst I helped her James got down on one knee behind me. Then I turned around and there he was, on the ground, asking me to marry him and he had this beautiful ring and Ellie was laughing because she had managed to keep it a secret, and I just found myself saying I would!" She was breathless.

"I can't believe you finally agreed!" I exclaimed. "Congratulations! I'm so happy for both of you! All of you," I added.

"I'm over the moon," she said. "This was the right time. It's been long enough since the ugliness with Neill, and James has been so patient."

"You're very lucky," I said. "James is a wonderful guy."

"I know," she gushed. "I can't believe this is happening."

"When's the wedding?"

"We haven't even talked about it yet."

"I'm really happy for you, Greer," I said. And I was. But what I didn't tell her was that I was feeling a wee bit melancholy, too. Sorry for myself. I once had a great guy, too, but something had gone terribly wrong and now I didn't know how our relationship was going to continue.

I rang up Mum and scolded her. "You let me think something terrible had happened!" I accused.

"I knew you'd want to know, and I was afraid Greer would wait to tell you until she saw you. I wanted you to share in her happiness from the start."

"I'm glad I talked to her right away," I said. "They're going to be so happy."

We were silent for a moment, both of us probably thinking the same thing: that we all thought Seamus and I would be happy, too, when we were first engaged. But it would be different with Greer and James. Neither of them had secrets they wouldn't share with the other. We hung up with promises to talk again soon.

I cleaned the shop before going to bed that night. I didn't like being by myself in the shop with the light on, because anyone out in the darkness could see that I was alone. But the alarm was on, and that gave me a welcome feeling of security.

When Seamus arrived the next morning to continue his work in the studio, I told him the news about Greer and James. It wouldn't be fair to leave him out of the loop. After all, Greer was still his sister-in-law and he loved Ellie. He beamed. "That's braw!" he exclaimed. "I'll ring them up today and congratulate them. The bairn must be thrilled!" Ellie, I was sure, was as happy as both Greer and James.

Eilidh came in shortly after Seamus. She was angry.

"What's wrong?" I asked. Seamus leaned around the studio doorway. He must have heard me.

"Something wrong, Eilidh?" he asked.

"Callum makes me so mad," she said, practically throwing her bag onto the counter. "He wants to move. Can you believe it? Move!"

I was confused. "Why does he want to move? Where does he want to go?"

She gave an elaborate shrug. "How am I supposed to know? He has no idea. He wants to live in a more posh place, he says. I told him we're not the posh types."

"He doesn't like Cauld Loch?" I felt somehow hurt by this revelation.

"I think he likes it, but he wants to move to a bigger village. Can you imagine me in a bigger place? I'll hate it!" she exclaimed.

"You don't know that," I said. "Maybe you should get more details."

"I don't care what the details are. I like my cottage, I like living near you, I like Cauld Loch, and I don't want to leave."

"Maybe he's just kidding," I said without hope. Somehow I knew Callum wouldn't joke about such a thing.

"He's not, as you well know," Eilidh said. She had seen right through my flimsy attempt to cheer her up.

"Give him some space. Maybe he's having trouble at work and he doesn't want to bother you with it."

Eilidh clearly hadn't thought about that. "Do you think he lost his job?" she asked, a sudden tinge of worry in her voice.

"I doubt it, or he wouldn't be talking about moving to more posh quarters," I said. "But maybe this is his way of expressing a desire to try working somewhere else."

"You could be right," she said. "I'll ask him about it at dinner tonight. I won't bother him about it now."

We spent the day changing some of the displays in the shop to reflect the colder season and the coming winter. Seamus and Eilidh left late in the afternoon. Chloe rang me up before I sat down to dinner alone.

"No new developments with Hagen," she reported. "I'm probably not going to see him for several days. I'm busy at work and helping Felix with a new show at the gallery and I just won't be able to get away." She told me a bit about the new show. I told her I hoped the artist would do as well at the Lundenburg as Seamus had done.

The next few days continued in much the same pattern—working in the shop and studio during the day with Eilidh and Seamus, then dinner alone in the evening. I was getting rather accustomed to it, though I had to admit that some company would be nice now and then. After the incident with Alice, neither Eilidh nor I was in much of a mood to go to the pub to watch people play darts or have a go at a game ourselves.

The constable came into the shop one day late in the week. "I wanted to give you an update on our progress with Alice McDermott."

"What have you found?" I asked.

"She has been examined by a psychiatrist and is now saying she was not in the right frame of mind when she broke into your house and attacked you. The psychiatrist agrees."

"I could have told you that," I answered frankly.

"She's been released to her home in London pending trial up here in Cauld Loch. She'll be required to return for that. For now she has to stay in London, so I don't think you'll have any more trouble with her."

"Thank you for letting me know," I said. What made him think Alice would stay in London? Her doctor apparently acknowledged that she wasn't mentally stable.

"What about the painting? Has there been any progress locating it? Or any progress in finding out who killed Florian McDermott?" I asked.

"I'm afraid there's been no progress on either count," he said. "Since Scotland Yard took over the investigation of Florian McDermott's death we haven't had too much to do with it—we've conducted some supplemental interviews, as you know, sent over transcripts of interviews and the like, but nothing more. And as for the painting, it appears to have fallen off the face of the earth. But once Scotland Yard determines the identity of the killer, I think we'll move quickly on finding it."

"It's that painting that has caused all the trouble for me and Seamus," I noted. "It's been at the root of the physical attacks, the nasty phone calls, the threats."

"I realize that, Mrs. Carmichael. It's just that our hands are tied. It's technically the Yard's case now."

"I understand. I just wish we all had more answers." I thanked him for coming by and saw him to the door.

As I locked the door behind him, then set the alarm system, I could feel the anger and anxiety rising in my chest. Why couldn't Scotland Yard give this case more attention? Surely the suspicious death of Florian McDermott, a prominent member of the London financial and art scene, deserved more attention than it was receiving. And surely the local police could do more to find the Leitch painting. It sounded like they were sitting on their hands waiting for Scotland Yard to find the killer before they made any attempt to look for the painting that was at the root of all the trouble we'd experienced in the last several months.

Suddenly I had an idea. I called Eilidh and asked if she and Seamus could mind the shop and the studio for a few days. Then I called Chloe.

"Do you think I could stay with you for a couple days?" I asked.

"Of course. That would be wonderful," she said. "What's the occasion?"

"I'm coming down there to talk to Hagen myself."

There was hesitation in her voice. "Do you think it'll do any good?" she asked. "I mean, do you think he'll talk to you?"

"I can only try," I admitted. "But I feel like I need to talk to him face-to-face to ask him more about the painting. Why he thinks we have it, where else he's looked for it, those types of questions. Scotland Yard doesn't appear to be getting very far, and I think Hagen might have some information that I know is important."

"That's fine." Chloe sounded doubtful. "I can take you to where he's being held as soon as you get here."

I thanked her and rang off after letting her know that I planned to take the train down the next day. I would be able to talk to Hagen in less than forty-eight hours.

I hastily packed a bag and went to sleep with a feeling of positive energy. I finally felt like I was taking steps to get to the bottom of the problems and threats that had plagued me, Seamus, and our friends and family for months.

Eilidh and Seamus came to Gorse Brae the next morning before dawn. I had already eaten breakfast, so I was ready to leave when they arrived. I waved to them as I pulled away from the house, anxious to be on my way. I had tried to get a ticket on the train, but there were no seats. I didn't want to wait for the next one, so I decided to drive. Though it was a long trip, it seemed to go quickly. I was focused on trying to distill the information I wanted most from Hagen—how he heard about the painting, what made him think it was still at Gorse Brae, and whether or not Thea had known anything about the painting. I didn't know how long I would have to talk to him, so I needed to make sure my questions were succinct.

It was lovely to see Chloe and Felix when I arrived late that afternoon. Chloe had left work early to greet me and help me settle into their gorgeous flat, and then she and I walked over to the Lundenburg to see Felix. He greeted me with a big hug and a wide smile, wanting to know how Seamus was doing and when I thought would be a good time for him and Chloe to visit us again. I told him reluctantly that Seamus and I were still living apart, but that maybe in the spring things would be better.

They took me to dinner at a posh restaurant near the gallery, then Felix went back to work. Chloe and I returned to their flat and sipped glasses of wine while I told her what I intended to find out from Hagen.

"You know he's not going to be very happy to see you," she warned. "He thinks you and Seamus are the cause of all his troubles."

"Hagen is the cause of his own troubles," I said wryly. "Seamus and I happened to get caught in the middle of everything. Have you told Hagen I'll be visiting him?"

"No," she said. "I thought it best if you just show up. That way you have a better chance of getting the answers you're looking for."

"Thank you," I said. I bid her goodnight.

The next morning we took the Tube to the place where Hagen was being held. When we got there we were told that his sister was visiting and that we would have to wait our turn and be quick once we were in. I had expected that, so I had made two lists of questions: a long list and an abbreviated one. I would have to use the shorter list. "Can he refuse to see me?" I asked Chloe in a low voice.

"I'm sure he can, but let's see what happens. He wants to get out of here, I know that. He has maintained his innocence from the very start. If he thinks you can help spring him from here by finding out something the police didn't realize, he might see the wisdom in answering your questions."

We waited in silence to be called into the room where I would see Hagen for the first time since he followed me in the woods along the shore of Cauld Loch. We sat in a large, rather crowded room facing the office, with our backs to the door through which visitors were admitted to the nether regions of the prison. After many long minutes enduring the room's stale odor and the pale yellow monotony of the walls, there was a loud clang and the door behind us opened. I turned around to see if I would be called back next, and I inhaled sharply.

Alice was walking through the room. She held her head high and looked straight ahead, and I was sure she hadn't seen me. Then the officer who had led her through the door called my name. Alice must have been the one visiting Hagen.

Alice was Hagen's sister.

I stood up hastily, dropping my purse and my lists on the gray cement floor. I waved my hand at the officer to let him know I was coming, then bent down to hiss at Chloe, "Did you see that?"

"See what?" she asked, turning around in her seat.

"Alice just came out of there," I whispered.

"Alice? You mean *your* Alice?" she asked, her eyes widening. "I wouldn't recognize her if I saw her. I've never seen her before."

She was right. She would have no way of knowing what Alice looked like. How many times had she been here to visit Hagen and seen Alice, not realizing she was looking at the woman who had terrorized me and Seamus? Not realizing what this could mean for Hagen and the rest of us?

Because of my injured arm, it took me several seconds to pick up my handbag and the papers that had drifted to the floor. That gave me a moment to gather my thoughts before going through the metal door. The officer stood with his hands on his hips, clearly impatient. He probably had better things to do.

I clutched my papers to my chest and followed him through the door, looking back at Chloe. She was watching me with worry in her eyes.

When I saw Hagen, I was surprised. I had expected him to look ravaged and scruffy, like prisoners on television and like I had last seen him in Cauld Loch. But he looked trim and clean, much like he had looked the first time I had seen him in London. His eyes narrowed when he saw me, and he made a move toward the door leading farther back into the prison. But a guard in the room held him back. He said something to Hagen, and Hagen turned around slowly to face me through the glass that separated us. I sat down tentatively.

"What are you doing here?" he asked in a rough voice, his tone belying his suave appearance.

"I've come to ask you some questions. I'm trying to get to the bottom of everything that's happened recently, and I think you might be able to help me if you can share some information about the painting. If you help me, maybe I can help you." Could I really help him? Did I really want to?

He stared at me, not answering.

"Is Alice McDermott your sister?" I asked.

He grimaced. "Yes. One can't choose one's family."

"So you two have been working together," I said.

He turned around and gave the guard at the door a hand signal. The guard came over to Hagen and bent down to his level. Hagen said something into the man's ear, then the guard looked up at me. "He's asked to return to his cell, ma'am. That'll be all for today."

Without giving me another glance, Hagen pushed his chair back and accompanied the uniformed officer out the door into the prison halls. I sat staring at his retreating back, wondering how this new information fit with everything I already knew.

Chloe was surprised that my conversation with Hagen had gone so quickly, but she wanted to know more about Alice.

"I can't believe I've been passing her all this time and I didn't realize it!" she exclaimed on our way out of the prison. "How does this change things?"

My mind was working furiously. "Well, for one, it may mean that Alice and Hagen have been working together this whole time. And it means that Alice and Florian probably both knew about the painting before Florian bought it. When Florian told us the painting reminded him of his childhood, he was probably just talking rubbish."

Chloe nodded. "What do we do with this information?"

"I guess we should tell someone," I answered. "Either Scotland Yard or the police in Cauld Loch."

"Will you call them today?"

"I don't think so. I'll visit the Cauld Loch police tomorrow when I get home and they can notify Scotland Yard."

Felix came home early that night and we discussed what we had discovered on our visit to the prison. He couldn't believe Alice was Hagen's sister.

"Are you sure she didn't see you at the prison?" he asked, a worried look on his face. "You know she's a bit daft, and if she saw you there'd be no end to the trouble."

"I don't think she saw us," I answered. Chloe nodded her agreement. "At least, she didn't show any recognition." Now Felix had me thinking. Was it possible Alice had seen us there, knew we made the connection between her and Hagen, and was now planning on stopping that information from getting out? I gave an involuntary shudder. "If she did see us, we'd both better watch ourselves." I turned to Chloe. "Promise me you won't go anywhere alone. Make sure there are always people around."

"I promise," she said solemnly. "Promise me you'll do the same."

"I will. I already know what madness Alice is capable of," I said.

I didn't sleep well that night. I was worried about the implications of what I had learned at the prison. When I stumbled out of bed groggily in the morning, the last thing I wanted to do was get in my car and drive for hours. I couldn't bear the thought of being behind the wheel for so long when I was so desperately exhausted, but I had to get back to the shop. I accepted a cup of coffee for the road, then drove away from Felix and Chloe's flat with a wave and a tired smile. I had promised Chloe I would pull over and text her periodically so she would know I was driving safely.

I didn't think anything of the car that pulled away from the curb behind me as I left.

Getting out of London on a busy weekday morning was dodgy. I fought the traffic while sipping my coffee, grateful that the caffeine would soon be working its magic and I would feel better. But until then there were the ceaseless noises of London traffic to keep me awake—honking horns, idling engines, the occasional shout from a street corner.

It was over an hour later when I finally got on the road headed north. The traffic dispersed as I drove father and farther from London, and by afternoon I could go several minutes without seeing another car on the road—except the one in my rearview mirror.

I pulled over at a deserted rest stop and the car behind me pulled in, too. Before I got out I texted Chloe that the trip was going well. Then I reached for the door handle, and as I opened the door it was yanked out of my hand.

I hadn't seen Alice standing next to my car, waiting for me to get out. I tried getting back in and pulling the door shut behind me, but she was too strong, even with the injuries Eilidh had inflicted upon her. She pulled the door open again and grabbed my arm, jerking me out of the driver's seat. I dropped the keys and she gave them a vicious kick out of the way.

"You just couldn't leave well enough alone, could you?" she asked through clenched teeth.

"What are you talking about?" I asked.

"You had to go down to London, poking around where it's none of your business. You had to go see Hagen. You had to ruin everything!" Her voice had gotten steadily louder, and now she was shouting. I tried backing away, but I backed into the side of my car.

"I don't know what you're talking about," I said, trying to speak in a reasoned tone so she would calm down. "I just wanted to ask him how he learned about the Leitch painting and how he found out Seamus had bought it."

"Does it matter?" she asked. "All that really matters is where the painting is now."

Until I realized Hagen and Alice were siblings I had continued to hold out hope that one of them had the painting and the other one was trying to find it. Knowing they were possibly in cahoots with each other made that assumption less likely.

"So you really don't know where the painting is?" I asked. I flinched, expecting an explosion of anger. But instead she gave me a thoughtful look that made her seem even more unglued.

"Of course I don't know where it is. Why do you think I came to your house looking for it? Why do think Hagen came?"

So the other person who broke in had been Hagen?

She made a good point. But if she was telling the truth—and I had no reason to think she was—where was the painting?

"I thought you came looking for it because I didn't know you were working together to find it. I figured one of you had it and the other was looking for it to try to throw suspicion away from yourself."

"That's stupid."

"No more stupid than attacking someone who knows nothing about the painting."

Without warning, she slapped me across the face. "I'm going to find that painting, and when I do neither you nor Hagen is going to be able to do a thing about it."

"What do you mean?" I asked. The realization that she didn't intend to let me escape from this was slowly dawning.

"I mean you're coming with me. In my car."

"You're mad if you think I'm going anywhere with you," I said, glaring at her in defiance.

"Oh, I'm afraid you don't have a choice," she cooed in a soft voice. She was becoming more frightening by the second. Her moods shifted like quicksilver.

I only hesitated a moment before running toward the restrooms. I would find safety inside, I hoped.

But Alice was as quick as she was strong. She caught up to me in no time, sticking out her foot and tripping me before my brain had a chance to process what she was doing. I sprawled onto the ground, my palms and knees stinging from the impact and my injured arm protesting in pain. She hoisted me to my feet roughly, then grabbed my good arm and marched me to her car, where she pushed me into the back seat and slammed the door. I tried to twist away from her, but her grip was too strong. My mobile phone was still in my car and my keys still lay on the ground somewhere in the parking lot. I had no way to contact anyone.

She gunned the engine and sped off in the same direction we had been traveling.

"Where are we going?" I asked.

"Cauld Loch. Where else?"

My hopes rose. If we drove into Cauld Loch, perhaps I could get the attention of someone who would recognize me. Then that person would know to alert Seamus, who would do anything to free me from this madwoman.

We drove in silence for a long time. We were still several hours from Cauld Loch. Alice alternated between heavy metal, classical, and pop music on the radio until I thought I would scream.

"You're not going to find the painting in my house," I finally told her. "You've searched, Hagen has searched, and you've both found nothing."

"I'll decide where to search," she said. "When I find it I'm going to follow the map, get the gems, and get out of Scotland." She gave a loud laugh. "I'm moving where no one will ever find me, and I'll live in luxury for the rest of my days on what those crown jewels are worth."

"I thought you had enough money to live in luxury for the rest of your days without the jewels."

"Not after Florian lost all that money. He practically wiped us out. Why do you think I sent him for that painting? It wasn't so we could hang it up and look at it. It was so we could sell it, obviously."

"You can't possibly think you can sell those jewels without people knowing where they came from. And that's *if* the jewels are still where they were originally hidden."

"They'll be there. They have to be. And I hope you're not foolish enough to think there aren't lots of people out there who would pay big money for those jewels." She was practically salivating with greed.

"Even if you find them, which is doubtful, there are other people with a claim to those jewels, too. The government, for example. The jewels belong to the nation of Scotland."

"Bugger off! The only people with a legitimate claim to those jewels are me and Hagen. That's because we are the heirs of the man who owned both the map and the painting." I realized with a jolt that Alice had just answered a question that had been tickling the back of my mind for a long time. How had Hagen known which Leitch painting hid Elizabeth's map? The answer had suddenly been made clear: as descendants of the man who had owned the painting and the map, Hagen and Alice would have grown up hearing the story. They would have known what the painting looked like.

Alice was still talking. "Thank God Thea is no longer a threat. If Hagen had married her, we would have had to share the money from the sale of the jewels."

A chill snaked its way up my back. "Did Hagen kill Thea?"

"Of course not," she scoffed. "The stupid sap loved her. The problem was that he didn't think things through. Why split the money three ways when we could split it in half and leave her out of it? I liked Thea at one time, but I had no choice."

Alice had killed Thea. I felt a stab of sorrow for a woman I had never known, who had done nothing wrong but fall in love with a man who had a crazy sister.

"Alice, you can't possibly think no one is going to find out that you did it." She didn't answer.

I was in the car with a murderer. If she killed Thea, whom she had once liked, would she hesitate to do the same to me? I had to find a way out. I tried reasoning with her again.

"You know, anyone who sees me in your car in Cauld Loch is going to know something's wrong, and they'll raise the roof to get me away from you."

"I should have made myself clear. I'm going to Cauld Loch. You won't quite make it that far."

I felt a chill start at the base of my skull and spread throughout my body. "Where are you taking me?"

"It's a surprise." I could see her grinning in the rearview mirror.

An hour later we turned off the road and went bumping down a poorly paved road to a small dirt lot. There were no other cars in sight.

"Good," Alice said with a sigh. "I was afraid there might be other people here. It's deserted." Her voice had an ominous tone.

"Alice, this is crazy. Whatever you have planned, you haven't thought it through clearly."

"By the time they find your body, I'll be long gone," she said, her smile sly. "Come along." She opened the back door and pulled my arm. I tried as best I could to stay where I was, but I couldn't match her strength. Besides that, she had the advantage of standing up, whereas I was seated. She had the leverage of planting her feet while she was pulling. She grunted with the effort of pulling me as I resisted.

Finally I landed on the ground with a thud. I flipped onto my back and started flailing my legs, hoping to knock her down somehow, but all I succeeded in doing was exhausting myself.

Then I remembered the last text I had sent Chloe. Though I had said the trip was fine, she was expecting me to text every hour. I hoped fervently that she had taken my silence over the past few hours as a sign of trouble. But how would anyone find my car? And even if they found it, where would they go to look for me?

Alice had grabbed my good arm and was pushing me toward a metal gate. I had been here before, but I couldn't think straight to remember the name of the place.

Then it came to me—Crainskellie Gorge. I had come here to take photographs on one of our trips to the Highlands before Seamus and I moved out of Edinburgh. It was beautiful—and dangerous. Having viewed the three-thousand-feet-deep gorge through a zoom lens, I knew there was no hope of surviving a fall into its depths. The booming sound of rushing water reached us from the bottom of the gorge. Alice propelled me forward in front of her. I struggled against her hold on my arm, but to no avail. We walked down a steeply sloping switchback path with hairpin turns until I glimpsed the suspension bridge over the gorge. There were tall spikes on either side of the bridge to keep foolhardy people from leaning too far over, but as with any dangerous place, if someone really wanted to get around the security precautions, they could find a way.

And Alice knew just where to go to bypass the suspension bridge. Pushing me ahead of her, we charged through the thick brush toward the edge of the gorge, stumbling over hidden rocks and tiny hillocks of grass. I didn't dare look down—I had seen enough of it when I took photos of it. The raw beauty of the photos flashed through my mind, but it was quickly replaced with images of a body lying along the bottom of the gorge, cold water rushing over it. My body.

I couldn't let that happen. Alice let go of my arm and gave me a shove toward the edge of the gorge. I moved my arm in large circles, trying to keep my balance. When I righted myself, I took a step backward, keenly aware that Alice stood just a meter away, lunging toward me. Then I dodged to one side and she rushed past me, stopping herself in time to avoid heading over the side of the gorge. The thicket where we were performing our deadly dance was wet from recent rain, and from moisture rising from the rushing water far below us. It was difficult to keep my footing.

My mind was entirely focused on staying alive, and when Alice hurtled her body toward me again I reached my hand out to try to push her toward the edge of the gorge again. But she stopped and swung her arm at me instead, trying to use her brute strength to push me to my death.

She lunged at me again and I slipped backward toward the gorge, grasping at a clump of long grass to keep myself from slipping over the edge. She stood closer to the gorge than I then, and suddenly there was a shout from above us. Several years as a nature photographer had taught me never to lose focus in order to get that perfect shot that might only last a second or two, and I was able to ignore the shout at first while I watched Alice, waiting for her next attack. But Alice hadn't had such training and she lost her focus. When she jerked her head to see who was calling, she lost her balance and fell backward, plunging over the side of the gorge.

I let out a scream of—what was it? Terror? Relief? Probably both. It was a long minute before I was able to collect myself enough to make my way toward the sound of the voices and away from the edge of the precipice. By the time I reached the path, the people who had shouted were rushing toward me, their faces betraying their horror and shock. I sank to the ground, sobbing, as they approached.

In bursts of words, I tried to explain what had happened. They had already alerted the authorities, they said, and the police should be here in short order.

They were tourists. They had seen me struggling with Alice at the top of the gorge. Through my tears I thanked them again and again for shouting and distracting Alice from her deadly quest.

When they asked if there was anyone I could call, I gave them Seamus's mobile number. He was the one I wanted, and they phoned him straightaway.

When the police arrived they set about the laborious process of retrieving Alice's body from the bottom of the gorge. It was going to require a helicopter, they said, so it would be a little while before they could reach her.

An ambulance had accompanied them to the gorge, but I refused to go to the hospital again. After all I had been through, I could certainly handle the bumps and scratches that had resulted from this last encounter with Alice. I sat in a police car while they questioned me, and I told them everything that had happened since I left London. I relayed the confession Alice had made in the car, and they promised to notify the authorities with the news.

They took me to the nearest police station to clean up and call Seamus. He was tearing up the road to get to me, he said, and Eilidh was with him.

I started crying again. I would soon be in the arms of my husband and my cousin, safe at last. The fear and the threats from Alice were over. Hagen would probably be released and the murder charge dropped, but he would face charges for attacking me in Gorse Brae, causing another concussion.

When Seamus saw me he cried like a bairn. He held me for a long time while Eilidh stood close by, watching and wiping the tears streaming down her face. My own tears had started the minute I saw them come in the door, but they were happy tears.

My car was still at the rest stop along the road where I had left it. The police sent a tow truck for it and promised to have it at the station by the following day. Seamus and I could drive up to retrieve it then.

I was never so happy to get in the back seat of a car. Eilidh sat in the front so I could stretch out on the back seat and rest, but I was too revved up. I wanted to talk.

Seamus told me he had gotten a call from Chloe. She was worried about me since I hadn't answered any of her texts, and she knew I wouldn't forget to text if I could. She knew something had happened. But since Seamus had no idea where I was, there was nothing he could do but wait. "It was fair agonizing," he said, glancing at me in the rearview mirror.

"Chloe called the police in London and told them everything," Seamus said. "She told them Alice and Hagen were brother and sister, which had somehow escaped the notice of Scotland Yard and the police in Cauld Loch."

"And apparently there was no reason to suspect that anyone in Hagen's family would kill Thea or the police would have looked into that possibility. Since they were sure Hagen had done it, they had stopped looking for suspects," I added.

"I don't understand, though," Eilidh said. "If Alice and Hagen really don't have the painting, where is it?"

None of us had an answer.

CHAPTER 20

There was something therapeutic about getting back to work. Back to the shop and the gallery, the studio, and my photography. I spent the next several days enjoying the peace and quiet of the cottage, waiting on the customers who came through the door and working on my photos. Seamus was back in the house, but for all we had been through together, he was still sleeping in the guest room. I had never been so happy to see him as I was at the police station after my encounter with Alice, but that didn't erase what he had done. We were slowly moving toward a real and lasting peace, but I didn't feel we were ready to live as man and wife again.

The day came when Seamus received a phone call. He found me in the kitchen when he was done talking. He at me somberly and said, "It's Rose's time. I need to go say goodbye. Do you still want to come?" I didn't know what to say. "I think maybe you should go," he said.

I was surprised. I didn't think he would want me there.

"Why?" I asked.

"For me. For moral support."

I couldn't say no.

We were on the road to Edinburgh in no time, with Eilidh minding the shop for us. We didn't intend to be long.

When I met Rose I was shocked by the sight of her. I had been with my father when he passed away, but he had died just a day after having a heart attack. He hadn't lost any weight and he wasn't gaunt or bony. He looked just like himself. But Rose—even though we had never met, I knew her illness had changed her from the inside out. She lay back against a dingy pillow, her long hair stringy and splayed across her shoulders. Her collarbone jutted against her nightgown, and her hands, white and almost translucent, lay on the bed against her side, almost lifeless.

I stood off to one side of the room while Seamus bent over and kissed her forehead. Rose's family was in the room, and apparently they were still fond of Seamus, for they cried and smiled at him when he straightened up from her bed. Then he motioned to me. I took a tentative step forward and Rose's mother nodded at me, encouraging me to approach the bed where Rose lay in her last minutes.

I cleared my throat. I hadn't really thought of what I was going to say. "Rose, you and I have never met, but my name is Sylvie. I'm Seamus's wife." Her eyelids fluttered. I thought she could hear me.

"I just want to let you know," I said, choking on a sob, "that I'm going to take good care of him. You don't have to worry about him. And if your family needs anything, he will be there. He'll help them. I promise." I stroked her hand, the hand of a woman I was just meeting for the first time, and felt a wave of grief wash over me.

I took a deep, quavering breath and walked over to Seamus. I looked up at him, my face streaked with tears, and he smiled at me. "That was beautiful, love. Thank you."

After we had both shared our sadness with Rose's family, we waited outside for one of them to tell us she was gone. When she died, I was sure it was with a feeling of love and peace surrounding her.

It was over the course of the time I spent in that room with Rose and her family that I realized what was important, what was holding me back. Yes, Seamus had deceived me. Yes, I felt betrayed. But what was money for Rose in the face of life and death? We could make that money back. Seamus had known all along what was important, and I had lost sight of it. It was time to start restoring our marriage. We would still have to talk things over, still have to make changes, but I was ready to be married again. And I knew Seamus was, too.

We talked about it all the way back to Cauld Loch. It wasn't the excited talk of two people in love, but rather the calm, reasoned, and hopeful talk of two people who had learned from their experiences and were ready to apply the new knowledge to their married lives.

When I rang up Mum to tell her that Seamus and I were back together to work things out, she cried with relief. So did Greer, and so did Chloe. I had been surrounded by the well wishes of my family and friends since Seamus and I separated, but I felt them most now.

Later that night Seamus and I decided to go to the pub for a late dinner. I was pulling on my coat when Seamus suggested we invite Eilidh and Callum.

"Good idea. I'll ring them up and tell them to meet us there," I said.

"Nay, let's surprise them. They don't know all we talked about on the way home from Edinburgh, so let's stop over there and tell them the good news. They'll be so happy to know I'm not going to be underfoot anymore," he said with a laugh.

He offered me his hand and we left the house after setting the alarm and making sure we had left several lights on.

We walked up the path to Eilidh and Callum's house and Seamus rang the bell. There was no answer. He rang it again.

We heard footsteps and I noticed something moving out of the corner of my eye. The curtain next to the front door had twitched. Someone was looking out to see who was at the door. I glanced at Seamus.

The door opened a crack and Callum stood facing us. He didn't invite us in.

"Is something wrong, man?" Seamus asked, concern in his eyes.

"Nay, everything's all right," Callum answered.

"Can we come in?" Seamus asked.

"I'd rather you didn't just now."

"Are you sure you're all right?" Seamus asked. "We just thought we'd come by and invite you two to a late dinner at the pub. We're celebrating."

"We've already eaten," Callum said. "But thanks for asking." He moved to shut the door.

"Now, listen here, Callum," Seamus said sternly. "I know you. Heck, I've even lived with you. And I know there's something wrong. Now let us in. We can help, whatever it is." He pushed the door open with his big hands.

The living room was a mess. Two large pieces of canvas and small bits of paper lay scattered about the floor. The remains of a wooden frame had been tossed near the sofa.

Seamus's eyes wrinkled in confusion. "What's this?" he asked. He walked over to one of the pieces of canvas and turned it over.

A woman's painted face looked away from us. She was bending down to pick tiny purple flowers that dotted the field in front of a church.

It was the Leitch painting.

"My God, man," Seamus breathed. "What have you done?"

Callum slumped down onto the sofa, his face in his hands. "I'm so sorry, Seamus. I'm so sorry," he said over and over.

"You've had it? All this time?" Seamus asked. Callum nodded.

"How did you get it?" Seamus asked. I was afraid to hear the answer, and I know Seamus was, too.

"I don't think I should say," Callum said. "You don't want to know."

"Did you kill Florian?" Seamus asked, his voice barely above a whisper.

Callum nodded again. "I didn't mean to. It was an accident," he insisted. "I was following him and I must have scared him and he went off the road."

I looked at Seamus. Someone had tampered with Florian's car. Either Callum was lying or there was someone else involved.

"Callum? Was it really an accident?"

Callum hung his head. "Eilidh's going to leave me," he said. "When she finds out what I've done she's going to leave me."

"Where is Eilidh?" I asked, my voice tense with uncertainty and fear.

"At the market. I sent her there so I could have a look at the painting and the map."

"What were you planning to do with the map?" Seamus asked.

"I was going to find the jewels and sell them. I need money, Seamus. My job doesn't pay enough, and I don't want Eilidh to have to work. But if she doesn't make more money we'll be broke. We'll lose the house."

"Why didn't you tell us this?" I asked. "We would have helped you."

Callum snorted. "Charity for a poor relation? I couldn't. I'd kill myself first."

"How did you know about the painting?" Seamus asked.

"I was there the night Florian told you he'd buy it, remember? So I knew it was valuable. But I didn't know about the map behind it. Not yet. Not only that, but I had gotten a call at the office about the painting. I was filling out requisition forms for artwork to go on the walls of an old house that the village is helping to restore, and someone called asking lots of very specific questions about the painting. They had heard it was in the Cauld Loch area and also that the local preservation office was looking for artwork. Whoever rang me up was willing to buy it from me at any price, and I was curious. So I looked it up online and recognized the picture from when I had seen it hanging in your shop."

It must have been either Hagen or Florian, searching for the painting, who had talked to Callum on the phone.

"So why didn't you just buy the painting?" Seamus asked.

"For three thousand pounds? I don't have that kind of money, Seamus," he scoffed.

"Was Florian's death really an accident, Callum?" Seamus repeated. Callum started to cry, shaking his head slowly from side to side.

Florian's death had been no accident.

Seamus shook his head. "What are we supposed to do now?" he asked me.

I couldn't bear the pain I was feeling for Callum, and especially for Eilidh. What would she do when she found out her husband had killed someone? "I honestly don't know," I answered.

"I do," Callum said. He pulled his mobile phone from his back pocket and dialed 9-9-9.

He was asking the officer on the other end to send someone to pick him up when Eilidh came into the house.

She stopped short in the doorway, frowning. "What's going on here?" She looked around the room, taking in the sight of Callum's tears, my drawn face, and Seamus's pained expression. "What's going on, I asked?" she repeated, more shrill this time.

"Eilidh," I said, taking a step toward her. "I think you should have a seat."

Callum hung up the phone. Eilidh sat down in an armchair across from him and he knelt down next to her.

"Eilidh, there's something you need to know," he said, then he bowed his head. "I'm so sorry, Eilidh."

"Just tell me, please," she pleaded. There was terror in her eyes.

"You remember the night Florian died?" he asked.

"No," she said, her eyes widening, her hand flying to cover her mouth. "No. Tell me it wasn't you. Tell me you didn't kill him, Callum."

He didn't answer. He couldn't. He pressed his lips together until they turned white. He closed his eyes and gulped.

"I'm so sorry, Eilidh. I did it for us. I did it so we wouldn't have to worry about money anymore."

"No!" she screamed, leaping to her feet. "Callum, it was an accident, right?"

"It wasn't," he said quietly.

"What's going to happen now?" she screeched. "You'll go to prison! What am I going to do without you?" She was hysterical.

"You'll be okay," he assured her, though I didn't know how that could be true. How could anyone recover from such a thing?

"No I won't!" she screamed. She started pummeling him with her fists. Instead of trying to stop her, he stood still and let her get out her aggression, her fear, and her hopelessness.

She was crying so hard I was afraid for her. The keening noises coming from her throat were horrifying and terribly sad. I wanted to hug her, to take her in my arms and make everything better, but I knew not to touch her. She had to calm down before she would be ready to accept hugs.

The next thing we knew she fainted. I rushed to her side, where Callum was already tapping her face gently, trying to bring her back to consciousness. Seamus stood over us, his face showing sadness, shock, and concern. And that's how the police found us when they knocked on the door just a few moments later. Callum called for them to come in.

They took charge of the scene immediately. They called for an ambulance for Eilidh and handcuffed Callum, despite my assurances that he wasn't dangerous and wasn't going to try to flee. Callum looked at me sadly and shook his head, as if understanding they were doing their jobs. Then two officers took Callum away while a third waited with us for the ambulance.

Seamus and I accompanied Eilidh to hospital. When she awoke in the ambulance, she panicked, screaming for Callum and hitting my hand as I tried to hold hers. "Don't touch me!" she cried.

"I'm sorry," I murmured.

She cried harder. "I'm sorry, Sylvie. I'm so sorry. What am I going to do? How am I going to live without him?"

I didn't know what to say, except to mumble that everything would work out all right, though I didn't believe it myself.

The orderly in the ambulance gave Eilidh a mask and pure oxygen started to flow into her lungs. She calmed noticeably and closed her eyes, probably hoping to dream and wake up to find all of this nothing but a nightmare.

But it was real. She was given something to help her sleep soon after she reached the hospital. I stayed with her overnight while nurses watched her for signs of agitation. I think they were afraid she would wake up and try to take her own life. That's what I feared, too, and that's why I spent the night in her room.

In the morning she was able to speak, but she wouldn't. She was lethargic and morose. She checked her mobile phone a hundred times, hoping, I'm sure, for a text from Callum. But none would come. I knew that. The police would have confiscated his mobile phone. Seamus arrived at hospital early in the morning. While I sipped the tea he had brought me, he sat with Eilidh and tried to explain what Callum would be experiencing as he waited to be formally charged. Knowing that seemed to bring a calm to her, though that surprised me. I expected her to be more upset.

"Do you think he'll be able to come home?" she asked Seamus in a pitiful voice.

He shook his head. "Not if he really did what he says he did. He'll probably go to trial. And it's anyone's guess what will happen after that."

"Eilidh, was there anything to suggest that he did this?" I asked quietly.

She was silent and I held my breath, waiting for her to speak.

"I never said anything because the idea was too horrible to put into words," she began. "But he left the house the night Florian died. I remember because I heard the sirens and I hoped he hadn't been in an accident. He wasn't gone long. When he came home he didn't say much, but I have secretly wondered about it ever since. But I never saw the painting in our house, and I began to relax and think my suspicions had all been in my mind. He must have hidden it well."

And so he had. As more information came to light about Callum's involvement in the death of Florian McDermott, we learned that he had indeed hidden the painting in his office to keep it from Eilidh. He had yearned for a better life for the two of them, one in which Eilidh wouldn't have to work and one in which they could afford their dream house and posh vacations.

"But I never asked for any of those things," Eilidh insisted one night when Seamus and I were staying with her. "I would have been perfectly happy just being married to Callum for the rest of my life, worrying about money and never having enough. The money wasn't what was important."

Callum and I had both learned that lesson the hard way.

EPILOGUE

Callum was indeed convicted of killing Florian McDermott and is now in prison. With good behavior, he should be out within six years, or so his solicitor tells him. Seamus goes to visit him regularly, since he knows what it's like to be in prison and how comforting it can be to see a friendly face. Since Callum is the brother Seamus never had, my husband misses the camaraderie they shared before Callum left.

Eilidh, on the other hand, has not been able to bring herself to visit Callum yet. She was devastated following his conviction and was terrified to see him face-to-face after that. Since she's been on her own she's changed a lot—she's become more pensive, but she's also shown a surprising willingness to get out of the house and meet new people. She even took a second job, in addition to her job at our shop, to pay the bills. When she talks about Callum it's clear that she despises what he did, and that she's embarrassed he kept insisting he did it for her. I do wonder what the future holds for the two of them when he is eventually released.

Seamus took a three-week break from visiting Callum in the spring. At Felix's request, he we back to London to be the first featured artist in the artist-in-residence program at the Lundenburg Gallery. I didn't go with him because he was going to be working every minute he was in the city and wouldn't have time to spend with me at all. Besides, business at our shop and gallery had picked up even more after Callum's trial, and it wasn't fair to ask Eilidh to answer questions that customers might have about the painting and the circumstances surrounding its disappearance and reappearance.

After the painting resurfaced, it was confiscated by the government and put in the custody of the National Trust for Scotland until its fate could be determined. Alice had left one heir when she fell to her death—her brother Hagen. But there were questions about his right to the ownership of the painting, the map, and anything that might be found when searchers followed the map to the place where Elizabeth had buried the gems centuries before. Hagen's solicitor came up with an intriguing plan—Hagen would give up his rights to the painting and the map in order to avoid imprisonment. In doing so, he would also give up any possible claim he might have to the jewels, if they should be located. Hagen agreed to the plan immediately and preparations began to look for the jewels.

The search for the jewels became a story followed by all of Scotland. To the nation's amazement and joy, when researchers from the National Trust for Scotland followed Elizabeth's map they found the jewels from the Honours of Scotland exactly where Elizabeth originally buried them. Seamus and I were invited to be on hand when the jewels were unearthed: it was an astounding and emotional discovery. We were pleased to learn that the National Trust for Scotland would keep them on permanent display with the Honours of Scotland. As much as Seamus enjoyed the artist-in-residence program in London, and as much as we both enjoyed participating in the exciting discovery of the missing jewels from the Scottish Regalia, we couldn't wait to get back to our peaceful day-to-day lives in our beloved Highlands. There is nothing that can compare to the breathtaking beauty of the mountains, the lochs, the forests, and the tiny villages of this rugged and pristine part of Scotland. Now, in the shadow of the mountain behind Gorse Brae, we work side by side in the studio, Seamus on his paintings and me on my photographs.

We've never been happier.

Author's Note

Photo by John A. Reade, Jr.

USA Today bestselling author **Amy M. Reade** is also the author of the Malice series, as well as the novels *Secrets of Hallstead House, The Ghosts of Peppernell Manor,* and *House of the Hanging Jade.* A former attorney, she now writes full-time from her home in southern New Jersey, where she is also a wife, a mom of three, and a volunteer in school, church, and community groups. She loves cooking, traveling, and all things Hawaii and is currently at work on the next novel in the Malice series. Visit her on the web at www.amymreade.com or at amreade.wordpress.com.

Trading the urban pace of Edinburgh for a tiny village overlooking a breathtaking blue loch was a great move for budding photographer Sylvie Carmichael and her artist husband, Seamus—until a dangerous crime obscures the view . . .

Sylvie's bucolic life along the heather-covered moors of the Highlands is a world away from the hectic energy of the city. But then a London buyer is killed after purchasing a long-lost Scottish masterpiece from Seamus's gallery—and the painting vanishes. As suspicion clouds their new life, and their relationship, Sylvie's search for answers plunges her into an unsolved mystery dating back to Cromwellian Scotland through World War I and beyond. And as she moves closer to the truth, Sylvie is targeted by a murderer who's after a treasure within a treasure that could rewrite history . . . and her own future.

"You are not wanted here. Go away from Hallstead Island or you will be very sorry you stayed."

Macy Stoddard had hoped to ease the grief of losing her parents in a fiery car crash by accepting a job as a private nurse to the wealthy and widowed Alexandria Hallstead. But her first sight of Hallstead House is of a dark and forbidding home. She quickly finds its winding halls and shadowy rooms filled with secrets and suspicions. Alex seems happy to have Macy's help, but others on the island, including Alex's sinister servants and hostile relatives, are far less welcoming. Watching eyes, veiled threats…slowly, surely, the menacing spirit of Hallstead Island closes in around Macy. And she can only wonder if her story will become just one of the many secrets of Hallstead House…

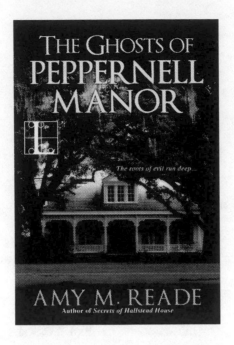

"Do you know what stories Sarah could tell you about the things that happened in these little cabins? They'd curl that pretty red hair of yours."

Outside of Charleston, South Carolina, beyond hanging curtains of Spanish moss, at the end of a shaded tunnel of overarching oaks, stands the antebellum mansion of Peppernell Manor in all its faded grandeur. At the request of her friend Evie Peppernell, recently divorced Carleigh Warner and her young daughter Lucy have come to the plantation house to refurbish the interior. But the tall white columns and black shutters hide a dark history of slavery, violence, and greed. The ghost of a former slave is said to haunt the home, and Carleigh is told she disapproves of her restoration efforts. And beneath the polite hospitality of the Peppernell family lie simmering resentments and poisonous secrets that culminate in murder—and place Carleigh and her child in grave danger...

A dark presence had invaded the Jorgensens' house. On a spectacular bluff overlooking the Pacific Ocean, something evil is watching and waiting . . .

Tired of the cold winters in Washington, D.C. and disturbed by her increasingly obsessive boyfriend, Kailani Kanaka savors her move back to her native Big Island of Hawaii. She also finds a new job as personal chef for the Jorgensen family. The gentle caress of the Hawaiian trade winds, the soft sigh of the swaying palm trees, and the stunning blue waters of the Pacific lull her into a sense of calm at the House of the Hanging Jade—an idyll that quickly fades as it becomes apparent that dark secrets lurk within her new home. Furtive whispers in the night, a terrifying shark attack, and the discovery of a dead body leave Kailani shaken and afraid. But it's the unexpected appearance of her ex-boyfriend, tracking her every move and demanding she return to him, that has her fearing for her life . . .

Printed in the United States
by Baker & Taylor Publisher Services